THE KNITTING NEEDLE MURDER
THE MIDDLE WAY MYSTERIES
BOOK I

MARIKO MCCARTHY

Copyright © 2025 Mariko McCarthy

Layout design and Copyright © 2025 by Next Chapter

Published 2025 by Next Chapter

Edited by Tyler Colins

Cover design by Lordan June Pinote

This book is a work of fiction. Names, characters, places, and incidents are the product of the author's imagination or are used fictitiously. Any resemblance to actual events, locales, or persons, living or dead, is purely coincidental.

All rights reserved. No part of this book may be reproduced or transmitted in any form or by any means, electronic or mechanical, including photocopying, recording, or by any information storage and retrieval system, without the author's permission.

For Mike, always

CHAPTER 1

Jenny steered the trolley round the end of the bookcase. The *R*s were done, now for the *S*s. She slotted the books into place, one by one. It was a peaceful, undemanding task. When she noticed a book out of alphabetical order, she replaced it in its proper home. *Stibbe, Nina* after *Stewart, Mary*. Before Jenny shelved each book, she flicked quickly through the pages as Valerie Raeburn, the library manager, had told her to do, just in case there was something unexpected hidden inside.

'Quite astonishing what people will use for bookmarks,' Valerie had said. 'I once found a rasher of bacon inside a Richard Osman.'

Cooked, or uncooked? Jenny had wondered, but hadn't asked.

'*Streaky*,' Valerie added, with a shudder of disgust.

There were no bacon rashers in any of the books today, although an envelope fluttered out of one of them. *Loo rolls, marmalade, sweet chilli sauce, cat litter* Jenny read. She had a lively curiosity about people and their hidden lives. This borrower evidently had a cat. Perhaps one that liked its Whiskas spiked with chilli.

Jenny found a home for her last book just as a bell tinkled.

This was Valerie's signal that the library would be closing in five minutes. In fact, it was nearly empty already. A brown-skinned woman with glossy hair coiled in a bun was heading towards the desk pulling a tartan shopper behind her. As Jenny watched, she lifted piles of books out, placed them on the desk in front of Valerie, and offered her a fan of library cards.

A family of readers, Jenny thought. *Or perhaps a book club or a reading circle.* She wondered if she should think about joining a book club. She loved reading, but for her it was a solitary pleasure, curled cosily in an armchair, allowing an author's words to transport her to another world. She didn't really want to talk about what she read with other people, no matter how friendly and welcoming they might be.

I've become very anti-social Jenny said to herself.

She scanned the library: the long table where the students sat with their phones and laptops out, earbuds in, secretly nibbling biscuits and swigging from cans of energy drink; the stand with the Recommended Reads colourfully on display; the circles of chairs in tucked-away corners, where people parked their shopping and rested their legs, and sometimes snored … Oh, there *was* someone still there. An elderly man with a large book splayed open on his lap, chin resting on his chest. As Jenny approached, she saw a ragged piece of paper—like something torn from a newspaper—lying on the floor next to him. Without thinking, she picked it up, folded it, and slipped it into her pocket.

'Excuse me,' Jenny said. 'I'm afraid the library's about to close.'

The man did not move or give any sign of having heard her.

Gingerly, Jenny placed a hand on his shoulder. 'I'm sorry, sir,' she said. 'But you'll have to leave soon.'

Still nothing. Jenny exerted a little more pressure. The man slid down in his seat, his head rocking slightly to and fro. Something long and shiny was sticking out of his chest. Jenny gasped and jumped back, and the man's body slumped sideways, then off the chair and on to the floor, landing awkwardly, limbs flung anyhow, with the book underneath him. Jenny must have made a noise, because suddenly the woman with the shopper was beside her. She knelt by the body and felt for a pulse at the neck—with what Jenny, even in her shock, could see was calm proficiency. Then she stood up.

'I'm afraid he's dead. We must call the police.'

'The *police*?' Valerie had appeared, and stood helplessly rubbing her hands together. 'Are you sure, Neeta?'

'Very sure,' Neeta said. 'He's been stabbed. With a knitting needle.'

Jenny felt the room, its endless rows of books, start to swirl around her. The next thing she knew, she was lying on the floor, its parquet cold against her cheek. Neeta was by her side, speaking gently to her.

'Now—Jenny, isn't it? It's all right—you've had such a shock. Let us help you up and we'll find somewhere for you to sit down and recover.'

She and Valerie put their arms around her and lifted her, and she sensed the indignity of it and tried to stand properly, but her legs were so weak, like a puppet's, and she was gasping for breath, shiveringly, noisily. The two women guided her to the office behind the desk where the staff and volunteers gathered for tea and biscuits and chat, and lowered her gently into an armchair.

'I will make us all a cuppa,' Neeta said. 'You will do the phoning, Val?'

Jenny heard Valerie speaking into her mobile, and Neeta filling the kettle with water. She was starting to feel a little better. She closed her eyes, but the image of the body kept intruding. She now remembered the patch of dark blood on the man's pullover where the needle had entered.

'The police are on their way,' Valerie said. 'They told us to lock the doors to make sure no one else comes in. I'll go down and do that now.'

Jenny watched Neeta making the tea: filling the mugs, mashing the teabags against their sides, pouring milk from a carton, then showering sugar into one mug, although not into the other two. It was too late to say that she hated over-sweetened tea.

'There you are, dear,' Neeta said, placing the mug on a raffia mat on the low table at Jenny's side. She perched next to her on an upright chair and sipped her own tea daintily.

'You were very calm,' Jenny said. 'I feel so silly the way I panicked.'

'You shouldn't feel silly,' Neeta said. 'I'm a nurse, I've seen it all before. Although not with a knitting needle. Not in the *chest*, anyway.'

Valerie returned and picked up her mug.

'Ooh, nice and strong. Just how I like it. Thanks, Neeta.'

Jenny took a quick gulp of tea. It was still too hot, it burned her mouth, and it was almost electric with sugar.

'Who *was* that poor man?' Valerie asked. 'I've seen him here quite a few times—always in the same corner. I think he rather claimed it for himself—he'd spread his stuff out and glare at anybody who tried to join him.'

'It was Mr Sykes,' Neeta said briskly. 'He used to teach English at Kerston Comp. He taught me, in fact.'

'Oh deary me. Who could have done that to him? A former pupil? Or a parent?'

'He was a good teacher, but he didn't always consider people's feelings. He could be very sarcastic, especially if he thought you'd said something stupid. We were all a bit scared of him, to tell the truth. But he retired ages ago. Or, rather, he *left*. Yes, it's coming back to me now. It happened after *I'd* left—gone to college—but one of my friends has a sister, Libby, who was still there and she told me about it. It was very sudden, right in the middle of term. Of course, there were all sorts of rumours flying about at the time …'

Jenny and Valerie both looked at her expectantly.

'I should not speak ill of the dead,' Neeta said primly, but they could tell she was bursting to do just that.

'Oh, go on, Neeta,' Valerie jogged her. 'It's not as if you can hurt him now.'

'Well, people said he'd been a little too touchy-feely. With some of his pupils.'

'With the girls?'

'Yes, I suppose so.'

'Were the police involved? Because that does sound like abuse to me.'

'No, no police. It was all a bit ...' Neeta set down her mug and twirled elegant fingers through the air. 'A bit ... *flimsy*. No one wanted to come straight out and make the accusation. But I suppose the head teacher had a word with him, and they agreed it would be best if he resigned.'

'He might have been innocent,' Jenny said. Somehow, she felt that she should speak up for poor dead Mr Sykes.

'Yes,' Neeta said. 'He might have been. Girls can be very *nasty*, you know. The young fellow who had to come in and replace him at short notice—they teased him so much, he nearly had a nervous breakdown. *He* left too, as soon as he could.'

'Why did they tease him?'

'Libby said he had a gap between his front teeth, and he whistled when he spoke. *Whoo-hee, whoo-hee,* like that.'

There was a loud knocking at the door downstairs. Valerie went down to answer it and reappeared with two uniformed officers, who introduced themselves as Police Sergeant Jim McBride and Police Constable Jack Hollis. Neeta got up and offered them a cup of tea.

'Perhaps later, Neeta,' Sergeant McBride said. 'We'll go and take a look at your body first.'

'You seem to know everyone,' Jenny said, once the officers had walked away.

'Not *everyone*.' Neeta smiled, as though Jenny's comment

wasn't that far off the mark. 'My husband is a doctor at the health centre, and I work part-time there as one of the practice nurses. And I'm a library volunteer—I take books to elderly people and others who are housebound. As a matter of fact,' she went on, gazing at her laden shopper, 'they'll probably be wondering where I've got to.'

'Jenny is a volunteer too,' Valerie said. 'So it's nice that you've met. Although, of course, not in *this* way.'

'Mm, *h'm?*' Neeta said, cocking her head to one side, obviously inviting Jenny to say more about herself. But Jenny didn't feel that she could. It would take too much out of her right now.

'I must phone George,' Valerie said. 'Tell him I'll be home late. I suppose the police will want to talk to us once they've looked at the body.'

'I'm sure they will,' Neeta said, taking her own phone out of her pocket, dabbing at the screen, and holding it to her ear. 'Oh Jonty, something rather dreadful has happened at the library ... No, I'm fine, but an elderly gentleman has been found dead ... No, not a heart attack—well, yes, in the sense that someone attacked his heart. They stuck a knitting needle through it. The police are here, and we have to wait and talk to them ... Could you ring my library biddies—Mrs Pycroft, Mrs Grundy, Mr Nettles, Mrs Scrivens—to tell them I'll bring their books round tomorrow? Just say I've been unavoidably delayed. Oh, and give Maisie her tea? Thanks, honey! I'll text you as soon as I know what's happening.'

'Is Maisie your daughter?' Jenny asked once Neeta had re-pocketed her phone.

Neeta smiled. 'Yes, she's eight. I'll have to tell her about Mr Sykes, or she'll pick up some garbled version at school—these things get around in no time. Actually, she might be more excited than anything—she's always reading detective stories, and I think she fancies herself as a little Sherlock. Do *you* need to phone someone, Jenny? You can use my phone if yours is out of battery.'

Jenny shook her head. 'Thanks, but no, there isn't anyone.'

Once again, Neeta gave her a questioning look, but she was spared by the reappearance of the two police officers.

'Right, ladies,' Sergeant McBride said, clearing his throat. 'I've called this one in, and a pathologist and the scene-of-crime folk will be arriving soon. I need each of you to give a brief statement, and after you've done that, you can be on your way. Although, of course, we may want to speak to you again later. Now, which one of you found the body?'

'That was me,' Jenny said, rising to her feet. 'I'm Jenny Meaden, and I'm a library volunteer.'

'We'll start with you, then, Ms Meaden. Constable Hollis will talk to you, Neeta, and ... and ...'

'Valerie Raeburn, library manager,' said Valerie.

Jenny followed Sergeant McBride out of the office. 'We have to be interviewed separately,' she thought to herself, 'so we're not influenced by what the others say.' That was logical, and she wanted logic, she wanted *sense*. The sergeant guided her to the long table where the students sat and pulled out a chair for her. Mr Sykes's corner—it would always be that now—was hidden by a double row of bookcases, but all the same she was glad to be sitting with her back to it.

The sergeant placed his notebook on the table and clicked his Biro. He was broad-shouldered with close-cropped badger-grey hair—fifties, she thought. About her own age.

'So,' he began, 'you are Ms Jennifer Meaden ...'

'No,' Jenny said. He looked up in surprise, pen hovering. 'I'm just Jenny—it's not short for anything,' she explained.

'Ah.' He smiled. 'My apologies. It must have been a shock, Ms Meaden, coming across a body. In a library, of all places.'

Was a library a particularly shocking place for a murder? There was a—very popular—crime section, but those murders were fictional, of course. Although there was also a healthy—no, an unhealthy—appetite for 'true crime' ... Jenny realized her thoughts were going completely haywire.

'It was a Mr Sykes,' she said, determined to ground herself. 'A retired schoolteacher. Neeta recognized him.'

Sergeant McBride's bristly moustache twitched. She thought he muttered something like *Neeta would* under his breath. He asked her for her address and phone number and wrote them down.

'And can you remember what time it was when you found Mr Sykes?'

'It was just before five o'clock. Valerie—Mrs Raeburn—had rung the library-closing bell, and I went to tell him he'd have to leave.'

'So, you spoke to him?'

'Yes, and when he didn't answer, I touched his … shoulder.' (*Just say the words. Don't let the pictures come back …*)

Sergeant McBride nodded. 'And then?'

'He slid off the chair, on to the floor. There was a book on his lap. I think I must have fainted, because Neeta and Valerie had to help me back to the office.'

'You said that Mrs Biddle—Neeta—recognized him, but had *you* seen him in the library before?'

'No—at least, I hadn't noticed him specially. But I've only been working here a couple of weeks. Valerie said he came in quite regularly, and always sat in the same spot.'

'And today, before you went to wake him up—because I guess you thought he'd just fallen asleep?'—Jenny nodded—'had you seen anyone near him—talking to him, for instance?'

'No.' Jenny shook her head.

Sergeant McBride closed his notebook and leaned back in his chair.

'Well, Ms Meaden, that will be all for now. Thank you very much for your time. Let's go and see how the others are getting on.'

Valerie was in the office, lifting her coat from its hanger.

'I suppose,' she ventured, 'the library will have to stay shut tomorrow?'

The sergeant nodded. 'You'll appreciate it's a crime scene. We'll let you know when you can re-open. If you can give me the keys, now?'

Valerie handed them to him as Neeta and PC Hollis walked back in. Neeta was pulling her shopper, and Jenny saw the two police officers look at one another.

'Just a moment, Neeta,' Sergeant McBride said. 'We are not accusing you of anything, but we need to make sure.' He and PC Hollis lifted the books out and piled them on the coffee table. Jenny saw the younger officer's eyebrows shoot up at some of the more lurid covers—a Godzilla-type monster belching flames at a girl wearing what looked like a fur bikini, a gaggle of Regency ladies in extremely low-cut frocks.

'They're not for me,' Neeta said crossly. She had also noticed the eyebrows. 'I take them round to the old and housebound. It's all part of the service.'

Sergeant McBride slid his hand into the now empty shopper and felt around inside it.

'All clear. I'm sorry to inconvenience you, Neeta, but knitting needles *do* come in twos. Someone might have slipped the other one in, rather than be caught carrying it out.'

Neeta, for once, was speechless. Jenny thought it most unlikely that the murderer had discarded a needle in that way, but it did raise a question: did whoever stabbed Mr Sykes bring in a pair, or just the one? She could just about visualize someone—a woman, surely?—carrying their knitting in with them, perhaps looking for a comfy chair so they could sit down and get on with it, and then, for some reason, becoming enraged at Mr Sykes and driving one needle—the one not loaded with stitches—into his chest. But if there was only ever a single needle, that made the crime more deliberate, more premeditated. Perhaps it had even been specially sharpened ...

'How are you getting home, Jenny?'

She realized, with a jump, that Neeta was speaking to her.

'Oh, I'll catch the bus.'

'No,' Neeta said, 'you won't do that. My house is just a few steps away. You come with me, and rest for a while, and then Jonty or I will drive you home.'

'That's very kind,' Jenny said. She was already learning that Neeta was not the sort of person to take *no* for an answer.

The distance to Neeta's home was a little more than 'a few steps', but not by much. It took the two women about five minutes to walk there. They were still close to the centre of Kerston, but away from the main road.

'This is me,' Neeta said, stopping in front of a white-painted wooden gate.

A little girl came running towards them down the garden path, unlatched the gate, and held it open so the two women, and the shopper, could pass through. She had fizzy brown curls and bright dark eyes.

'Thank you, darling. Jenny, this is Maisie. Maisie, this is my new friend, Jenny.'

'Hello, Maisie,' Jenny said, smiling. *Friend!* The word sat inside her like a warm pearl.

As Neeta trundled the shopper towards the house, between a pocket-sized lawn and flowerbeds with clipped rose bushes, a man appeared at the open front door.

'And this is Jonty. Dr Jonathan Biddle, to give him his proper title.'

'Pleased to meet you,' Dr Biddle said to Jenny as Neeta introduced her. He was in his forties—perhaps a few years older than his wife—with blunt, cheerful features and unruly fair curly hair. He pulled Neeta's shopper up over the red-tiled front step and away down the hall.

'Now, Maisie,' Neeta said, 'I need to talk to Daddy about something. Can you entertain Jenny for a minute or two?'

'Yes,' Maisie said eagerly. 'Shall I do a handstand?'

'No, not that sort of entertaining. I mean *make conversation*.'

'Oh, I can do that too.' She led Jenny into the sitting room at the front of the house and plonked herself down on a flowery sofa. Jenny seated herself next to her.

'Would you like to see my rats?' Maisie asked, wriggling to get comfortable and punching the cushion behind her.

Rats! Were they stuffed toys?

'They're called Bill and Ben,' Maisie added.

'Do they live in a flowerpot?'

Maisie wrinkled her nose and looked puzzled. 'No, of course they don't. They live in a big cage with a rat gym and hammocks to sleep in.'

Jenny tried—and failed—to picture rats doing press-ups. 'Perhaps I could see them another day. Do you like other animals too?'

'Oh *yes*.' Maisie squirmed again, this time so she could reach into her trouser pocket and pull out a card. She handed it to Jenny, who read,

Maisie Biddle
Pet Detective

The card was decorated with a border of rabbits and mice (or possibly rats). At the foot, Maisie had written her address and also, in a balloon coming out of the mouth of one of the rabbits, *Reckomended by the Police!*

'I accept all cases,' Maisie explained. 'My last one was rescuing a hamster that had escaped and gone under the floorboards.'

'Really? How did you solve that?'

'I found the hole it had squeezed through, and I laid some bait a little way away from it. Peanut butter spread on a slice of apple. Then I just sat and waited, and when it came nosing out, I pounced on it.'

'You sound like a very good detective,' Jenny said.

Maisie nodded. 'Inspector O'Keeffe says I have great ... pencil.'

'Potential? Although, of course,' Jenny went on hurriedly, 'pencils are a very important part of detective work. You definitely need—great pencil.'

'Yes, and I have a notebook where I write about all my cases. Shall I show it to you?'

Jenny was saved from having to reply by Neeta reappearing.

'A drink, Jenny? Another cup of tea, perhaps?'

'Oh, no thank you, I'm fine.' She was afraid that even if she told Neeta she didn't take sugar, it would still be served lethally sweetened.

'Perhaps something a little stronger? Sherry? Or we have a Christmassy bottle of sloe gin—*last* Christmas, that is, but I don't believe it goes off.'

Jenny smiled. 'I suppose you wouldn't happen to have any whisky?'

'Oh, we do! Whoopee! Highland Park—is that all right? And I can join you because Jonty will be driving you home.'

Maisie disappeared up the stairs to her bedroom, and Jenny and Neeta sat side by side, sipping their whisky from heavy crystal glasses.

'Such a strange thing to happen,' Neeta mused. 'I mean, Mr Sykes being stabbed is weird enough, but with a *knitting needle*. It must mean it was a woman who did it, don't you think?'

'Unless it was a man, and he *wanted* us to think that.' Jenny could feel the tensions in her muscles dissolve as she sank back into the cushions, warm, relaxed.

'My goodness, that's true! We should try to approach this like detectives. Well, man or woman, it must have been quite a *strong* person. I did notice it was a thin steel needle—a number eleven perhaps.'

Jenny closed her eyes and tried to organize her thoughts. If you wanted to stab someone, it would be much easier to use a knife, or even a skewer. Unless the murderer hadn't intended attacking Mr Sykes when they'd entered the library, and when the urge came upon them, a knitting needle was their only weapon to hand. (So, they'd have had *two* needles ...) What had Mr Sykes done, though, to incite such fury? Was it something that had flared up there and then, between him and his attacker, or were the reasons buried somewhere in the past?

And why kill someone in a *library*, where there were people moving about all the time? Mr Sykes wouldn't have been moving, though; he'd have been sitting in his out-of-the-way corner, absorbed in whatever he was reading. The whisky had dulled Jenny's sense of shock, and she was able to picture the attacker bending over Mr Sykes, then driving the needle through clothes, through skin, through flesh, straight into the heart. To keep pushing—that needed strength, but it needed something else too. *A terrible, implacable hatred.* Jenny shivered. The needle had been a *statement*. And so too had the scene.

'A top-up?' Neeta was asking.

'It was lovely, but I've had enough, thanks. Any more and I'll be falling asleep.'

'Why don't you stay and have supper with us? Just Jonty and me—Maisie's had her tea already. It's only a beany casserole but you're more than welcome.'

'That's really kind, Neeta, but I'm starting to feel absolutely exhausted. But don't worry—I can easily catch the bus from here.'

'No way—I'll get Jonty.'

They said goodbye on the doorstep.

'Ah well, library run tomorrow,' Neeta said, stifling a yawn.

'Would you like me to come with you?' Jenny asked, on impulse.

'Ohh, er—yes! That would be lovely. If you don't mind a bit of a tramp round town.'

'Not at all. It's about time I saw some more of it.'

'I'm at the health centre in the morning, but I'm free after lunch—meet you here about two?'

Afterwards, Jenny had a vague memory of climbing into Dr Biddle's car, and of him talking to her about this and that while she tried to make appropriate responses. In no time, it seemed—*had she actually nodded off?*—the car was gliding to a halt outside her own house, and she was scrambling out on to the pavement, murmuring, 'Good night! Thank you!' and delving in her pocket for her keys. It was dark—*when had that happened?*—and the chilly autumn air woke her up.

In the hall, she shrugged off her coat and hung it on its peg. Then she pushed open the door of the sitting room.

'Hello, darling,' she said. 'You wouldn't believe the sort of day *I've* had!'

CHAPTER 2

She had spoken to him nearly every day for well over thirty years. First thing in the morning, last thing at night. There was nothing she couldn't share with him, and she knew he felt the same way. There'd been difficult periods—her depression after Melanie was born, the time he was shot in the course of duty—but they'd come through them together. And then they had faced the greatest challenge of all: his diagnosis of pancreatic cancer. But they'd gone on talking, through the fear and the hope—which was almost worse than the fear—and the battery of hospital appointments and consultations. Eventually he fell quiet, as the drugs took hold, but she'd carried on speaking to him as she sat at his bedside, holding his hand. Although she'd seen one or two of the nurses shake their heads sadly, she knew that, at some deep level, he was still listening to her.

All those years together, all those memories ... Why should she stop now? Jenny paused in front of the silver-framed photo showing him in his uniform—Detective Chief Inspector Alan Meaden, recipient of the Queen's Commendation for Bravery. She reached into her pocket for a tissue to wipe away a spot on the glass, and as she withdrew her hand a folded piece of paper dropped to the floor. For a moment Jenny was puzzled, and then she remembered: it had been lying by Mr Sykes's chair, and it was only an instinct for tidiness that had led her to pick it up. She sat down at the table and smoothed out the paper—a half-page of newspaper, ragged at the edges. Should she have mentioned this to the police officers? Perhaps it wasn't too late: Sergeant McBride had said they might want to talk to her and the others again. Would he be annoyed? You weren't supposed to tamper with a crime scene. But she hadn't *known* it was a crime scene then ...

In the centre of the piece of paper was a crossword, nearly completed. Quite a wide margin had been torn around it. Jenny bent over it with interest; she enjoyed solving cryptic crosswords and allowed herself one or two a day in breaks from her work as a freelance editor. *Which newspaper did this come from?* she wondered. The *Guardian*, she concluded, recognizing the font. Mr Sykes had presumably been poring over the clues, so absorbed that he hadn't noticed his attacker approaching him. He'd done really well; there were only a few blank squares. Jenny felt a fresh wave of sadness for him. The nearly completed puzzle made him all too human, a person she could relate to.

The crossword page had been lying on the floor by Mr Sykes's chair—it must have slipped from the book he'd presumably been using as a rest. *But*—might there be another explanation? Jenny took a quick short breath. Perhaps the puzzle *wasn't* his—perhaps he really had been reading his book, and it had been dropped there by his attacker. On purpose? In which case, it might contain a hidden message. *No*, Jenny thought, *that's ridiculous*. Nevertheless, she scrutinized the grid even more closely, to see if the answers *were* as accurate as she'd taken them to be. They were. She also noted the name of the compiler: Tarantula. No way of knowing what he or she was really called—by convention, setters chose an alias. *Tarantula*—a poisonous spider. Jenny's brain was full of random facts, and she remembered that people had once thought that the bite of a tarantula made the victim start dancing madly and uncontrollably—a dance that came to be called a *tarantelle*.

She exhaled and laid her hands, palms down, on the table, either side of the newspaper page. 'I need you to tell me this is all rubbish, Alan,' she murmured under her breath.

Jenny suddenly realized that she was very hungry. A fish-finger sandwich! While the oven was heating up, she poured herself a large glass of white wine and stood by the counter sipping it. Despite all that had happened during the day, she didn't feel despondent. Curiously, she was brighter, more energized, than she'd been for some time. And tomorrow, there was the library trek with Neeta to look forward to! Once she'd finished her supper, though, tiredness swept over her again, and, after a warm, scented bath, she slept soundly for almost eight hours.

The *burr* of the central heating switching itself on woke Jenny up. As usual, she made herself tea and toast, and ate sitting at the table, the radio softly playing in the background. Then she carried her tea over to the French windows and stood looking out at the garden. She realized that she'd hardly been out in it since she'd moved in three months ago. Summer had gone by unnoticed, and now leaves were drifting from the trees into the long, uncut grass. She finished her tea, opened the doors, and stepped outside.

The grass, still wet with dew, brushed her trouser legs, and snail shells splintered under her feet, as she made her way to the end of the garden to the pair of old apple trees standing by the wooden fence that marked the boundary of her property. She'd known they were there —in fact, the enthusiastic estate agent had pointed them out specially —but she hadn't really *noticed* them before. Now she saw the apples had ripened. There were so many that a branch had broken under their weight; another was propped on an ancient wooden crutch. Fallen apples lay scattered here and there. Jenny picked one up. It was bruised and pocked with one or two scuzzy holes—*but*, she thought, *I could easily cut out the bad bits*. She walked back to the house, returned with a carrier bag, and spent the next ten minutes or so filling it.

In the kitchen, she tumbled the apples into the sink and turned the tap on them. While they were draining in a colander, she took down a few of her cookbooks and searched for recipes. Apple pie, of course, and apple crumble, but there were others she'd never tried before. *Parsnip and apple soup ... apple and ginger chutney ...* While Alan was alive, Jenny had loved cooking for the two of them, but since it had been just her, she'd stopped bothering about what she ate. *Ready meals, cheese on toast, eggs every which way ...* She felt a sudden urge to start cooking again, to fill the house with wonderful, warming aromas. Perhaps she'd start with a Dutch apple cake, and take it to the library to share with Neeta and Val ...

Now, how to spend the rest of the morning? She had work to do: a book about economics that she was proofreading on her computer. Jenny's career had been in publishing, her last full-time job as commissioning editor for a small academic press. She'd resigned from that when Alan needed her constant care, but she'd kept in touch with her colleagues, and now they regularly provided her with copy-editing and proofreading work. It wasn't terrifically well paid, but it was enjoyable, and well within her capabilities.

But Jenny found herself rebelling against the idea of sitting in front of a screen for a couple of hours, closed off from all that was happening in the world outside. It was far too early to go and meet Neeta, but she could get a bus to the town centre, walk around, look at the shops, people-watch, have a coffee ...

Kerston High Street was bustling with shoppers. A man was playing a banjo—rather badly—outside Specsavers, and Jenny smiled at him and dropped a few coins into his hat. The library doors were locked, and an elderly couple were standing reading the notice taped to them: CLOSED UNTIL FURTHER NOTICE.

'Well,' the woman said crossly, 'I'd like to know what we pay our taxes for.'

There was no quick answer to that.

Jenny bought herself a sandwich and a carton of juice, made her way to the riverside path, and found a seat. Sunlight gleamed on the water and a flotilla of ducks (drakes—they always seemed to hang out in gangs) drifted past. She and Alan had often driven to the Cotswold town of Kerston from their North London home. It wasn't such a tourist hotspot as places like Burford and Castle Combe, but in their eyes it was just as attractive, with its rows of honey-coloured houses and cottages, its Norman church, the old arched bridge over the river. And the High Street—the main shopping street—still had a number of independent shops wedged between the inevitable chain stores. Yes, they'd decided, this would be the perfect place to retire, close to glorious countryside but not too far from their daughter Melanie in Isleworth.

After Alan died—four years ago now—Jenny had often thought about Kerston. Even more once she began to emerge from the fog of grief. She was fond of their London home, but she had never been a city person. She started browsing websites for houses in the area—she liked some of them very much but never took things any further. And then Melanie happened to be looking over her shoulder as she studied the description of a three-bedroomed cottage—tiled roof, that lovely stone, 'a delightful garden'.

'Right, Mum,' her daughter had declared. 'We're going there this weekend. We'll check out houses on the Saturday—I'll make an appointment to view this one—stay in a hotel overnight, and have a fantastic dinner. And raise our glasses to Dad!'

Melanie had always been decisive, energetic, focused. *More like Alan than me*, Jenny had often thought. She worked as a history lecturer at her local further education college. After she left university, she had married Paul, who had been her tutor, but that marriage only lasted a couple of years. Melanie had been mortified when she'd discovered his affair with an even younger student, and Jenny thought her feelings of anger and shame stamped out any remaining sparks of affection. *How could I have been such an idiot, Mum?* Jenny herself had never liked Paul—and neither had Alan. Too full of himself, with an air of tolerant condescension when he spoke to you. And absolutely no sense of humour.

After the Kerston trip, Jenny found herself making an offer for the dream cottage. Then things moved fast: her offer was accepted, she put her own house on the market, arranged viewings with an estate agent. Before she knew it, she was packing books into boxes, wrestling with the yards and yards of bubble wrap the removals firm had supplied.

Had she made the right decision? She asked Melanie that as they stood in the now-empty kitchen on their final evening there. Melanie was going to stay with her in the cottage for a few days to help her unpack and 'settle in'.

'Of course you have, Mum! You're going to a place where you and Dad were happy together, and you're taking him with you.'

Yes. She'd never have trusted Alan's framed photo to the removal van; it was safe in her shoulder bag. It would be the first thing she'd set up in her new home.

When Alan and Jenny had talked about moving to Kerston, they'd started to make a list of all the things they'd do there: the walks they'd take, the stately homes—and the pubs!—they'd visit. Now Jenny was free to do all those things. Her editing work wasn't so demanding that she couldn't take a day or two off. Yet she found that she didn't want to—in fact, in those first few weeks, she only left the house to walk to the supermarket. Instead, she closeted herself with her work, taking comfort in its regular, undemanding routine. It was the sobering realization that she was in danger of becoming a recluse that led her to volunteer in the library after she'd seen an article in the local newspaper asking for helpers. Chatting with Valerie, answering queries from borrowers—it was a step out into the world again.

It was time to go and meet Neeta. Jenny crumpled her sandwich wrapper and juice carton, dropped them in a bin, and retraced the walk she'd taken yesterday. As she arrived at Neeta's house, Neeta emerged, pulling her tartan shopper behind her. They set off down the road together.

'I sometimes take the car if the weather's not looking too bright,' Neeta said. 'But I walk if I can—it's good exercise. Have you been living in Kerston long, Jenny?'

And Jenny found herself telling Neeta about their plans to retire here, about Alan's illness ...

Neeta stopped, and laid her hand on Jenny's. 'I'm so sorry, Jenny. Cancer is a horrid, horrid thing. I won't say any more, but you are very brave, you know, to take up your life in a new place.'

They walked on in silence for a little while.

'Mrs Pycroft first,' Neeta said. 'I hope she likes what I've chosen for her—she's very particular.'

'What does she like?'

'It's more a question of what she *doesn't* like. I have to choose detective stories—murder mysteries—but they absolutely mustn't have any bad language. Last time, she told me one of the books had four buggers and six f-words—she was very offended.'

'She must have read to the end, though,' Jenny said. 'To count the buggers.'

'Yes, she must,' Neeta said, and started giggling. 'Anyway, here we are. I don't see how she can possibly object to these.' She removed a couple of books from the shopper. *Kittens, Cupcakes and Murder*, Jenny read. The smug-looking kittens were clustered round a tea table, gazing at a pyramid of iced cakes. The other book was titled *Adolphus Works It Out* and was No. 7 in the series *Adolphus: Dog Detective*. Jenny wondered if it would interest Maisie.

'He looks constipated, doesn't he?' Neeta commented.

Jenny thought that Adolphus, a morose dachshund, had good reason to be annoyed by the wire-rimmed spectacles someone had balanced on the end of his nose.

Mrs Pycroft opened the door, leaning heavily on a stick. She was in her late seventies or her eighties, Jenny thought, with severely cut grey hair, a receding chin, and bottle-glass spectacles.

She examined the books suspiciously, staring particularly hard at Adolphus.

'Are you sure this isn't for *children*, Neeta?'

'Oh no, it was in the adult section—crime and thrillers. Why don't you try it? I can always find something different if you don't like it.'

'Ah well, I suppose it can't be worse than the last one.' Mrs Pycroft sighed, accepted the books from Neeta, and toddled back down her hallway to fetch the ones she was returning.

'Thank goodness they're not all like her,' Neeta whispered after they had said their goodbyes and were heading off down the road.

'Perhaps you could persuade her to try some of the classic detective novels,' Jenny said. 'I expect she's read all the Agatha Christies and Ngaio Marshes and Margery Allinghams, but lots of other writers—from the forties and fifties, say—are having their works reprinted. I can send you some suggestions.'

'Thanks Jenny, That's a really good idea. After all, you don't get Sherlock Holmes saying "Oh, sod it, my dear Watson", do you?'

No, you don't! Neeta's wayward historical sense added to the fun, Jenny thought, as she laughed along with her.

The next two deliveries were to Mrs Grundy, who was overweight, with swollen legs, and favoured books about animals, including a series set in a vet's practice, and Mr Nettles, a jolly old man in a wheelchair, who welcomed the ravening monster book with open arms.

'Ah, Neeta, you're a treasure, you are! This one looks like it's going to be a cracker!'

'So,' Neeta said, manoeuvring the shopper back on to the pavement, 'there's just Mrs Scrivens to go.'

Mrs Scrivens's home was a modern brick bungalow—a short, paved path led up from the road to her front door. Several things caught Jenny's attention. First, a police car was parked outside the house opposite. Second, a wooden board propped in the front garden announced *EGGS FOR SALE* in wonky writing with a blobby picture of a hen painted above it. And third, they were being watched—a pair of binoculars in the front window swivelled as they walked up the path.

Neeta thumped on the front door with her fist, then bent down and shouted through the letterbox, 'Yoohoo Ruby, it's me!'

'She's seen us anyway,' she whispered to Jenny, and then, as shuffling footsteps approached, '*Don't buy any eggs from her!*'

Before Jenny could ask why not, the door was pulled open and Mrs Scrivens—Ruby—appeared. She was an imposing figure, nearly six foot tall, with a lined brown face and close-cropped white curls. She wore a summer dress printed with gaudy flowers, and an emerald-green cardigan, and on her feet were a huge pair of hairy slippers studded with pretend toenails.

'Come in, come in!' Ruby Scrivens led the way slowly to her front room, the site of her observation post.

'This is my friend Jenny,' Neeta said. 'She's helping me with the deliveries today.'

'I am so pleased to meet you, Jenny! Any friend of Neeta's is a friend of mine. You like me Yeti feet?'

'They look very comfy,' Jenny said.

'Ah, I'm all for comfort at my age. That is all I need. Well, that and sex, of course.' She snorted with laughter as Neeta tutted. '*Ruby!* Behave yourself!'

'There is nothing wrong with sex,' Ruby continued. 'It is natural. After all, I still have me *juice*.'

'That is *way* too much information, Ruby. Here are your ...' Neeta broke off as Ruby turned her back on them, hobbled to her seat at the window, and lifted her binoculars.

'What on earth are you looking at now? The police car?'

'*Mm h'm*. Waiting to see them drag him out. In handcuffs, I expect.'

'*Who?*'

'Old fella across the road. Mr Sour-Puss Sykes.'

Neeta and Jenny exchanged glances.

'You won't be seeing *that*, Ruby. Mr Sykes is dead.'

'*Dead?* I must tell 'em. *Heyyy!*' She leaned forward, rapped on the window, and waved her arms about.

'*No*, Ruby,' Neeta said. 'The police know that already. I expect they've gone into his house looking for clues. Did he live by himself?'

'Course he did. No one want to marry *him*.' Ruby turned towards Neeta and her eyes narrowed. 'You said *clues*. Someone *murder* him?'

'Well ... yes ... *but*,' Neeta went on as Ruby swivelled all the way round and folded her hands in her lap, looking up at her expectantly, 'we can't tell you any more than that. I'm sure you'll hear the full story soon.'

'Who tell me *that*?' Ruby wailed. 'Poor old lady, living on her own. Never a visitor from one day to the next—well, *hardly* any,' she added, as she caught Neeta's eye.

'I expect it will be on the local news,' Neeta said briskly. 'And in the local paper. I know you can make it down the road to the corner shop. Now then, let's see what books we have for you.' She unloaded a pile on to Ruby's table. Ruby picked up the top one, with its cover of beach-ball-bosomed lovelies. *And a couple of Darcy-style young men lurking behind a pillar*, Jenny now noticed.

'Ahh, Skye Savory! Me favourite author! You should read her too, Neeta. She don't stop at the bedroom door, you know!' She beamed at both of them. 'Now, let me just check on the murder scene.'

'It wasn't—' Jenny started, then broke off as Neeta laid a hand on her arm. They joined Ruby at the window. A police officer was standing by the door of his car, while his colleague had moved to the house next door to Mr Sykes's and was talking to a woman who had appeared at her garden gate. Jenny saw her raise a hand to her cheek in evident distress.

'That Mrs Wedderdale,' Ruby said. 'Well, she will be missing Mr Sykes for sure.'

'They've been neighbours a long time?'

'Oh yes, Jenny. A very long time. But she will miss him specially because they been having sex.'

'*Ruby!*' Neeta scolded. 'You shouldn't say things like that. Even if it's just to us.'

'Why not? It is true. She is in and out of that house like a jack-in-the-box. Or a cuckoo clock. Daytime, night-time. I seen it all. You think I should tell the police?'

'No, I don't,' Neeta said firmly. 'I'm sure they'll talk to her, and she'll explain things to them. Now, we must be getting on. I'll see you next week, Ruby.'

'Would you like some eggs? Fresh today.'

'No thank you—I have lots at home. And so does Jenny.'

'What's wrong with her eggs?' Jenny asked, once they were out of Ruby's earshot.

'Nothing's wrong with them. They're just very expensive.'

'Well, if they're free-range, it's OK for her to charge a premium, isn't it? She has feed to buy, and so on.'

'Jenny,' Neeta said, halting with the shopper at the end of Ruby's path, 'did you hear the merry cluck-cluck-cluck of chickens while we were talking in there?'

'No, but ...'

'That's because there *are* no chickens. She gets eggs delivered from Aldi or Tesco's—whichever's the cheapest—puts them in plain boxes and charges double the price. Tourists get taken in—the rest of us are wise to her.'

'Goodness! Isn't she breaking the law?'

'Apparently not. Her notice doesn't say anything about the eggs being *organic*, or *free-range*. People just *assume* that.'

Jenny laughed. There was more to life in Kerston than she'd ever have imagined. Opposite them, the police car was moving off, but Mrs Wedderdale stood frozen at her gate, staring into the distance, evidently at a loss.

'Let's go and have a word,' Neeta said. 'We can offer our condolences about Mr Sykes.'

'You don't think ...?'

'No, of course not. As you probably noticed, Ruby has sex on the brain.'

From a distance, Jenny thought Mrs Wedderdale could have passed for fifty. But once they got close, she could see the tired lines radiating from her eyes, the slack skin beneath her chin. She was wearing a white blouse with a pie-crust collar adorned with a cameo brooch, a pale pink angora cardigan, and a pleated skirt. Her hair was determinedly blonde, sprayed and backcombed to increase its volume, with the ends flicked up. *Seventies?* She turned to gaze at Neeta and Jenny with a forlorn expression as they approached.

'Mrs Wedderdale?' Neeta held out her hand. 'I'm Neeta Biddle, and this is Jenny Meaden. We just wanted to say how sorry we were to hear about Mr Sykes. I gather you were ... good friends.'

'Oh—yes.' She held out a limp hand with coral-painted nails. 'The policeman just told me. Such a shock. I saw him only the other day, and he was fine.'

'Mrs Wedderdale,' Jenny said, 'it was me who found Mr Sykes. In the library. I'm afraid it looked as though someone had attacked him.'

'Yes, yes, they did say something ...' She seemed hopelessly vague, confused, but then she gave a little start and seemed to pull herself together. 'Oh, I do apologize. Where are my manners? Do come in. I can offer you tea?'

'That would be very kind,' Neeta said. 'We've been tramping round delivering library books, so a sit down would be lovely.'

They followed her up the path. At the front doorstep Mrs Wedderdale paused, and Jenny realized she was looking at the shopper.

'Would you mind terribly leaving it outside? It's just that I vacuumed the carpet this morning, and those wheels will have picked up ... I'm sure it will be quite safe, behind this bush.'

'No, that's fine,' Neeta said, and moved the shopper.

If anyone did steal it, Jenny thought, *they were going to be very disappointed—not to say surprised—at their haul of returned library books.*

Once they were inside, and standing on a deep-pile beige carpet, Mrs Wedderdale removed her shoes and placed them side by side against the wall. Neeta and Jenny obediently did the same, their trainers joining Mrs Wedderdale's patent leather sling-backs. Jenny had a sudden urge to giggle. She stole a glance at Neeta, which was a mistake. She muffled a snort in a tissue hastily pulled from her sleeve.

'Oh, bless you!' Mrs Wedderdale smiled at them. She seemed much more at ease in her own domain. 'Do come through.' She waved them into her sitting room, where they padded across more soft pastel carpet and seated themselves on a pale grey sofa. 'Now—Earl Grey or camomile?'

What Jenny really wanted was a good strong mug of builder's tea, but that didn't appear to be on offer.

'Earl Grey would be lovely,' she said, and Neeta nodded too.

'I will go and put the kettle on. Oh, I should have said—I'm Dorinda. But I am Dora to my friends, so do please call me that.'

Jenny gazed round the sitting room. It was, of course, spotlessly clean, and the scent of polish hung in the air. There were a few pictures on the walls—fairly anonymous countryside scenes—a standard lamp with a fringed shade, and a bowl of potpourri on top of a walnut bureau. Neeta nudged her.

'It's all very ... *clean*, isn't it? I suppose she was afraid we might have pulled the wheely-bug through some dog poo.'

After a few minutes, Mrs Wedderdale—*Dora*—reappeared, pushing a tea trolley, from which she dispensed cups of very weak Earl Grey tea. She also handed round plates and paper napkins, and a bone china cake stand, from which Jenny and Neeta helped themselves to malted-milk biscuits.

'I'm afraid these are shop-bought,' Dora said. 'I was about to start baking when the police arrived with their dreadful news.'

Her guests made sympathetic noises through mouths full of crumbs. Dora turned to Jenny.

'I believe you said it was you who found Avery? In the library?'

Avery! 'Yes,' Jenny said. She hoped very much that Dora wouldn't ask her for more details.

'He did love to go there,' Dora said fondly. 'To be surrounded by books. He was a very educated man, you know.'

'I do know, actually,' Neeta said. 'He was my English teacher, and I remember him well.'

'Oh yes, that's right. He'd been retired for a while, but he kept up all his ... intellectual pursuits. Crosswords and reading, and he did some tutoring too.'

'And you'd been friends for a long time?'

'Well, yes. We didn't live in each other's pockets—not at all—but I did go in and help him to, well, keep his house in order. Dusting, polishing, that kind of thing. You know what men are like'—she smiled confidingly at them—'not the slightest bit of sense in that department, and after my dear Frank passed, I had the time to spare. Time to be *neighbourly*.'

'I'm sorry to hear you lost your husband,' Jenny said, secretly wondering about the kind of life Frank had led in such a pristine environment. But perhaps it *wasn't* so pristine then ...

'Thank you, my dear. It's many years ago now, but I still *speak* to him. Say goodnight at the end of every day.'

Jenny must have flinched, because suddenly Dora's gaze sharpened.

'I can see that *you* know what I'm talking about, Jenny. We never forget them, do we?'

'No,' Jenny said, blinking hard. She felt trapped somehow, and angry, as if she'd been tricked into exposing something extremely personal. She was relieved when Neeta took up the conversation, chatting about anything and everything—the weather, her work at the health centre, the library run ...

'I know where the library is,' Dora said. 'In the shopping mall. But I have never been there.'

'Well, why don't you try it?' Neeta said. 'There's a very good selection of books, for all tastes. And if you have mobility issues, we can bring the books to you. Here's my card—it's my practice nurse one but it has my email and phone number. And this is a leaflet about the library, with information about the volunteers' scheme. It's Valerie Raeburn you need to contact about that—she's the library manager.'

Dora accepted the card and the leaflet, gazing at them curiously. And then they were saying their goodbyes, and Neeta was retrieving the shopper from its hiding place.

'Do call again, any time,' Dora said. 'I will always be so pleased to see you.'

'*Not likely*,' Neeta muttered as they made their escape. 'Are you OK, Jenny?'

'Yes, I'm fine.' Jenny smiled at her. 'Thanks for the distraction.'

'She was a bit *tactless*, wasn't she? Do you know, I think she's one of those people who *loves cleaning*.' Neeta made Dora sound like a member of some strange, exotic tribe. 'I watched a documentary about them once—it's a form of OCD. They're obsessed with germs, and they can't relax until they've scrubbed everything to within an inch of its life.'

'Poor Mr Sykes—Avery.'

'Yes, funny name, isn't it? I wonder if *Avery* had any say in the matter.'

'He could have locked his door, refused to let her in.'

'But he didn't. Perhaps he liked having his carpets vacuumed for free—because I'm betting he didn't pay her anything. All the same,' Neeta mused, 'I don't believe they were having an *affair*. She would just find that too *messy*. She was in and out to polish his furniture, not to have mad passionate sex.'

'On the bright side,' Jenny said, 'I don't think you'll have to add her to your library round. I didn't see any books at all on her shelves.'

'No, nor magazines. And, come to think of it, I didn't see a single photograph of *dear Frank*, either.'

They walked on in companionable silence, heading back towards Neeta's house.

'Let's go and have a *proper* drink,' Neeta said suddenly. 'I don't mean alcoholic, just a really good coffee. I need something after that awful piddly tea. Also, I know just the place.'

CHAPTER 3

Dani's Café was in a small parade of shops in a part of Kerston Jenny hadn't yet visited. Inside, it was brightly lit, with most of the tables occupied by chattering customers. On display, behind glass, was a tempting array of cakes and pastries, bright with jams and glazes, and the rich, enticing smell of freshly brewed coffee filled the air.

'*Neeta!*' The woman who emerged from behind the counter folded Neeta in a hug. She was in her early sixties Jenny thought, with short grey hair and rosy cheeks.

'*Dani!* Lovely to see you! This is my friend Jenny. We're both dying for a coffee—and perhaps something nice to nibble too.'

'Welcome Jenny!' Dani extended her hand—warm, creased, just how you'd expect a baker's hand to be. 'You choose whatever you like; I'll bring you coffee.'

'Now, Jenny,' Neeta said. 'This is on me. *No*, you're not allowed to protest. Everything is delicious, but I specially recommend the Polish apple cake. Or the Krakow cheesecake—that's unbelievably yummy.'

Jenny and Neeta both chose the apple cake and seated themselves at a table in one of the quieter corners.

'Dani is Polish?' Jenny asked.

'Yes, her full name is Daniela. I went to school with her daughter, Hanna—in fact, she was my best friend. Hanna lives in Bournemouth now—she's married and she has two little boys—but we still keep in touch.'

The coffees arrived and a minute later the cakes, with a dusting of icing sugar and a piping of cream on top.

'My goodness, this is wonderful,' Jenny said. 'I can taste cinnamon, and perhaps some other spice ...'

'*Mmm*. You won't get Dani to give you the recipe though—it's her secret.'

The doorbell jangled. A man stood outside carrying a large cardboard box—evidently unloaded from the van that had drawn up, blocking half the pavement. Dani hurried to let him in.

'Mrs D. O'Keeffe?' Jenny heard him say, reading from the delivery document, and Dani nodded, taking the box and carrying it away, behind the counter. *She'd heard that name before ... when she was talking to Maisie ...*

'Neeta—Maisie talked about an Inspector O'Keeffe. Is he Dani's husband?'

'No—son. Mr O'Keeffe died in a road accident a long time ago.' Neeta's mouth was semi-full, and Jenny waited for her to say more, but she didn't seem inclined to.

Jenny reached into her pocket and took out the folded crossword page. It had become even scruffier. 'I haven't shown you this before, but I found it lying next to Mr Sykes in the library. I forgot about it when the police were talking to us.'

Neeta laid down her pastry fork and took a quick sip of coffee. She flattened the page with her hand and studied it carefully. 'I don't understand this at all. Do you think he's put in the right answers?'

'Yes, he'd nearly finished it.'

'Well, look at this clue: *Doctor stupidly cuts organ with piles*. What does that even *mean*? And why is the answer *plastic surgeon*?'

'It's a cryptic crossword,' Jenny said. 'Part of the clue is the definition of the word to enter, and the rest is a puzzle version of it that you have to untangle. Here, the definition is *doctor*—a plastic surgeon is a *doctor*—and then *stupidly* is a hint that the letters that follow will be jumbled up—an anagram. So, if you take the letters in *cuts*, *organ*, and *piles* and re-mix them, you get *plastic surgeon*.'

'Wow! Are you thinking the crossword as a whole is some sort of *clue*?'

'Well, I did wonder. But I can't see how that would work. If it was a message to Mr Sykes, it would mean the setter—Tarantula —was involved. But there are heaps of easier ways of passing on information. I'm afraid I just make things more complicated than they need to be—it's a bad habit of mine.'

'No, Jenny,' Neeta said. 'Your instincts are right. This *is* a clue.'

'But how ...?'

'This is from one of the newspapers Val provides for readers. There's a rack of them by the issues desk. For some time now, she's been getting complaints that someone's been tearing pages out, but so far she hasn't been able to identify the culprit. Well, it was Mr Sykes! No wonder he hid away in his corner.'

'How is that a *clue*, though?'

'Jenny, I have seen enough on TV, I have read enough whodunits to know that, in cases of murder, the character of the victim is very often key. And now we know more about Mr Sykes. He was *mean*—why couldn't he buy his own paper? *And* he was extremely inconsiderate.'

All true, Jenny thought. *But lots of people are mean or inconsiderate, and they don't end up getting themselves stabbed with a knitting needle.*

'Jenny,' Neeta went on with a sly sideways glance at her, 'wouldn't you like to find out more about him? About *Avery*?'

'Well, I suppose so, yes. But how are we going to do that?'

'We can go round to his house. *Tonight!*'

'Neeta, are you suggesting we *break in*?'

'Oh no, that would be against the law. We can creep down the side passage and take a look at his garden—you can tell a lot about people from their *gardens*. And sneak a peek through his windows. The ones on the ground floor,' she added hastily. 'I bet they're really clean, what with Dora swooshing Windolene all over them.' And then, when Jenny still looked dubious, 'Oh, come on! It will be *fun*!'

Afterwards, Jenny was not quite sure why she'd said 'yes'. It had something to do with enjoying her new friend's company, wanting them to go on doing things together. Also—although she found this harder to admit—she had started to realize that she was deeply cautious by nature: someone who would always choose the safer option. The tamer one. Here was a chance to break out of that mindset and do something that was truly adventurous. Truly *daft*, to put it plainly!

'I'll pick you up at 8,' Neeta said. 'We'll wear dark clothes—although I don't think we actually need *masks*. That would be very suspicious if someone happened to spot us.'

'What are you going to tell Jonty?'

'Oh, that I'm meeting you. He'll think we're going out for a drink somewhere.' Neeta looked a touch shamefaced, Jenny thought. 'I can own up later,' she added.

Neeta parked round the corner from Mr Sykes's house. After they'd scrambled out of the car, she and Jenny stood and looked each other up and down, and Jenny fought an urge to giggle. What on earth were they doing—two thoroughly respectable, middle-aged women—prowling the mean streets of Kerston, kitted out like burglars?

'Did you bring a torch?' Neeta hissed, and Jenny nodded, pulling her black beanie down over her fair-and-greyish hair.

'Right,' Neeta continued, 'we don't want Ruby spotting us, so we'll go along the back alley and through the gate into his garden. I just hope he didn't lock it—I don't fancy having to climb over his fence.'

Jenny didn't fancy it either.

Neeta shone her torch down the alley. It was lined with bins, some with angled lids squashing down rubbish. Jenny thought they looked strangely sinister in the darkness. *Like Daleks.* The alley was gravelled, but lanky weeds had sprung up here and there. Suddenly, there was an unearthly yowl, and the two women clutched one another.

'Oh, it's just a cat,' Neeta breathed, bending to pick up her dropped torch. Jenny caught a glimpse of a lithe form leaping up one of the fences and heard the *tack* of its claws on the wood.

'Now then. Which house is Mr Sykes's?' Neeta swung the torch to and fro. 'He's number 28 and I reckon he must be about six houses in.'

The trouble was that there were no numbers on the back gates. 'Bother it,' Neeta said. 'Do we have to go back down the road and count?'

'That would be safest,' Jenny said. 'If Ruby's at her window, her light will be on, and we can just walk straight past, without stopping, and then return a few minutes later.'

'Too much of a faff,' Neeta grumbled. 'Let me think ... Yes, you've just given me an idea. Most people will still be awake—it's not *that* late—but there won't be anyone in Mr Sykes's, since he lived by himself. So, we search for a *dark* house. In fact—look! There are rooms lit either side of this one, *and* it's in the right place. Roughly speaking.'

Jenny couldn't help thinking that Neeta's plan was not exactly foolproof. *Excuses for being caught in someone's else's garden in the middle of the night ... Looking for a lost cat?* However, Neeta had already clicked the latch and was holding the gate open for her.

They walked up the garden towards the back door of the house.

'I don't think Dora has been at work here,' Neeta said. The

grass was long and uncut and spattered with fallen leaves. The few flowers in the borders were straggly, uncared-for.

At the door, Neeta stood on tiptoe and directed the beam of her torch through the window.

'Kitchen,' she said. 'Very clean and tidy. Just as you might expect.'

As she stepped back to let Jenny take a look, her foot caught on something that fell over with a *clunk*. '*Bugger!* What was that?' Jenny shone her torch on a pottery gnome. Its bearded head had come off and was still rolling to and fro.

'*Aaargh!* I have killed Grumpy.'

Jenny picked up the gnome's body. There, taped in place where the head had been, was a door key. She and Neeta stared at one another. Then ...

'Neeta—we *mustn't*. It really would be breaking the law. And we're not even certain this *is* Mr Sykes's house.'

Neeta said nothing, but smiled serenely, extracted the key, and slid it into the lock. It turned smoothly.

'I don't think we'll find much in the kitchen,' she whispered once they were both inside. 'Let's look in the other rooms.'

Sweeping her torch beam ahead of her, she walked through the kitchen into the hall and picked up a couple of envelopes that were lying on the mat by the front door.

'Addressed to Mr A. A. Sykes. We *are* in the right place.'

Unlike Dora's house next door, the two rooms leading off the hallway had been knocked through to create a spacious living area, with a dining table at one end, a sofa and a couple of armchairs at the other. A further difference was the profusion of books—shelves along the walls were crammed tight, and more books were piled haphazardly on the low coffee table.

'Very un-neat. Dora can't have liked *this*,' Neeta commented.

'I expect he didn't allow her to touch them.' Jenny moved over to the shelves and played her torch over the titles. She was curious about Mr Sykes's taste in reading matter. By and large it was what you would expect of a retired English teacher—all the classics: Thackeray, Trollope, the Brontës, Jane Austen, George Eliot, a complete leather-bound set of Dickens. There were also nature books—guides to birds and butterflies, wildflowers and mosses—and a number of paperback whodunits. Jenny felt a pang—there was something painfully intimate about seeing what he had liked. As though she was standing at his shoulder, watching him turn the pages as he relaxed in his armchair—the one with the reading light poised above it.

But not everything was predictable. 'Look here, Neeta,' Jenny called, and Neeta, who had been lifting the cushions on the sofa and peering underneath them, came to see what she had found.

It was a row of raunchy romances. Jenny pulled one out—the cover showed a ringleted young woman smiling coyly as she lifted a flounce of petticoats to display her lace-gartered legs, spread wide apart.

'Wowee!' Neeta said. 'Well, we shouldn't point the finger. Each to his own. Hey—this one is by Skye Savory. You remember—Ruby's favourite author. I wonder if they got together to compare notes.'

They both giggled.

'Did you find anything interesting?' Jenny asked.

Neeta shook her head. 'Nothing under the cushions. Not even a crumb. Which is very different to *our* house.'

Jenny swept the torch beam over the walls. There was not much space, because of the bookshelves, but a few black-and-white photographs were on display: artfully composed landscapes featuring tors on Dartmoor, a cascading waterfall, storm-tossed seagulls above churning waves. Striking, but rather impersonal—there were no people in any of them.

Her roving light picked out a framed photograph on top of a small desk—Arts and Crafts she thought, oak with inset stained-glass panels like boiled sweets. It was by far the nicest piece of furniture in the room. The picture showed a man holding a plaque and smiling. Some award or other? She peered more closely. Was it Mr Sykes—*Avery*? She hadn't really noticed his face in the library. The man in the photo appeared to be several years younger, and was quite nice-looking ... but there was something strange, unsettling about the image ...

Jenny's thoughts were cut short by the unmistakable sound of a key turning in the front door.

'Oh my God!' Neeta squealed. 'He's come back!' She grabbed Jenny's hand and pulled her towards the sofa. They scrambled behind it and crouched down, Jenny's breath throbbing painfully in her throat.

The door opened and someone came in. A torch beam moved slowly around, questing, probing. Jenny realized with a shock that Neeta had dropped her torch in panic, and its light was leaking out onto the carpet. And then a man's voice said, 'Stand up, please.' Neither of them did. The voice went on, 'Come on, Neeta. You can hide but you can't run.'

Neeta and Jenny rose slowly to their feet and stood holding on to the back of the sofa, blinking at the light that was directed into their eyes.

'For heaven's sake, Marek,' Neeta said, 'turn that torch *off*.'

The beam faded, and the electric light was switched on. Jenny saw a dark-haired young man—late twenties perhaps? He was scanning them with an amused expression.

'What are *you* doing here?' Neeta was still annoyed.

'Investigating a report of an intruder. A neighbour rang it in, and as it happened to be the house of a murder victim, I thought I'd come along.'

'And how did you know it was us—*me*?'

'Telepathy, Neeta. Though I did notice your car parked round the corner. Er, who is ...?'

'Jenny Meaden,' Jenny said.

'Address, please, Ms Meaden.' She recited it and he wrote it down in a notebook. He evidently knew Neeta's already.

'Back door was open, sir.' A uniformed officer had entered the room.

Marek raised his eyebrows and seemed about to say something when, once again, a key turned in the front door. He walked out into the hallway and Jenny heard him say, 'Detective Inspector Marek O'Keeffe. And who might you be?'

A flustered voice twittered something they couldn't catch, and then Marek reappeared, shepherding Dora Wedderdale in front of him. Jenny concluded it was she who'd reported them to the police.

Dora was wearing a voluminous fleecy cardigan (a *bedjacket?* Jenny wondered) over a long, flower-patterned nightdress. Her bouffant hairdo was sadly mussed. She was breathing quickly, tremblingly, and Marek hastily guided her to one of the armchairs. Jenny and Neeta took the opportunity to move to the front of the sofa and sit down on it.

'Are you all right, Mrs Wedderdale? A drink of water?' He gestured to the other officer, who disappeared into the kitchen.

'Thank you, sergeant.' Dora took the glass offered to her and sipped gratefully. 'I just want to make things clear. So you don't misunderstand. I thought I heard someone in the house—I live next door—so I asked my friends here if they wouldn't mind checking for me. I'm a widow living alone and I'm afraid I'm of a rather nervous disposition—and you do hear about so many burglaries nowadays ...'

Marek's glance flicked from Dora to Neeta and Jenny and back again.

'And you let them in through the back door?'

'Oh no, through the front door. Mr Sykes let me keep a key.'

'And these *friends*—they just happened to be passing your house?'

'Oh yes, they were. I saw them from my window. So fortunate!'

Marek stared hard at Neeta and Jenny. Then he sighed and

said, 'I haven't the slightest idea what's been happening here. And I don't have the patience to find out. I would like you all to leave —immediately. Sergeant Jenkins and I will lock up. Mrs Wedderdale, here is my card. If there are any more incidents of this kind, don't hesitate to contact me.'

They walked back through the house and out the kitchen door to avoid Ruby's scrutiny. Dora tripped along after them. Neeta turned to her. 'Well, Dora, you certainly saved our bacon there. That'll teach us to be so nosy.'

Dora gave a simpering smile. 'It was Mrs Scrivens over the road who rang the police. I saw her squinting through her binoculars and then reaching for her phone. They arrived very promptly, I must say. And when I saw it was *you*—well, I couldn't leave my friends in the lurch, could I? Or give that nosy old witch the satisfaction!' She pressed their hands, then tottered back down the hallway on heeled slippers with a pink fur trim.

Neeta said nothing as she drove Jenny back home. When the car came to a halt, she drew a deep breath. 'Why did it have to be Marek? He's never going to let me forget this.'

'If it had been someone else,' Jenny ventured, 'they might have taken it further. We could have been arrested.'

'For breaking and entering? But we didn't *break* anything— not even Grumpy. I must say, Dora came up trumps. That was quick thinking on her part. I suppose she wanted to get one over on Ruby. But I can't say I like the idea of being best buddies with her now.'

'I don't think she's going to *blackmail* us, Neeta,' Jenny said, trying to lighten the mood. And then, when Neeta still looked sulky, 'Marek seems very young to be a detective inspector.'

'He's thirty-two. Eight years younger than his sister. And me, for that matter. He was *the* most infuriating little brother. And he still is, in a lot of ways.'

'But good at his job?'

'Yes. Despite his *reputation*.'

'His reputation for what?'

'Hanna told me what his nickname is down at the station. *Lock-up.*'

'But if he has a good arrest record ...'

'I'm sure he does, but that's not it. No—it's Lock Up Your Daughters O'Keeffe.'

CHAPTER 4

Jenny made herself a mug of hot chocolate to take up to bed. After a moment's hesitation, she added a tot of whisky. The events of the day swirled around in her brain, and she knew there were one or two things she'd need to figure out properly in the morning. *Disturbing, puzzling things* ... She tried to focus on something soothing, relaxing, pictured herself walking down the garden, gathering apples from the grass and from the low branches of the trees. *She could take some to Dani ...*

She woke later than usual, feeling bleary and unrested. She was strongly tempted to turn over, curl up, and doze some more (*a top-up snooze*, Alan had called it), but she knew that if she did that, her rhythm would be broken and she'd find it all the harder to sleep that night.

She heaved herself out of bed, showered, dressed, and put the kettle on for coffee. She had started to slice bread for toast when her doorbell rang. Jenny quickly ran her fingers through her hair and went to answer it. Neeta? She'd said she'd come round after lunch, but perhaps she hadn't been needed at the health centre in the morning.

However, it was Marek O'Keeffe who stood on the doorstep.

Jenny stifled a gasp—and wished, at the same time, that she'd brushed her hair properly—but he smiled at her.

'May I come in, Ms Meaden?'

'Yes, of course,' she said, stepping aside.

'It's all right,' he said, taking a seat at her table. 'I'm not going to say anything about last night. I'm sure Neeta inveigled you into ... whatever it was she was up to.'

Which she did, Jenny thought. But she had gone along with it willingly. And it had been *fun*. Parts of it, at least.

'Would you like some coffee? I was just making a pot.'

'Can I be very fussy and have tea instead? I'm still full of my mum's breakfast brew.'

'Of course.' Jenny was secretly relieved her efforts weren't going to be compared with Dani's. She made the drinks and joined him at the table.

'The reason I've called on you, Ms Meaden,' Marek said, circling his teaspoon in his mug, although he hadn't taken any sugar, 'is that I'm investigating the death of Mr Sykes. I know you found the body, and gave a statement at the time, but sometimes people remember things after the event that could be of use to us. I'm very sorry to have to take you back to what must have been a very distressing experience ...'

'No,' Jenny said. 'It's all right. I'll try to help. Could you call me Jenny, by the way?'

'Of course. And I'm Marek. As Neeta calls me—when she's not calling me other things.'

He sat back and smiled at her. He really was strikingly good-looking—thick dark wavy hair, blue-grey eyes. He didn't have the action hero's carved profile—his features were gentler—but she sensed a sharp intelligence. It wouldn't be easy to fool him. Expressions flickered across his face: you could see that he was constantly reacting, taking things in, but you couldn't be quite sure what he was actually thinking. And he had that gift—rare, she'd found—of being absolutely in the moment, of concentrating on whoever he was talking to—as he was to her now.

'OK,' Marek said. 'Just take me through what you were doing, up to the time you found him.'

Jenny repeated what she had already told the other officers—shelving the books, hearing Valerie ring the closing bell, speaking to Mr Sykes, placing her hand on his shoulder, watching him tumble to the floor … She'd thought it would be a straightforward task, but by the end her voice had started to tremble. Marek, who had been jotting down the occasional note, reached across the table and grasped her hand firmly in his.

'Thank you, Jenny. Once again, I'm so sorry I have to put you through this. And—just to be clear—you'd never seen Mr Sykes in the library before?'

'No—but that doesn't mean he wasn't there. Valerie—Ms Raeburn—said he often came in and sat in the same place.' *I've been really unobservant*, Jenny thought. *Focused on my book trolley, not on any of the visitors.*

'And, has anything else come back to you? Even the slightest thing sometimes proves to be helpful.'

'Well …' Jenny got up and retrieved the crossword page, which she had parked between a couple of her books at the other end of the table. 'I found this on the floor next to the … next to him. It was before I realized … I think he must have dropped it.'

Marek studied the crossword, then looked up at her. 'It all helps build up a picture of Mr Sykes. He definitely liked doing crosswords—there was a book of them on his bedside table. I expect you know he was an English teacher. Actually, he taught me, briefly.'

Jenny wondered how Marek had got on with the reportedly sarcastic Mr Sykes. She imagined he'd been a livewire—cheeky, but not malicious. As if he'd been reading her thoughts, Marek said, 'I thought he was always picking on me, but, to be honest, I was just a badly behaved kid.' He pushed back his chair and stood up. 'Well, Jenny, thanks for the tea. Now I have to go and make an appeal for witnesses—someone's coming to the station to film me, and it'll go out on the local evening news. Meanwhile, I'll leave you my card—it's got my mobile number, and you can contact me any time.'

'I suppose you don't have any CCTV?'

'Not anything that's likely to be useful—there's none inside the library, and the entrance to it is in the shopping mall, as you know. We can check people going *into* the mall—dozens of them —but there's nothing to show which of them were visiting the library. My sergeant suggested checking on loans and books returned, but honestly, you're not going to stab someone and then calmly choose your next Agatha Christie.'

Marek smiled, turned towards the door, and then stopped in front of the framed photograph on the sideboard.

'This is your husband?'

Jenny nodded. 'Alan.'

'And the medal—the Queen's Commendation for Gallantry?'

'Yes. He was shot disarming a gunman.'

'You must be very proud of him. He's ... no longer with you?'

'No. He died a few years ago. From cancer.'

'I'm so very sorry.' His eyes met hers and held her gaze. *People hadn't known what to say to her*, Jenny thought to herself. *After the diagnosis, when it was 'palliative care only'. And they hadn't wanted to look at her—not properly, not in the face. Some had even crossed the road when they saw her coming. They didn't think she'd noticed—but she had.*

'Neeta told me your father died. In a traffic accident,' she said. 'I was very sorry to hear that.'

'He was murdered.' Marek's eyes were cold blue steel. Then he seemed to recover himself, to soften. 'He was knocked down by a hit-and-run driver. *Kind of* an accident—he was walking home from the pub late at night and there was no pavement; he was on the grass verge. On an unlit road. But he wasn't killed by the impact—if the driver had stopped, even just called an ambulance, he might have survived. That's unlawful killing, in my book.'

'And the driver was never identified?'

'No. He—if it *was* a man—hit a metal post after he'd injured my father and smashed a headlight. He also left some paint scrapings. Enough for a match if his car was ever found. But it wasn't. He needn't have been local; he could have driven off anywhere.'

'That must be so hard,' Jenny said. 'The not knowing.'

'It's better that way.' Jenny must have looked confused, because Marek added, 'What scares me is that I don't know what I'd do if I ever did find my dad's killer. I'm pretty sure I'd forget all about being a police officer.'

After Marek had left, Jenny sat at the table for a few minutes, simply absorbing what he had told her. Then she fetched a pad of paper and a pen and started to write down letters, repeating them, crossing them through, moving them around. *Yes! She'd had an inkling, but now she was sure ...*

Neeta appeared at about two o'clock. Jenny made them both coffee.

'Did you tell Jonty about last night?'

'*Mm.* As soon as I got back. He was really cross—and Jonty hardly ever loses his temper. He said I'd put us both in danger—that there was a murderer out there, and he could well have been keeping an eye on his victim's home. I didn't think that was likely, but I could understand how he felt.'

'In any case, we're not going to go there again, are we?'

'Er—no. Just look across the road, I suppose, when we call on Ruby again. I hope she didn't recognize us, by the way. I don't see how she could have done—we never turned round to face the window when the light was on. And Dora's not going to tell her.'

'Marek was here earlier,' Jenny said. 'No—not about last night'—because Neeta had visibly tensed—'he just wanted to see if I'd remembered anything else that happened in the library.'

'And did you?'

'No, nothing. He's recording an appeal—it'll be on the local news this evening.'

'*Hmph.* A lot of good *that* will do. If anyone saw anything useful, they'll have gone to the police by now. Unless they were the murderer, of course. *Or* their accomplice.'

That was a new angle, Jenny thought. If there were two people acting together, one of them could have created a distraction—drawn attention away from Mr Sykes in his corner. Because whoever stabbed him took an enormous risk ...

'Marek did a TV appeal about a street robbery a few months ago,' Neeta went on. 'Dani told me two people phoned in afterwards to ask if he was married.'

Jenny laughed. 'And is he?'

'No way! Why would he want a wife? He has the pick of the ladies of Kerston. And a mother who absolutely adores him and waits on him hand and foot—he has a flat above the café, on the top floor.'

A thoroughly spoilt young man, then? But Jenny knew there was more to him than that. She guessed that he was certainly aware of the effect he had on others, and not above using it to his own ends, but he was also intuitive, thoughtful. And there was the unhealed hurt of his father's death ...

'He mentioned the accident that killed his father. Hit and run. He called it murder, because the driver didn't even call an ambulance—if he *had*, Marek thought his father would have been OK.'

'I'm not sure about that,' Neeta said. 'It was a bitterly cold night, and Shaun O'Keeffe died from a combination of his injuries and hypothermia, as I remember it. So, yes, if the driver *had* stopped to help him ... Marek found his father's body—did he tell you?'

'Oh no! How awful for him! He must have been—just a boy.'

'He was twelve. Shaun hadn't come home after visiting the pub and Dani thought he'd just slept over there—he'd done that before. She sent Marek to go and fetch him. Afterwards, she blamed herself for that—said she should have gone herself, but Hanna was sick and running a temperature and she hadn't wanted to leave her. And Marek was keen to go—he was very close to his father.'

Jenny and Neeta sat in silence for a few moments. Then ...

'He went very wild after that,' Neeta said. 'Skipping school, getting into fights—Dani and Hanna were terribly worried about him. But one of the police officers who investigated the accident kept in touch with him and he was a really good influence. Marek calmed down, went to university, got a first-class honours degree, and after that he joined the police as a graduate entrant. He's done very well since then—Dani told me he's being interviewed for DCI soon.'

After another pause, Neeta added, 'I know I complain about him, Jenny, but I'm really very fond of him. I promised Hanna I'd look out for him after she left home—not that I've been able to do very much in that line. He's very good with Maisie—talks to her and explains things, which she loves. But—he's always known how to wind me up. Must be the Polish-plus-Irish mix—after all, they *are* the two craziest nations in the whole world.' (*Where did she get that idea?* Jenny wondered.) 'Anyway, do you reckon we found out anything useful last night?'

Jenny laid a sheet of plain paper on the table, and wrote:

AVERY SYKES
SKYE SAVORY

She turned the paper round and passed it across the table to Neeta, together with her pencil.

'OK,' Neeta said. 'What am I looking at here? Apart from the obvious?'

'Start crossing out the letters that match.'

Neeta picked up the pencil and started scratching.

'Ohh! I *see*. The names are *anagrams*. Like in the crossword.'

'Nearly. The *O* in Savory doesn't match the *E* in Sykes.'

'So perhaps it's just a coincidence. A very big one, though.'

Jenny thought of the Persian flaw—the tiny mistake, the hitch in the pattern, that carpet-makers would weave into their carpets, to show that they were only human, and that perfection belongs to God alone. She wouldn't be at all surprised if Avery Sykes had known about this ...

'I don't think it's a coincidence,' she said.

'So, what are we thinking?' Neeta asked. 'That Mr Sykes made up his name from the letters in Skye Savory's name—with one little mismatch? We know he liked reading her books—they were on his shelves. That would mean his real name was different altogether—and he wanted to keep it hidden. He was running from something—and his murderer tracked him down.'

'I think it's the other way round,' Jenny said. 'Having *Savery* with an *e* instead of *Savory* with an *o* would have been just a bit too obvious with the rhyme with Mr Sykes's first name. He loved puzzles, he wanted to tease. And *Savory* is a good name for a writer of sexy romances, as it also means *tasty*. With a *u*,' she heard herself add, pedantically. 'Avery Sykes *was* Skye Savory—he wrote all those books, under a penname.'

Neeta's eyes opened wide. 'Heavens! All those bouncing bosoms, and ... and ...'

'Yes!'

'But is that the *reason* he was killed? Was someone super-offended at all the sex? Which, according to Ruby, is pretty explicit.'

'It doesn't sound like much of a motive. There are masses of these steamy romances, so why pick him out?'

'Perhaps he wrote *about* somebody in one of the books? In disguise, but the person recognized himself. Or herself. He could have described them committing a crime, in a way that was dangerously close to something they really had done.'

'That's a *little* more probable. We need to tell Marek about this. If he hasn't already worked it out for himself.'

'I don't see how he could have. He didn't shine his torch over the shelves, only at us. And it was different officers we saw at the house earlier. OK, we tell Marek. And our investigation can run in parallel to his.'

'*What* investigation, Neeta?'

'Into Mr Avery Savory. Oh, come on, Jenny. Don't you want to know what happened?'

'Well, yes, I do,' Jenny said. 'But isn't it up to the police ...? They're not going to welcome us interfering.'

'We won't be interfering. Like I said, our enquiries will be running *parallel* to theirs. Parallel lines don't meet!'

'Neeta, I am not going back ...'

'No, no, no. Of course not. Although I'm sure Dora would let us in ... No, there are other angles we can investigate. We can find out more about Skye Savory and her—or should I say *his*?—books. There's probably a website. Also—and I've thought about this, and I reckon it's the best angle—we can look into the reason Mr Sykes left his teaching post. He was accused of touching up some of the girls—let's talk to those girls, the ones who made the accusations, and get the true story. He might have gone a lot further than *touching*, and someone could have wanted revenge for what he did then.'

'But Neeta, that all happened twenty years ago. Would someone have waited so long before killing him?'

'Well, who's to say he didn't *continue*? Sexual predators do tend to, I believe. It could have been a much more recent assault.'

'All right,' Jenny said. She felt she was being dragged at speed in the wake of Neeta's enthusiasm. Perhaps the responsible thing would be to go along with her, so she could put a brake on her madder schemes ... 'But how are we going to find those girls? And—shouldn't we tell Marek what we're doing?'

'Well, I already know who the girls were. I think I mentioned that my friend Angela's sister Libby was at the school then, and I rang her this morning—in between giving flu jabs—and she gave me their names. I couldn't trace one—she might have changed her name after getting married—but the other was Pat Brudenell. I actually know her quite well—she works in one of the High Street pharmacies. I vote we go and talk to her—tomorrow morning, say?'

'But what about telling Marek?'

'Marek will get to it another way. He'll look into Mr Sykes's history, and he'll find out about his hasty departure. Then he'll talk to anyone who taught there at the time, and that will put him on to the girls. We are really only cutting a corner. Parallel paths, you know!'

Although geometry had never been her strong point, Jenny was pretty sure you couldn't cut a corner and still be on a parallel path.

'Neeta, if those girls really were seriously abused by Mr Sykes —if *Pat* was—I'm not sure we have the right to bring it up again. She's bound to find it incredibly upsetting, and we're not qualified counsellors, or anything.'

'I do in fact have a counselling diploma,' Neeta said. 'But I appreciate what you're saying. I'm assuming the police will eventually get round to speaking to Pat and possibly the other girl as well, and we can start by simply alerting her to that. So it doesn't come as a shock, and she has time to compose herself. If she wants to say anything more to us, we will listen, obviously. But we won't put any pressure on her.'

'All right.' Neeta gave Jenny the address of the pharmacy, and they arranged to meet there at eleven o'clock. After she'd left, Jenny walked down the garden and collected a few more apples. This time, she looked more closely at the flowerbeds on either side of the lawn. The summer perennials had died back to blackened leaves and stiff stems, but the bronze head of a chrysanthemum nodded here and there. 'I'll wait and see just what's been planted,' Jenny said to herself, because it was plain someone had once laid out these beds and cared for them. She rubbed the leaves of a still-green bush between her fingers and sniffed. *Lemon balm!* She could add it to salads ...

Jenny re-entered her kitchen with a feeling of happy anticipation. She found the novel she was currently reading and settled in an armchair by her front window. A couple of chapters, and then she'd make herself tea. With lemon balm! She saw herself snipping the sharply fragrant leaves ... A minute or two later the book had slipped from her lap, and she was asleep.

She woke an hour later, disoriented at first, her mouth dry. Not really rested either. Outside, the light was changing, the autumn day drawing to its close. *There was just time to pick the lemon balm!*

She cut a handful and laid it on a worktop. She was still a little muzzy from her sleep, but she knew there was something she'd promised to do. The card Marek had left her was also on the worktop, and it jogged her memory—she had to tell him about Mr Sykes and Skye Savory. His email was on the card—that would be the best way. Then she also remembered that he would be on the local news, making his appeal for witnesses, so she turned her TV on and sat down to watch.

'As we reported earlier this week,' the newsreader began, 'on Monday, the body of a man was discovered in Kerston Library. The police are appealing for witnesses—over to Detective Inspector Marek O'Keeffe.'

Marek appeared. He'd changed into a suit and looked smart, handsome, professional. A police van in the background suggested he was standing in the station car park.

'Good evening. As you've heard, a man was found dead in Kerston Library, in the Northgate shopping centre, on Monday afternoon. He'd been the victim of an assault. If you visited the library at any time after two o'clock that day, please get in touch with the police. It's very important you do this, even if you don't think you saw anything useful. As ever, we rely on you to help us do our job. Thank you.' He recited a phone number, and it scrolled past at the foot of the screen.

Jenny climbed the stairs to her study and opened up her computer. First, she read an email from Valerie Raeburn: the library was reopening tomorrow, and Val would be 'glad to see her' then. Jenny replied to say that she had a commitment in the morning but would be there after lunch. Then:

Dear Marek

(*Get straight to the point!*)

While Neeta and I were in Mr Sykes's house yesterday (and I really am sorry about that), I saw he had a number of books written by an author called Skye Savory. That's a virtual anagram of his name, Avery Sykes, and I think it's likely he wrote them, under a penname. I don't know how useful that information is, but Neeta and I thought we should mention it.
 With best wishes,
 Jenny (Meaden)

Jenny paused. Had she said enough—or too much? She'd revealed that she and Neeta had gone on discussing the case, but surely that wouldn't surprise Marek? She *hadn't* said anything about their planned visit to Pat Brudenell tomorrow ... Before a twinge of guilt could waylay her, she pressed SEND. Now for a glass of wine, and an omelette with fresh herbs! And oven chips!

CHAPTER 5

After breakfast the next morning, Jenny searched for Skye Savory on her computer. She quickly found a Skye Savory website, with a cartoon of a pixie-faced girl with tumbling curls. *Skye Savory,* Jenny read, *loves to create sexy romances with super-hot heroes and heroines who just love to say YES!* There were enticing offers of 'exclusive content' for readers who followed the author. Jenny grinned. *If only they knew!*

Amazon revealed a long list of books published over the last twenty years or so. They were all of a kind, with titles like *A Duchess Undone, The Sins of Aurelia, The Wicked Captain*, and the covers showed women adorned in the standard Regency frills and flounces being ogled, snogged, or straightforwardly undressed by a succession of firm-jawed young men with brooding eyebrows. The books were certainly popular, each with a readership of thousands, and page after page of admiring, if sometimes badly spelled, comments: *Great fun and frolicks in Chatau Debochery* ... Jenny noted down the publisher's details. The samples on the Amazon website didn't include the author's Acknowledgements, which were probably at the end of the text. They'd be interesting to read and might include an agent's name.

She'd look at a library copy when she went in—provided they hadn't all been borrowed by Ruby.

The pharmacy where Pat Brudenell worked was on the High Street—not very far from the library. In the window was a large red glass flask, surrounded by random medications—bottles of Dettol, tubes of hand cream, foot cream, boxes of painkillers. Jenny thought there might be a special name for the flask, and was musing about this, as well as whether the glass itself was red or just the liquid inside it, when Neeta appeared beside her.

'*Right*,' Neeta said. 'I have my little speech worked out.'

A bell tinkled as they entered, reminding Jenny of Val and the library. The warning bell that had started everything off ... Neeta marched straight up to the counter.

'Hello, Pat, my dear. How are you today?'

Pat Brudenell looked up from the counter, where she had been sticking price tags on packets of cough sweets with a hand-held labeller. She was a heavy-set woman in her mid-to-late thirties, with a doughy, rather sulky face and brown hair scraped back from her forehead and clipped into place.

'Morning, Neeta. What can I do you for?'

'Well, I'll take some of those sweeties—they're very soothing when I get a frog in my throat. This is my friend Jenny, by the way.'

Pat regarded Jenny without any real interest and gave a slight nod.

'Now, Pat,' Neeta continued, 'I expect you've heard about this awful thing in the library. The man being found dead. We were there at the time—in fact, Jenny was the one who found his body.'

This time Jenny noted a spark of interest in Pat's pale blue eyes as she scanned her again.

'I did hear that, yes,' Pat said, laying down her labeller. 'There was an item on the news, and yesterday the police made an appeal for witnesses.'

'That's right! They didn't give out his name, which I guess is because they want to contact his family first. That seems to be taking them a long time—I mean, he died on Monday and it's now Thursday. He perhaps didn't have anyone close, which is very sad. Anyway, Pat, I recognized him. It was Mr Sykes, who used to teach us English.'

Pat gave a little gasp and blinked once or twice. 'Are you *sure* it was him?'

'I'm afraid so. Pat, the reason we've come here to tell you this is because the police will be looking into his background, to find a motive for his murder—because it *was* murder. They'll check his employment history, and they'll discover he left the school very suddenly, after some accusations were made. I think … I think that you … Oh dear—are you all right?'

For Pat had slumped forward, spreading her hands just in time to stop her head hitting the counter. Jenny and Neeta exchanged anxious glances. After a few moments, she pushed herself upright again and stared at them with bewildered eyes.

'I'm so sorry,' Neeta said. 'We just wanted to alert you. So it didn't come as a total shock.'

Pat brushed her palms over her cheeks. 'Can I talk to you?' she said in a hoarse voice.

'Yes, of course.' Neeta looked round as the bell gave another *ting*, and an elderly lady pushing a walking frame appeared in the doorway. 'After you've seen to customers.'

'I'll get Mandeep—he's checking stock.' Pat disappeared through a curtain drawn over an arch behind the counter and returned with a bearded young Sikh.

'Mandeep, would you mind just holding the fort for a while? I have to go and talk to these ladies.'

'Sure, no problem.'

Pat pulled her coat off a peg, shoved her arms into its sleeves, and led the way out of the door. On the pavement, she took a couple of deep breaths, as though the confines of the pharmacy had been constricting her lungs.

'Shall we go and have a coffee?' Neeta asked. 'There's a Costa just along here.'

Pat nodded.

Inside the Costa, Jenny and Pat slid on to cushioned leather seats in an alcove while Neeta ordered drinks: lattes for Jenny and herself, an espresso for Pat, who tore open packets and showered sugar in as soon as it was placed in front of her. She moved her spoon round and round, staring at the black liquid. Jenny wondered whether she needed a sympathetic prompt, but Pat stopped stirring and looked up at them.

'It was Zara Newton,' she said. 'It was Zara ... accused Mr Sykes. I just backed her up.'

'How do you mean, *backed her up*?' Neeta asked gently. 'Did you see—um ...'

'I didn't see anything. There wasn't anything *to* see.' Pat took a sip of her coffee.

'Pat, are you saying that Zara made a false accusation?'

Pat nodded. 'Mr Sykes was always on at her—talking in class, not handing in her homework, wearing make-up. Then one day, she had a date after school with a boy she was really keen on, but Mr Sykes put her in detention at the last minute, just for giving him cheek.'

'And she decided to get her own back?'

'She told our form tutor that he'd put his hand up her skirt, and ... I said I'd seen him do it.'

'But, *why* ...?' Jenny asked, although she already had an inkling of the reason. Zara, the rebel, the star delinquent, probably attracted others to her like moths to a flame. And Pat—plain, awkward—must have found her irresistible.

Pat sighed. 'I dunno. I've asked myself that loads of times. Zara was popular, and I wasn't. I guess it was a way of ... getting close to her. Afterwards, I wanted to tell the truth, but Zara said that if I did, we'd *both* be expelled, and I couldn't bear the thought of laying *that* on my mum.'

'So, what happened, Pat? Were the police involved?' Neeta laid her hand on Pat's.

'No. There was talk of it, but Zara started to scream and shout and said she'd kill herself if she had to talk to the police. I think she realized she'd gone too far, and the police would pull her story apart. She just wanted a way out. I was asked if Mr Sykes had ever *touched me inappropriately*, and I said he hadn't. Anyway, he left the school, and it all blew over.' Pat looked up, her gaze moving between Jenny and Neeta. There were tears in her eyes. 'I'm so sorry,' she choked.

'It's OK, Pat,' Neeta said, stroking her hand. 'We all remember how easy it is to be influenced at that age. Are you still in touch with Zara?'

Pat shook her head. 'No! She moved away—her father got a job up in Glasgow, and as far as I know she's still in Scotland. Will the police want to talk to her? Will they want to talk to *me*?'

'I think so,' Jenny said, smiling, and taking care to keep her voice low and gentle. 'They're trying to gather as much information as possible about Mr Sykes's life, so they'll find out that he left his teaching post under a cloud. You see, Pat, if you *don't* speak up and clear his name, they're going to head down the wrong path and start looking for more victims—women and girls he might have assaulted. And that will cost them time and effort.'

'We can come with you to the police,' Neeta added. 'I know the detective inspector who's in charge of the investigation, and he's really very approachable. He won't scold you for what happened all those years ago.'

Pat drew a deep breath and started to get to her feet.

'I'll do it. It's OK—you don't need to come with me. I'll go to the station as soon as the pharmacy closes.' She looked down at Jenny and Neeta and half smiled. 'It's a way of making things a little bit right, isn't it?'

They both nodded.

'*Whew!*' Neeta said after Pat had left them. 'We need to talk this over, don't we? Let's go to Dani's—it's practically lunch time and she does really nice sandwiches and wraps and stuff.'

'Sounds good,' Jenny said. 'And then I'm due back at the library—it's reopened today.'

'Do you feel OK about that? I mean, I'm sure Val could really do with your help, but ...'

'I'll be fine. And I thought I might see if there are any Skye Savory books on the shelves: I looked her—*him*—up on Amazon and he's published loads. And they've sold very well.'

'He must have made plenty of money then. So he had no reason at all to be snaffling a newspaper. Still, I suppose some people just have that meanness gene.'

Dani's Café was as warm and welcoming as before. It was only a few minutes after 12, so they had no difficulty finding seats. They had just ordered their sandwiches at the counter and had sat down again when the door opened and Marek came in. He was wearing a black raincoat and a long, multicoloured scarf was looped round his neck. Jenny was reminded of Tom Baker's in *Doctor Who*. He caught sight of them, smiled, and eased himself into one of the spare chairs at their table, unwinding his scarf as he did so.

'Aha! My two favourite housebreakers!'

Neeta glared at him, but he just grinned at her, his eyes sparkling with mischief. He was on home ground; he seemed to have put aside his professional dignity.

Dani walked over with their sandwiches. Then she ruffled Marek's hair. 'What would you like, darling?'

'Oh, anything, Mum. Just give me whatever you've got too much of.'

'I will make you your favourite—tuna with mayo.'

Once she'd retreated, he had the grace to look sheepish. 'I'm afraid she spoils me.'

'Yes, she does,' Neeta said decisively. 'Shouldn't you be at the police station? Interviewing all those library visitors?'

'Neeta, I have been doing that for the past three hours. Even police officers are allowed a break, you know.' Marek stretched and shrugged his shoulders.

'So, you had a good response to your appeal?' Jenny asked.

'Certainly a lot of people have come forward.'

'With absolutely nothing useful to say, I'm betting.' Neeta bit into her chicken and avocado sandwich.

'Ah, that's where you're wrong, Neeta. True, a lot of people didn't spot anything out of the ordinary—and didn't even notice Mr Sykes—but there were a couple of interesting sightings.' Apparently absentmindedly, he picked up one of Neeta's crisps and crunched it—then, when she made to slap his hand, 'It's OK, you can have some of mine!'

'Well, are you going to tell us? Or is it a big police secret?'

'No, it's not a secret. I'm going to have an identikit made up once I've gathered all the information. I just hope there'll be *more* of that this afternoon.'

'You don't have enough info already?'

'No. Identikits are useful because they show someone's *face*, and while they may not be particularly accurate, they can spark recognition in someone who knows the person. We have some details of age, sex, clothing, but that's all.'

'The person hid their face? Well, that's suspicious straightaway, isn't it?'

'Yes, *possibly*. I'll explain.'

Dani appeared with Marek's sandwich, and he scooped up a handful of crisps and transferred them to Neeta's plate.

'You have time for coffee, darling? And for Jenny and Neeta too. It is on the house!'

They all nodded eagerly.

'Two people', Marek said, 'saw an oldish, shortish man talking to Mr Sykes. I say *talking*, but they didn't hear anything. It's possible this person was speaking in a low voice, because they were in a library, or he may have been bending over Mr Sykes *as if* he were talking to him.'

'While he was actually *killing* him!' Neeta said. 'What did this person look like?'

'The witnesses said he wore olive green corduroy trousers, a bit long in the leg. Navy duffel coat, grey woollen beanie hat, spectacles. The frustrating thing is that they all say he was wearing a black face mask that covered the lower half of his face.'

'Everyone wore those masks during Covid,' Neeta said. 'And I've noticed a few people have kept on wearing them. Specially when they come into the surgery—I suppose they reckon there are lots of germs floating about in the waiting room.'

'Exactly,' Marek said. 'So, he may have been super risk-aware, or possibly someone with a special vulnerability that meant they needed to go on taking precautions. You'd know about that, Neeta?'

'Yes—there are a whole range of pre-existing health conditions that are associated with a poor outcome if the patient happens to contract Covid. Obesity, diabetes, chronic kidney disease, active cancer, receiving an organ transplant in the past … It would make sense for a person in one of those categories to carry on wearing a mask in public places. But, Marek, it *could* simply have been a disguise.'

'Yes, it could. I suppose neither of you recognizes even a part of the description?'

'Friday Fred wears a beanie,' Neeta said. '*And* spectacles. But I've never seen him in a duffel coat. Or olive cords.'

'Who is this Fred?' Marek reached for his notebook.

'Oh, he's an old gent who comes in every Friday, and sometimes other days too. Settles down and has a snooze next to the DVDs. I think he's just lonely—Val often invites him into the office for a cup of tea. And, of course, the library's warm, which is a godsend if you're struggling to pay your heating bills. He doesn't wear a face mask, though. It would be a good thing if he *did* put one on—he has breath that could strip paint. Oh, you don't need to bother about *him*,' Neeta added, as she saw Marek's pen hovering. 'He's very tall, over six foot, and he *shuffles*. Your witnesses would have noticed that.'

'Did they notice if this person was carrying anything?' Jenny asked.

'That's a good question,' Marek said. 'According to them, he was carrying a rucksack. Not on his back; he was holding it by a strap. So, a needle could have been concealed in there.' Dani delivered their coffees. 'Thanks Mum! I'm not sure when I'll be back tonight—I'll send you a text.'

'You work too hard, darling,' Dani said, ruffling his hair again. 'Whatever time, I will have your supper waiting.'

'The strangest thing is the *needle*,' Jenny said. 'Why not a knife? I suppose it makes us think a woman was the killer—which doesn't seem to have been the case.'

'That is definitely very odd,' Marek said. 'I've never come across one being used to attack someone before. The only reason I can think of is that a knitting needle isn't, on the face of it, an offensive weapon. It wouldn't arouse suspicion if you happened to be searched—in the way a knife would, for instance. Especially if it was one of a pair. It's also harder to retrieve prints from, as it doesn't present a flat surface, although this needle was absolutely clean, so perhaps the killer wore gloves. Oh, I should add that, although we're sure the victim was Mr Avery Sykes, retired schoolteacher, we haven't yet been able to arrange a formal identification. So, please, if you could keep his name to yourselves for now.'

'Can't Mrs Wedderdale do it?' Neeta asked. 'She lived next to him for ages.'

'We did ask her, but she almost passed out with shock and then she started hyperventilating. No point trying again—we didn't want *two* bodies on our hands. The house on the other side is full of students—they've only been there a couple of months, and they don't know any of their neighbours.'

'Could I do it?'

'Thanks for offering, Neeta, but we need somebody who was in touch with him recently. You hadn't seen him for more than twenty years—although full marks for recognizing him, of course.'

'And I suppose Ruby is too batty.'

'The lady with the eggs? I had a job escaping from her, I can tell you. But she does notice a lot of what's going on in the street. I'll send my sergeant to have a proper chat ... Oh, Jenny, thank you very much for your email about Mr Sykes's double life as an author. From a quick look on Amazon, his books seem to be quite —what's the word?'

'*Spicy! Salacious!*' Neeta and Jenny spoke at the same time.

'Mm, yes. Have you read any of them?'

'Of course not!' Neeta said. 'Not my sort of thing at all. Ruby has, though. She told us that Skye Savory is her favourite author.'

'Ah. That kind of removes Ms Scrivens from the suspects list, doesn't it? Which, I have to say, is pretty empty at the moment. And you don't kill someone for writing sexy novels. If you're on a clean-up-Kerston campaign, there are lots more obvious targets.'

Neeta lifted her eyebrows enquiringly, but Marek simply smiled at her. 'Well,' she said, 'it might not be the *fact* that Mr Sykes wrote those books—it might be something inside them. He could have described a crime being committed and based it on something that really happened. And given enough details for the person to be recognized.'

'H'm. It would have had to be a serious crime. And those books don't look to be big on murder. More about dukes getting their kit off, from what I can gather. Also, killing Mr Sykes wouldn't stop his stories circulating—if anything, it would give his sales a boost.'

'It might not be one of his published novels,' Jenny said. 'He could have been working on a new one and been murdered so he'd never finish it.'

'OK,' Marek said. 'That's certainly one line of enquiry—and we need all the help we can get. We have Mr Sykes's mobile and laptop, and our tech team are in the process of unlocking them. If he *was* working on his next masterpiece, the files will be on his computer. I'll get the search team to go back to his house and look for anything like a typescript, too. And I'll talk to his publisher. Presumably, he had an agent, and they might know more about his personal life—which is something of a closed book to us at present.'

'We've helped, haven't we?' Neeta asked.

'Yes, you certainly have. Even if you came by the information in a slightly dubious way. So, thank you, both. More crisps?'

'No. There's another thing we can help you with—not in the way of suspects, but we can stop you going down the wrong track. You know Mr Sykes left his teaching job very suddenly, about twenty years ago?'

'Yes. That, again, is something we're looking into.'

'Well, we can save you a lot of trouble. There were rumours at the time that he'd been asked to leave because he was ... behaving inappropriately with one of his students. But those rumours were entirely false—he *wasn't*.'

Jenny watched Marek's face. His expression changed—it was suddenly sterner, his blue-grey eyes colder.

'And you know this—how?'

'Jenny and I talked to one of the girls who made the accusation, and she admitted she'd told a lie. She said she'd seen Mr Sykes put his hand up the skirt of another girl, Zara Newton, but she'd only done it to be in with Zara, who was the queen bee, and a bit of a scamp, by all accounts.'

'You talked to someone who's a potential witness to an event in Mr Sykes's past? Neeta—*you* are not the detective here. It's up to the police to interview this woman, and the fact you've already been in touch with her may have compromised the investigation.'

'I don't see how, ' Neeta began, but he cut across her. 'Did you tell her any details? The method? I'm assuming you told her who the victim was.'

'Yes, I told her it was Mr Sykes. But I'm sure that's getting to be common knowledge. I didn't say anything about the knitting needle.'

'And how did you find her? What's her name?' Marek spread open a page of his notebook.

'She's called Pat Brudenell. I knew her already: she's the manager of a pharmacy on the High Street. I asked—er, I *talked* to someone who was in her class at the time. You remember I went to that school too, although I'd left by the time you started.'

'Yes—you and Hanna.' Marek seemed to relent a little.

'Pat was very upset, Marek,' Neeta went on. 'Very sorry for what she'd done. She's going to go to the station after she finishes work this afternoon and make a statement, so you'll see her there.'

Marek drew a deep breath and closed his eyes for a moment. 'OK. OK. We'll try to track down this Zara person too. But Neeta —no more playing detective. There is a murderer out there, and as we have no idea about motive, it's possible there might be further attacks. Take care—both of you.'

They nodded obediently. Marek finished the last of his coffee. 'Ah well. Time to dive back into the library interviews.' He stood up and lifted his raincoat and scarf from the back of his chair.

Then a new thought seemed to strike him. 'Do you really want to help in the investigation—Jenny, Neeta?'

'Of course we do,' Neeta said.

'Well then, there *is* something you can do.'

They looked up at him eagerly.

'You can read all of Mr Sykes's novels and tell me if there are any clues hidden there.'

'*Marek!* There are masses of them. It'll take ages.'

'It will keep you out of trouble then, won't it, Neeta?'

'Jenny and I will go and collect the books, but I can't promise ...'

'*Oh* no! You're not setting foot in that house again. I'll get an officer to pack them up and deliver them to you. Half each— that's fair, isn't it?'

He had his coat on and was looping his scarf round his neck.

He was suppressing a grin, possibly a laugh, and Jenny knew they'd been outmanoeuvred. 'Good afternoon, ladies.' He stopped at a table Dani was clearing, bent to kiss her on the cheek, and then disappeared out of the door.

'*Well!*' Neeta fumed, but Jenny caught her breath. Something that had been hidden in the recesses of her memory had suddenly surfaced.

'Neeta—Marek's scarf. Did Dani knit it for him?'

'Yes, she likes to knit, and I gave her some leftover wool once I'd finished knitting baby clothes for Maisie. She's not terribly good at it though, so a garter-stitch scarf is about all she can manage. You're not thinking that *Dani* ...?'

'Oh no, of course not. It's just that I've remembered what Mr Sykes was wearing. A sleeveless pullover. It was all different colours, like Marek's scarf. There was a photo in his house of a man holding some kind of award and wearing the same pullover. It must have been him—he looked younger, so quite a few years ago, probably. I felt a bit queasy when I saw the photo, because the last time I saw it, it had that patch of blood in the middle.'

'Interesting,' Neeta said. 'But maybe not significant. You're thinking that the pullover was special to him because he kept on wearing it for so long? But men are like that—they have favourites that they hang on to until they're falling apart. Jonty has a horrible old rugby shirt he wore at university—it's covered in stains and the moths have been at it, but he cries blue murder if I try to throw it out.'

'I'm sure the pullover had been hand-knitted, not bought from a shop. It had a rather odd pattern on it. And knitting something for someone to wear—isn't that a sign that you care for that person? Like Dani and Marek.'

'Now you mention it, the pattern *was* peculiar.' Neeta closed her eyes, trying to visualize it. 'It was like Fair Isle but *not* Fair Isle. There were rows of little figures that looked like Space Invaders. Or possibly spiders. And a row of llamas. With rather short legs—perhaps they were dachshunds.'

'I think it was a pattern the person made up,' Jenny said. 'I'm sure you wouldn't be able to buy it anywhere. I wonder if the design meant something to Mr Sykes. And to the knitter, of course.'

'Perhaps it was like those QR codes—you might be able to *scan* him with your phone and discover some vital information.'

They looked at each other and started laughing.

'There *is* a connection, though, isn't there?' Jenny said. 'Mr Sykes was stabbed with a knitting needle. And, several years ago, someone knitted something very personal for him.'

'A jilted knitter! But he was stabbed by a *man*.'

'We don't know that for sure. The man who was seen with him in the library might just have been talking to him—asking Mr Sykes if he'd mind removing his coat from the empty chair, for instance. Perhaps he'll be visiting the station this afternoon to explain that. Also, men knit too!'

'*Or* the knitter might have been devastated by Mr Sykes spurning them—even though he went on wearing the pullover they'd knitted,' Neeta said. 'And someone close to them could have decided to punish him for that. This is a good line, Jenny. And not one we're going to share with Marek.'

It was worrying that Neeta still seemed set on pursuing her rivalry with Marek, Jenny thought. But the knitting theory probably *was* too fanciful to bother him with. They said their goodbyes, and she made her way towards the library.

CHAPTER 6

The library was buzzing. Val and the two other members of staff on duty were looking decidedly harassed.

'Oh Jenny,' Val said, clasping her hand, 'thanks so much for coming in. You can see it's like bedlam in here. Obviously, I didn't say anything to people about where Mr Sykes's body was found, but they seem to have figured it out for themselves. Either that or there's a sudden interest in the Chemistry and Mechanical Engineering section.'

There was a gaggle of visitors over there, only half pretending to look at the shelves.

'I removed the chairs,' Val said. 'They're in the storeroom. Otherwise, I had a horrible feeling people would be sitting in them and posing for selfies. We've been inundated with questions, but of course we're all keeping shtum. I don't think we're even allowed to confirm that the victim was Mr Sykes.'

'That's right,' Jenny said. 'I've been told the same by the police. Apparently, they can't find anyone to formally identify him.'

'How sad,' Valerie mused. 'What a lonely person he must have been. Anyway, Jenny, perhaps make a start on shelving? The returns are in the trolley.'

As Jenny pushed the trolley along, it seemed incredible to her that it was only three days ago that she'd been doing exactly this. Since then, her world had been turned upside down. Her discovery of the body had been horrible, and the sight of that seeping, soaking blood, and the needle standing proud, still haunted her. But Val and Neeta had been so kind. And her new friendship with Neeta had taken her on a whirlwind ride—one that, she suspected, wasn't over yet. Her safe, uneventful life, with only her books and her work for company, was a thing of the past —and, to her surprise, she found that she actually liked waking up each morning not knowing exactly what the day would bring.

Jenny's hands resumed their familiar rhythm, lifting books from the trolley, settling them in place on the shelves. It was a bit like knitting, she thought: a task that engaged just a part of your brain, allowing the rest of it to muse, to daydream. She was suddenly aware that a man was standing watching her—had been, perhaps, for a while. *Not another rubbernecker!* She turned to him and said, a touch coldly, 'Can I help you?'

He shifted on his feet, uneasy. He was in his forties—tortoise-shell spectacles, receding fair hair, a fresh pink-and-white complexion.

'I'm sorry to disturb you,' he said, 'but the man who was found dead here ...'

'I'm afraid I can't say anything about that,' Jenny said briskly.

He stared at his feet, then took a long breath and lifted his eyes to meet hers.

'Was it Avery? Avery Sykes?'

'As I said,' Jenny began, but something in his face made her pause. He wasn't simply curious—he was *pleading* with her.

'Did you know him?' she continued, more gently. 'Is that why you're asking?'

He gulped, choked, a tear ran down his cheek. He took off his glasses to wipe it away.

'He was my fiancé. We were going to get married.'

'Oh *no*! I'm so sorry.' Jenny reached out and touched him on the arm. 'Wait a minute, wait just there. I'll find somewhere for us to talk.'

Val was arranging the Recommended Reads display. 'What do you think, Jenny? I thought we'd have a nature theme—squirrels and hedgehogs and things, all bright and happy. It didn't seem right to carry on with True Crime.'

'Val,' Jenny said, 'there's a man over there who says he's Mr Sykes's fiancé. He's very upset—I wondered if there was somewhere private we could go.'

'His *fiancé*? Oh, of course, Jenny. Poor man! Use the office—it's empty now, and I'll make sure no one interrupts you.'

'Colin Ingram,' the man said, once he was seated in one of the armchairs. Jenny introduced herself too. 'I had to come—I had a dreadful feeling it *was* him, but I needed to be sure. We'd arranged to meet on the Tuesday, but he didn't turn up, and when I tried ringing him, his phone just went to voicemail. And then I searched the South-West area news online and found this report ...'

'You don't live in Kerston?'

'No, in London. Chalk Farm. Avery would travel down on the train. I was hoping he'd invite me to his house here, but never seemed very keen.'

Too many nosy neighbours, Jenny thought to herself.

'Do you know ... how he died? I gather it was a suspicious death, as there was an appeal for witnesses.'

'He was stabbed,' Jenny said. Surely it was OK to reveal that, as she hadn't said *with what*? 'I'm sure he died very quickly,' she added. 'It was actually me who found him.'

Colin's eyes opened wide. 'Oh dear—that must have been a shock. I can't take it in, though. He was a lovely guy; he had no enemies at all. It must have been some random mad person.' His voice trembled, on the edge of breaking.

'Let me make us both some tea,' Jenny said, getting up, and he nodded.

When she had placed his mug in front of him, she asked, 'Had you known Avery long?'

'About five years.' *He was not the knitter, then.* 'We met in London—in Tate Britain, actually. We were at the Van Gogh exhibition, and we were both looking at the same picture—*Starry Night*, as a matter of fact—and we got talking. We *clicked*—just like that.'

'Can you tell me a little about him?' Jenny sensed it would help Colin to keep on talking, rather than relapsing into a grieving silence. 'He seems to have been quite a private person, although I do know that he loved reading. And crosswords.'

'Ah yes, his blessed crosswords! I used to tease him about those. He was really very clever—much cleverer than me. And you're right: he was private—reserved. He was sometimes a bit of a grump, and he had his little foibles. He could be very generous —especially to me—but he hated shelling out money unnecessarily. He used to get me to drive up and down the streets looking for a free parking spot rather than pay in a car park, and if he saw a coin on the pavement—a 5p, for instance—he could never resist picking it up. *Germs, Avery!* I said, but he just laughed.'

That would explain the library newspapers, Jenny thought.

'But underneath it all,' Colin continued, 'he was a lovely, lovely man.' He sniffled again and reached for a tissue.

'He was an author too, wasn't he?' Jenny said tentatively, hoping that Avery Sykes hadn't concealed his writing career from his lover.

Colin laughed fondly. 'Oh, his *romances*! Have you read any of them?' Jenny shook her head. 'They're rather naughty—a bit X-certificate. He wrote the first one just for a laugh, but when he sent it to an agent, they went wild over it and got him a publishing contract. Then, of course, he had to go on writing more. He actually made a lot of money from them.'

'And he wrote as Skye Savory? I do think that's a brilliant penname.'

'Yes, it's an anagram, of course. All his readers thought he was this sexy young thing—his agent would pass on their messages, and we'd have a good laugh about them.'

'Colin,' Jenny said gently, leaning forward, 'I'm afraid so far, the police haven't found anyone to identify Avery. Did he have any family?'

'No—his parents died a while back, and he was an only child. I believe there are some cousins in Canada, but he was never close to them. Does that mean that I ... that I ...?'

'I think you should talk to the police first. I can ring them, if you like—I know the detective inspector who's in charge of the case.'

Colin nodded and sat back, which was Jenny's cue to take out her phone. She rang Marek's number, expecting it to go straight to voicemail, but he answered promptly.

'Marek, I'm in the library, and we've had a visitor called Colin Ingram, who knows Avery Sykes—in fact, he was engaged to be married to him. I'm sure you'd like to talk to him—can I bring him round?'

'Of course! You know where the station is—about ten minutes' walk from where you are?'

Jenny thought she'd passed it but checked with Val before leaving.

'Did you come on the train?' she asked Colin as they set off down the High Street.

'No, I drove. My car's parked at Waitrose.'

Otherwise, he offered no conversation—probably gathering his strength for what would be a painful interview, Jenny concluded.

Inside the police station, Marek was standing by the front desk. He smiled and extended his hand to Colin.

'Mr Ingram—many thanks for coming in. I'm Detective Inspector Marek O'Keeffe and I'm the senior investigating officer.

May I ask you to show me some ID first? ... OK, that's fine,' when Colin produced a driving licence. 'Now, may I take a look at your phone? I'm assuming that you and Mr Sykes texted one another —I'm not at all concerned with the content of those messages, it's just extra confirmation.'

Colin meekly handed over his mobile, unlocked.

'Fine. Let's find somewhere to talk. Jenny—thank you again. You're free to go, of course.'

Colin cast her a forlorn look. 'It's OK,' Jenny said. 'I'll wait.'

'It could be a while. Give me your phone number and I'll text you when we're through.'

Jenny didn't want to go back to the library, so she spent the next half hour or so wandering round the shops, returning to the station when her phone pinged with the message '*All done*'.

Colin was leaning against the front desk, looking wan and tearful.

'I've told Mr Ingram,' Marek said, 'that in all likelihood the body *is* that of Avery Sykes. We'll conduct a formal ID tomorrow, 10 o'clock. Mr Ingram wondered ... whether ...'

'It's OK,' Jenny said. 'I'll come with him.'

'That's good of you, Jenny. The mortuary is in the basement of Syrenham General—they'll give you directions at Reception.' He shook hands again with Colin and touched his arm gently. 'I'm sorry. I truly am.'

Colin nodded. He seemed dazed, unfocused. Marek steered Jenny aside. 'Is he going back to London now? I'm worried about him driving safely.'

'No, don't worry,' Jenny said. 'I'll make sure he's OK.'

'Thanks.' Marek was obviously tired—Jenny imagined he was looking forward to going home and being cosseted by his mother. 'I still have Pat Brudenell to see,' he continued. 'Perhaps it would simplify my life if I just handed you my appointments diary, Jenny!'

Outside the station, Colin paused, undecided, gazing up and down the street.

'What will you do now?' Jenny asked.

'I don't really know. Drive back to London, I suppose. I haven't brought anything for an overnight stay; otherwise, I'd look for a B&B or something.'

'You can stay with me,' Jenny said impulsively. 'I have a spare room. Then we can both go to the mortuary tomorrow.' *Is that sensible?* one half of Jenny asked the other half. She knew next to nothing about this man. Marek had seemed confident he was who he said he was, but it also crossed her mind that he was about the same height as Avery Sykes's mysterious visitor in the library. His clothes—blue anorak over a grey jumper, chinos—were different, but then, they would be, wouldn't they? A falling out between lovers? She was certain that Marek would have vetoed her offer— he must have been too exhausted to even consider it a possibility.

'Are you *sure*?' Colin was saying. 'I don't want to impose, and you've been so kind already.'

'Yes, I'm sure,' Jenny said. 'It'll be no trouble at all.' She knew about grief, and she was convinced that Colin's was real. He was genuinely devastated at his loss. *Sometimes*, she thought, *you simply have to trust.*

They walked to the Waitrose car park, and Jenny waited in Colin's car while he hastily bought a few toiletries. And a bottle of wine and a box of chocolates, which he presented to her once they'd arrived at her cottage. She showed him the spare bedroom, the bed already made up for when Melanie visited, and left him to rest while she walked to the end of the garden and collected a few more apples. Now she had her eye in, she could see there were several more, tantalizingly out of reach. *I could stand on the kitchen chair*, she thought.

Colin appeared, crossing the lawn towards her.

'I haven't lived here very long,' Jenny said. 'That's why the garden's still a bit of a mess.' (*Although, if she'd stirred herself earlier, there was a lot she could have done.*)

He smiled. 'You need to live with a garden for a while before you make plans for it. See what it's saying to you.' He looked appraisingly at the flowerbeds. 'Most of those perennials will come through next year, but I'm thinking those straight borders don't do them any favours. Something more *twirly*'—he waved his hand through the air—'less geometric. More cottage style. You could have a path leading through the lawn—a mown one perhaps, if you let the grass grow long. You'd get all kinds of meadow flowers seeding themselves—it'll look gorgeous, like a painter's palette.' Jenny's eyes opened wide, and he laughed and said, 'Sorry—I got carried away there. It's my job—I'm a garden designer.'

'No, that's really interesting,' Jenny said, trying to see her familiar plot through his eyes.

He handed her a card. 'That's me. Not that I'm touting for custom—in fact, if you like, I can draw up a plan for you, free of charge.'

'Oh no,' Jenny said, 'that wouldn't be right. I would pay you —perhaps we could talk about it sometime.' *('Sometime' being when all of this was over.)*

She made them spaghetti carbonara for supper, and Colin opened the bottle of wine. After his second glass, he looked up at her and said, 'I've been thinking about the last time I saw Avery. It was a fortnight ago—he came down to London, the way he usually did. We went out for a nice meal, we were talking about the wedding—close friends, no fuss—and then he said there were a couple of things he wanted me to know about him. I made some sort of joke, but he was serious. He said there were things in his past that he was deeply ashamed of—two things in particular— and he wanted us to start our life together without any secrets coming between us. Naturally, I wanted to know what he meant —I imagined some past relationships that went badly wrong— but he said he had to talk to another person first, that they were involved and he—he *owed* it to them. I asked him if it was a lover, and I assured him I could handle that—after all, *my* history isn't exactly spotless—but he said no, it was nothing like that.'

'And he didn't give you a clue about who this person was?'

'No. It also seemed odd to me that he seemed to be talking about two separate incidents, but they were connected to the same man.'

'Did you mention this to Marek?'

'The nice Inspector? No, I didn't think about it until just now. I suppose I was so uptight then, and being able to relax a little has brought it back to me.'

'I think you should mention it when we see him tomorrow.'

'Jenny—you don't think ...? Could this mystery man have *killed* Avery?'

'I don't know. We just don't have enough information, and there's no point speculating—it would only be upsetting. Marek is very competent—he'll get to the bottom of this.'

The next morning, they both woke early. Jenny brewed coffee and made scrambled eggs on toast. Colin was quiet, obviously apprehensive about what was to come. He drove them to the hospital in Syrenham, about fifteen miles away, where Marek was waiting for them. Marek greeted them both, then looked half-questioningly at Jenny. She wondered if he'd noticed that Colin was wearing the same clothes as yesterday, suggesting that he *hadn't* returned to his London home ...

Behind glass, in a softly lit room, a body lay covered with a sheet. Marek nodded, and an attendant lifted the sheet, exposing the face. Colin gulped, edged closer to Jenny, and she instinctively clutched his hand.

'I need you to speak,' Marek said gently.

'That is Avery. Avery Arden Sykes.'

'Thank you. I am *so* sorry. It's an awful way to see—a person you love. But he is cared for here—treated with respect. And you have my word that I will do everything I possibly can to find the person who did this to him.'

'What happens now? To *Avery*?'

'Our pathologist has completed the postmortem, which shows us that he died from a stab wound to the heart. He would have died almost instantly—wouldn't have suffered. We'll soon be able to release the body to you, as I imagine there aren't any other close family?' Colin shook his head. 'Then you can arrange his funeral—there's a funeral director in Kerston, very highly thought of, that I can put you in touch with. And at all stages, we'll keep you informed about how the investigation is going.'

'Thank you. Oh, Detective Inspector, Avery said something to me a short while ago that Jenny said I should mention to you.'

'OK. Let's go and sit in the hospital café and have tea or something, and you can tell me there.'

At a table in the café, over cups of tea, Colin repeated what he had told Jenny about the confession that Avery had wanted to make to him—*after* he had spoken to another person.

'And you have no idea at all who he could have meant?'

'No. I got the impression that he was talking about something —some *things*—that happened quite a long time ago. He didn't really have a lot of friends—assuming this person was a *friend*.'

Marek looked thoughtful. 'We're looking at his emails, and his phone history—texts and calls—so we may pick up a lead from there. Otherwise, there might be actual *letters*—did he keep those, do you know?'

'Yes, he did. He had a lot of correspondence about his novels —from his agent and his publisher and the marketing people and all that, not to mention letters from fans that were passed on to him. He kept it all in box files, labelled with dates and subjects.'

'That's going to be a great help. We'll examine all that material.'

'You've spoken to his agent? I've met her a couple of times, at receptions given by his publisher. She seemed very nice—she'll be terribly upset too.'

'Yes—Catherine Esson. She did mention that Avery received the occasional abusive letter or email—but I believe that's par for the course. Some people were offended by the sex—it didn't seem to occur to them that they could choose *not* to read his books—and one or two insisted he'd lifted his plots from something *they'd* written. Catherine said they'd investigated those claims and they were utterly groundless: the resemblances were just the kind of details you'd expect in that kind of fiction—that *readers* expect, in fact. Lord So-and-so unzipping his mistress's corsets—un-*hooking* them, I suppose—that kind of thing.'

'I don't think Avery's murder can have had anything to do with his *books*,' Colin said.

Marek caught Jenny's eye, and she suppressed a smile. 'Do you know if he was writing anything new?' she asked.

'I think he had a plot in mind, and he'd probably started making notes—that's how he worked—but I don't think he'd got any further than that.'

'So, he didn't tell you any details of the plot?'

'No. But even if he'd written more of it than I think he had, it wouldn't have *incriminated* anyone. All his stories are set in the Regency period, and they're about members of the nobility *having their wicked way*, as the phrase goes. With women, of course—they're not gay at all.'

'How are you getting on with your identikit picture of the man in the library?' Jenny asked Marek. 'It's of a man seen talking to Avery,' she explained, as Colin looked curious. 'It doesn't necessarily mean that he was involved in—what happened.'

'Well, one more person confirmed the other sightings, but they didn't see his face either. There'll be an item on the local news this evening.'

As they left the mortuary and Colin headed towards his car, Marek drew Jenny aside. 'I'm guessing he spent the night at yours?'

'Why would you think that?'

'Oh,' Marek said, tilting his head to one side, 'because it's the sort of thing you'd do. Kind, but perhaps not without risk.'

'Is Colin a suspect?'

'No, he isn't. I checked out his movements on the day of the murder, and he was visiting a client in Barnet. Designing a rockery for them—he was there all afternoon.'

'Well then, there *wasn't* any risk.'

'But you didn't *know* that, Jenny. Not at the time.' He smiled, and walked towards his own car.

Colin dropped Jenny off outside her cottage.

'Thanks so much, Jenny, you've been great. I'd have gone to pieces if you hadn't been there. Keep in touch, won't you? My contact details are on the card. If you can bear it, I'd really like you to come to Avery's funeral. You didn't know him, but—I feel there's a *connection* now. With both of us. And not just because you found him.'

'Of course. Here's *my* mobile number, and I'll write down my email too.'

'Someone loves you!' He pointed to the carrier bag on Jenny's front doorstep. 'And think about what I said about putting together a design for your garden.'

Jenny waved him off and then peeked inside the carrier bag. As she'd guessed, it was full of Skye Savory paperbacks. She imagined Neeta receiving the same gift and silently cursing Marek. Surely he didn't expect them to read *all* of them? Or even a couple? She lugged the bag inside and dumped it in the hallway. Then she phoned Neeta with her news.

'A *fiancé*?' Neeta said. 'What a dark horse he was! I'm sure nosy Ruby didn't know anything about *that*. I wonder if Dora did. Perhaps this Colin was planning to move in with Avery. All that extra cleaning—*yippee*!'

'Maybe they were thinking of buying somewhere new together,' Jenny said. She imagined that Colin had his round of gardening clients in London and might find it hard starting from scratch in Kerston, where he wasn't known.

'Come round to coffee tomorrow morning,' Neeta went on.

'We can talk about how things are going. And Maisie is dying to show you her rats. Oh—are you rat-phobic?'

'No, I'd love to meet them,' Jenny said, not entirely truthfully.

'Good! They really are quite sweet, and she's training them to do tricks. Well, one of them—the cleverer one.'

Was that Bill or Ben? Jenny decided to bet on Bill.

'Have you got all those books from Marek?'

'Yes,' Jenny said. 'But I'm sure he was just teasing us. Colin said he didn't think there were any clues in them, and I guess he'd read most of them.'

'Typical Marek,' Neeta snorted. 'Well—see you tomorrow!'

Jenny settled down to her editing work, since she'd neglected it for the past few days. When the news came on, she watched the local segment, which featured the identikit of the man seen talking to Avery in the library. It was pretty nondescript, as the newsreader acknowledged. That black mask was surely part of a deliberate disguise ...

What had the meeting with Colin told her? It had altered the picture she'd formed of Avery Sykes as curmudgeonly, tight-fisted, determinedly anti-social. He'd been *loved*, after all. Perhaps he'd withdrawn to protect himself from gossip—even if there had been no outright taunts, there could still have been malicious whispers about his sexuality. In a sense, he'd chosen to lead a double life once he started to write as Skye Savory, and maybe that habit of concealment gradually infused his character. And what of those past deeds that he needed to confess to his lover? There was a lot to puzzle over here, but Jenny's overriding impression was that people are invariably more complex than you might at first imagine.

CHAPTER 7

Saturday morning was fine and dry. Jenny stood in the garden with a mug of tea, listening to the muffled thumps as apples dropped from the topmost branches of the trees. She'd given up on her kitchen-chair idea, after struggling yesterday to plant it firmly on the bumpy ground. There were *apple-pickers*, weren't there—cotton bags on long poles? Perhaps Colin could advise. She gathered the windfalls to take round to Neeta's.

As she approached Neeta's house, she saw Maisie standing in front of a fence a few doors down, with her hands clasped to her chest. Closer, she saw that she was studying a notice tacked to the wood.

'Hello, Maisie!'

Maisie turned, and beamed at her. Now she could see she was holding a large black and white rat.

'Hello, Jenny. Could you hold Bill just for a moment?'

Before Jenny could say anything, Bill had been thrust at her and was clinging to her jumper with his tiny paws. She instinctively slid her free hand under his bottom to stop him dropping to the ground. Meanwhile, Maisie pulled a notebook and pencil out of the pocket of her blazer and started to write.

Jenny looked down at Bill. She had no strong feelings about

rats—certainly she wasn't repulsed by them—and he was definitely rather handsome. Delicate pink ears, bright boot-button eyes, a quivering spray of sensitive whiskers. She placed her bag by her feet and ran a finger over his smooth, glossy fur.

'Bill is a hooded rat,' Maisie said, pausing her pencil for a moment. 'That means he has these markings—a black head and a stripe down his back. I was going to bring Ben out, because he's a bit dim and needs *extra stimulation*, but he was asleep, and Bill was awake and asking to come.'

'He seems very bright,' Jenny said, smiling down at him.

'Yes, he is. He can't *see* your face—rats are very short-sighted—but he can sense you in other ways, like feeling your jumper and sniffing it. Anyway, he likes you.'

'What are you writing about?'

'Look at this, Jenny. It's a case for the Pet Detective!'

Jenny studied the notice. Below a photo of a small sandy-and-white dog, she read:

LOST!
Please help to find FIGARO
He is a Jack Russell puppy, four months old. Wears a green leather collar. He disappeared on 4th October from 37 Hawthorn Drive, Kerston.
Our little boys miss him terribly!
Reward offered!

At the foot were an email address and a mobile phone number.

'Hawthorn Drive, Hawthorn Drive,' Maisie muttered to herself. 'I need to speak to Mummy.' She stuffed her notebook back in her pocket. 'It's OK, I can take Bill now.'

Neeta's husband, Jonty, opened the door to them. 'Hello Jenny, good to see you again. I see you've met Burglar Bill.'

'*Don't* call him that, Daddy! Where's Mummy?'

Neeta appeared from the kitchen. '*Jenny!*' They hugged. 'Now, we have lots to talk about—'

'Mummy!' Maisie, still holding Bill, was jogging from foot to foot.

'Maisie, please don't interrupt. It's not polite. And put Bill back in his cage.'

'But Mummy, this is an *emergency*. I have to save a *life*.'

'*Save a life?* Whose life?'

'Figaro's. He's a lost puppy and there's a notice about him outside. Jenny saw it too.'

Jenny nodded.

'Maisie, you mustn't let this detective business go to your head. I'm very sorry to hear about Figaro, but the most likely thing is that he's been stolen. Unfortunately, that does happen nowadays if pets are left unattended. Let's hope whoever's taken him is kind to him and gives him a nice new home.'

'*Mummy*, people don't steal *Jack Russells*. They go for *unusual* dogs, like ... like chocopoos and bitching frizzies.'

'Bichon frisés?'

'Yes, Jenny, that's what I just said. Now, Mummy, where is it that Gracie lives?'

'Hawthorn Drive. But what's that got to do with ...?'

'I *thought* it was the same road. I have to go there. Straightaway, before it's too late.'

'Maisie, you are not making any sense at all. Now, I'm going to make some coffee and sit down with Jenny ...'

'No, it's OK,' Jenny said. She could see that Maisie was close to tears, frantic with anxiety and frustration. 'If Hawthorn Drive isn't too far away, I can walk there with her, and ... we can do our detecting together.'

'But you've only just come ... Oh, Jenny, if you really wouldn't mind? She gets these bees in her bonnet ...'

'I *don't*,' Maisie said. But she had already begun to cheer up. 'I'll just put my detection kit together.' She went off, carrying Bill.

'I brought you some apples from my trees,' Jenny said, handing her bag to Neeta.

'Ooh, lovely! Thanks so much. And thanks even more for helping Maisie. There'll be coffee and cake waiting for you when you get back. Hawthorn Drive is about ten minutes' walk—Maisie's friend lives there so she knows the way.'

After a couple of minutes Maisie reappeared, equipped with a backpack. She and Jenny set off at a brisk pace, down streets that Jenny hadn't yet explored.

'What do you think's happened to Figaro?' Jenny asked.

'I will explain,' Maisie said self-importantly. 'Jack Russells are *hunting* dogs. In the olden days, they were used to hunt foxes, and they remember that so they're always trying to go down *holes*. Now, there's a common behind the houses in Hawthorn Drive. There are rabbits there—Gracie and I watch them out of her bedroom window. Figaro must have escaped from his garden and chased one of them down a burrow and got stuck.'

Jenny thought that sounded plausible, but unlikely.

'And how are you going to find him? If he's underground?'

'I have bait. I was going to use Bill or Ben to tempt him out, but I thought that might be a bit risky if he shot out and tried to grab them. So, it'll be like the hamster, only with a sausage. The reason a rat would have worked very well is that—did you know this, Jenny?—dogs like Jack Russells used to take part in *rat-catching* competitions. The rats were put in a pit, and it was covered with wire so they couldn't escape, and ...'

Jenny must have sighed audibly—she hated hearing about cruelty to animals—because Maisie paused, before continuing in a softer tone: 'You don't need to get upset, Jenny. Those rats were just nasty *common* rats. Not *nice* rats like Bill and Ben.'

Jenny sighed again. Sadly, Maisie was a rat snob. A couple of turns later, she spotted the sign for Hawthorn Drive.

'We'll go down the side of Gracie's house,' Maisie said. 'There's a lane that leads on to the common.'

The common was an unkempt piece of ground encircled with houses, overgrown with seeding grasses, brambles, arching sprays of buddleia. And hawthorn bushes with crimson haws, which Jenny reckoned might account for the name of one of the roads bordering it. It must be protected in some way, she thought; otherwise, it would have been snapped up and built on. Perhaps the owner couldn't be found, so the local authority was responsible for it. It was wild, it was untidy, but she found it a refreshing change from the fussily manicured town gardens she and Maisie had passed on their walk.

Maisie stopped, shrugged off her backpack, and unzipped it. They were next to some bramble bushes, and Jenny could see where blackberry pickers had trampled the grasses flat. A few low runways led into the thorny tangles, probably made by small animals. Maisie unpeeled clingfilm from a cooked sausage and started to trot to and fro, waving her lure in the air and trilling *Figaro! Figaro!* Jenny followed her, assuming, correctly, that she was supposed to look after the backpack. Gradually, Maisie worked her way across the common, stopping every now and then to listen. Suddenly, she froze.

'Don't say anything,' she hissed.

'I *wasn't* saying anything.'

'You did, just now.'

'*Sorry* ...'

'*Jenny!*'

Maisie was standing next to a scrubby young oak tree. Jenny watched her kneel and part the grasses around it with her fingers, revealing the smallest of holes, and, quite unbelievably, a tiny nose, whiffling frantically. She sprang into action at once, tipping an armoury of knives, forks, and spoons from the backpack. Jenny knelt too, and they began digging and forking and spooning the earth away. It was a minuscule hole, too small for a rabbit burrow, and definitely too small for Figaro to squeeze out of. Jenny thought he must have gone underground somewhere else, perhaps chasing a rabbit as Maisie had suggested, and got lost.

The whiffling had now been replaced by a high excited whining and the scratching of small paws.

'Look, Jenny, he can't get out because there's this tree root in the way. You'll have to cut through it.'

Maisie produced a large chef's knife with a serious-looking blade.

'Daddy keeps it very sharp, so it ought to do the trick ... Oh,' she added, '*I'm* not allowed to touch it.'

Jenny sawed away, imagining that she was probably ruining the knife for good. Then the stubborn root split, Maisie wriggled under her arm and reached in, and out came a tiny, filthy dog, squeaking with excitement and relief and scrabbling up to lick her face as she cradled it.

'*There now*, Figaro, you're safe now! Hee-hee, you're tickling me!' He was still wearing his green collar, with a little silver bone dangling from it, engraved with his mobile number. Maisie cuddled him for a few moments, savouring her triumph. Then it was back to business.

'Here, Jenny.' She thrust Figaro into Jenny's arms and rummaged in her backpack again, this time bringing out a couple of towels, a water bottle, and a soup bowl. She poured water into the bowl, reclaimed Figaro, and lowered him to the grass, where he lapped splashily. Then he gobbled up the sausage, which was lying close by. It didn't stay down very long, as he sicked it up into the soup bowl.

'His tummy is probably delicate, because he's been without food for so long,' Jenny said, wondering at the same time how she was going to explain the knife to Neeta—not to mention the soup bowl.

'Yes, poor Figaro, only those old bones for him to eat,' Maisie said.

'*Bones?* What bones?'

'Those over there,' Maisie said casually, pointing to a disturbed patch of earth.

Protrusions from the dark soil. Fanned, like the ribs of a

broken umbrella. Jenny stared at the tapered joints and was sure, beyond doubt, that these were human. She breathed through her mouth, shallowly, a pulse beating in her ears. Perhaps it was just *a hand*? That would be awful enough. Should she try to uncover more? She turned to check on Maisie, but Maisie was fully occupied with Figaro. As Jenny watched, she poured water from her bottle on to a towel and started to clean the earth off him while he wriggled and squirmed, trying to reach the soup bowl and eat the sausage again.

The bones were stained—old ivory. They could be very old indeed. Jenny clung to that thought. The common could be an ancient burial place, left undisturbed because of some folk memory? But were people ever buried without coffins, without even *shrouds*? (Although any fabric would have rotted away.) There were medieval *plague pits*, she recollected, where the bodies of victims of the Black Death were unceremoniously flung. But surely a pit was *deep*, and this was quite a shallow burial. And—as far as she could see—a solitary one.

No point speculating, Jenny told herself. Reassuringly, the actions she now had to take unrolled in front of her, a series of steps back to normality. First, she took her phone out of her pocket and photographed the bones, in close-up and then from further away, with a final shot including the oak tree as a marker, with Maisie and Figaro beside it. Next, she brushed loose soil over the bones, hiding them from view again. Finally, she texted Neeta:

Figaro found!!! See you soon!

Maisie was reloading her backpack, an awkward task as she had Figaro clutched under one arm.

'I'll hold him for you,' Jenny said.

'Thanks! He's still a bit dirty. And wet now. I thought I'd wrap him in the clean towel.'

'You've thought of everything, Maisie!'

'Yes! Attention to detail is a very important part of being a detective.'

'Did Marek—Inspector O'Keeffe—tell you that?'

'He did. And I'm going to tell *him* about finding Figaro!'

Jenny found herself extremely impressed by Maisie's ingenuity, composure, general all-round competence. *Detective Chief Superintendent in about thirty years' time*, she thought to herself, with a secret smile.

The next step was to restore Figaro to his anxious owners. (There was no hurry about the bones—they'd lain there for a good few years already, so a little extra delay wouldn't matter.) Maisie shouldered her backpack and clasped Figaro in her arms. Jenny understood that she wanted to be the one to return him. He had stopped wriggling and was very quiet—when she folded the towel back to look at him, he had fallen fast asleep.

Maisie led the way back, down the alley at the side of Gracie's house and then left along Hawthorn Drive.

'This is Number 37,' she announced, stopping at a white-fronted semi-detached house with a child's trike parked in the front garden.

A young man in sweatshirt and jeans answered their knock. He opened his mouth to say something, and then he saw what Maisie was carrying.

'Is that ... is that ...?'

'It's Figaro,' Maisie said. 'We found him on the common. He'd gone down a rabbit burrow and got stuck.'

'That's—that's fantastic!' He reached out for the bundle, stared at it wonderingly, and then called over his shoulder, 'Toby! Nathan!'

Two little boys—about six and about four, Jenny thought—ran down the hallway to join him.

'Look who I've got here!'

'Figaro! Figaro!' they squealed, jostling one another and pulling back the towel. Figaro woke and yawned pinkly.

'Gently, now,' their father said, and then to Jenny and Maisie, 'Won't you come inside? Then you can tell us the whole story.'

'I'm afraid we have to be somewhere else,' Jenny said quickly. 'But it was Maisie who found Figaro, so she can explain.'

'I *thought* he'd escaped to the common,' Maisie said. 'He's a Jack Russell, and they like chasing rabbits. We had to dig him out because he got stuck in a very small hole. I had a sausage, you see,' she added, 'and he smelled it and made a noise, but it made him sick when he ate it.'

'He seems fine,' Jenny said. 'He was very lively before he fell asleep. I guess you should take him to the vet, just so he can be checked over. And only give him a little food, to begin with.'

The man nodded. 'I can't thank you enough. We put up a reward, you know. Can I fetch that for you now?'

'No thank you,' Maisie said, standing up very straight. 'I am a pet detective, and I don't charge anything for my services. Instead, I ask people to give some money to a wildlife charity or an animal rescue centre. This is my card.'

She pulled it out of her pocket and handed it over. The man examined it, grinned, and showed it to the boys. 'We'll definitely do that. And, once again, we're *so* grateful to you. Terrific detective work,' he added as Maisie smiled graciously.

'I'm not sure you should have put that bit about the police on your card,' Jenny said, as they walked back along Hawthorn Drive.

'Oh, it's OK,' Maisie said, still glowing from her triumph. 'Inspector O'Keeffe said he would be sure to recommend me the next time anyone reported a lost hamster to him.'

'Mummy!' Maisie shouted, as she marched into her house. 'I rescued Figaro!'

'You *did*?' Neeta winked at Jenny. 'You must tell me and

Daddy all about it. Would you like a drink? I'm making coffee for the grown-ups.'

'Yes please! Apple juice. I'll just go and feed Bill and Ben.'

'Neeta,' Jenny said, 'it's true—she did find that little dog, down a burrow. She was brilliant—and his owner was over the moon. But while we were digging him out, we also uncovered what looked like bones. Human ones.' She showed Neeta the pictures she had taken.

Neeta studied them. 'Come and look at this, Jonty.' Her husband took the phone and held it close to his face. (*Needs specs*, Jenny thought.) 'These are the bones of a human hand. Phalanges, metacarpals—no doubt about it. *Where* did you say you found them?'

'In the middle of the common. I wondered if they could be ancient—perhaps it was a burial site?'

'I've never heard of anything like that,' Jonty said. 'We should let the police know—they can test them.'

He's going to think I'm stalking him, Jenny thought, as she rang Marek. She first apologized for disturbing him, but he assured her he was on duty at the station. When she explained about the bones, she expected him to dispatch a junior officer to investigate them, but he said he'd come straight away and would be with her in about ten minutes.

'*Inspector O'Keeffe!*' Maisie squeaked excitedly, standing in the open doorway as he strode up the drive. 'Did Jenny tell you about me rescuing Figaro?'

'She did mention something along those lines. But I would like you to give me a full report. Including *all* the details.'

He sat next to her on the sofa while Neeta served coffee and banana cake. Jenny noted, approvingly, the way he listened to Maisie —actively, unhurriedly, prompting her in places to expand on this or that. 'Well,' he said once she'd finished, 'you put my efforts in the shade, Maisie! You really are shaping up to be an excellent detective.'

'Jenny helped too.'

'I'm sure she did. And now I have to talk to your assistant about something entirely different. Here's some peanut biscuits for Bill and Ben.' He reached into his pocket and spread them in front of her.

'Thank you!' Maisie scooped them up and disappeared.

'Mum's always loading me with snacks. I try to palm them off round the station, but no one was very keen on those. Still, I'm sure the rats will appreciate them. Now, let's go and look at your bones. I'll drive—it'll be quicker. Jonty, do you have a trowel or something like that I could borrow?'

'Sure. You don't want a spade?'

'No thanks, I'm only going to have a little poke, not dig up the whole thing. If it *is* a whole thing.'

Jonty supplied a trowel and a gardening fork, and Jenny and Marek walked to his car. It only took a minute or two to reach Hawthorn Drive.

'This is where we went through to the common.' Jenny pointed to the alleyway next to Gracie's house. 'I hope I can remember the way after that.' She took out her phone and scrolled through the photos. 'Yes, that oak tree over there. That's where Maisie found Figaro.' She led the way, following the path with increasing confidence.

'OK,' Marek said, looking down at the bones revealed after Jenny had brushed off their topsoil covering. 'A hand all right. Clean, no flesh, so it's been in the ground quite a few years.' He knelt and tore up clumps of grass a few inches away, then worked the fork into the earth, freeing the roots. Soon, he laid it aside, dug with the trowel and then with his fingers. Jenny watched as he smoothed soil in a straight furrow.

'Well, there's an arm. See—radius, ulna? Remember your biology lessons, Jenny?' He stood up and rubbed his hands on his trousers.

'I suppose you can't tell how old it is?' Jenny asked.

'No, but my first impression is that this is suspicious. It's not a deep burial at all. Perhaps somebody didn't have the tools, or the strength, to dig any deeper. Or the *time*.'

He stepped back and looked at the exposed bones. 'So—the body is lying *this* way. Which means that the head—if there *is* a head—must be about *here*.' He knelt once again and started digging with the trowel. Soon he had delved several inches deeper than the arm, and Jenny shivered at the thought that the corpse might be headless. Then, 'Ah,' Marek said. 'Here we are. The skull.'

Jenny bent over and saw the rounded bowl shape, stained and aged like the other bones.

'My guess is that the body was originally buried *this* deep,' Marek said. 'The arm is an anomaly: probably animals burrowing under the soil displaced it and pushed it up. I'll phone this in and get scene-of-crime onto it. Not that we're sure a crime's actually been committed, but it's starting to look that way. I'll wait for them here, guard the site. Would you be able to walk back to Neeta's house, Jenny? I'll come and update you as soon as I can. And are you feeling OK? Finding *two* bodies is very cruel luck.'

'I'm fine,' Jenny said. This second body hadn't become *real* to her in the way that Avery's was. She glanced at Marek, but he wasn't looking at her. Instead, he stood perfectly still, eyes focused on the boundary of the common, about twenty-five yards away. A row of houses facing on to a narrow lane.

'Over there,' Marek said, pointing.

'What are you looking at?'

'You don't remember? I suppose it was dark. The road the other side of those houses. That's where Avery Sykes lived.'

CHAPTER 8

'Wow! Kerston is becoming the murder capital of the Cotswolds!' Neeta said. 'So, the body was close to Avery Sykes's house? That *must* be significant.'

'It could be just a coincidence,' Jenny said. 'It wasn't right at his back door, and there are houses that are even closer than his.'

'But not belonging to murder victims—as far as we know.'

I'd better tell her, Jenny thought. 'Neeta, you remember I met Colin Ingram, Avery's fiancé?'

'Yes, in the library.'

'That's right. Well, I let him stay at my house on Thursday night—he was very upset and he didn't have anywhere else to go. Then I went with him to the mortuary yesterday.'

'Did you tell Marek about him staying with you?'

'He'd worked it out. Anyway, Colin is not a suspect; he has an alibi. He said a strange thing to me and Marek though: that Avery had a secret—*two* secrets—that he wanted to confess to him before they were married. Colin thought he was talking about some past love affairs, but Avery said it wasn't anything like that. The reason he hadn't told him before was because the secrets involved another person and he needed to speak to them first.'

Neeta's eyes opened wide. 'And there's a body buried just a few yards from his back door! That has to be one of the things he meant—but what's the other? Does Kerston have its very own serial killer?'

'I think you'd need a few more victims! And we still don't know anything about the body buried on the common. It might be very old—historic. Marek couldn't tell just by looking at it.'

'I bet it's *not*, though.'

'Also,' Jenny said, 'even if it is a suspicious death, it might not have been murder. An accident that somebody wanted to cover up? And what about this *other person* Avery said was involved in whatever it was he'd done?'

'Perhaps the other person was the murderer, and Avery knew they were but for some reason he didn't say anything at the time. *Yes*, Jenny—this is starting to make sense. Avery wasn't the murderer himself, but he knew who was—he might even have helped them bury the body. Especially if the killing took place *in his house*. Then he tells this person he's going to come clean, and they murder *him* to stop their secret getting out.'

Possible, Jenny thought to herself. Who could this mystery man be, though? Was he the man in the library seen talking to Avery? 'But why would Avery have agreed to keep such a massive secret?' she said. 'If the killer was a lover—perhaps, yes. Only he wasn't—Colin was certain about that.'

'Family? A close friend?'

'Avery didn't have any family. Just some cousins, and they're in Canada. He doesn't seem to have had many friends either.'

'Perhaps this person—our killer—offered him money to stay quiet. Avery might have accidentally witnessed the murder—he might not even have known the person who committed it—but they realized he saw them and they bought his silence.'

'It must have been a lot of money! And why didn't they just kill him too?' *A sure-fire motive in detective stories*, Jenny thought to herself. *The second victim has no connection with the first one: they simply happened to be in the wrong place at the wrong time.*

'I don't know,' Neeta said. 'Perhaps they couldn't quite gee themselves up to do it. They might have killed the first person in a fit of rage, and they couldn't summon that up for Avery.'

'But if your theory's right, they *did* manage it—they stabbed him in cold blood. In the library.'

'H'm. I suppose their resentment might have built up over the years—because this must have happened a long time ago. Especially if Avery kept demanding more and more money from them. I believe that's typical of blackmailers.'

'Well,' Jenny said, 'Marek will probably find out who it was. He's going through Avery's phone records and everything on his computer. Also, all the letters he wrote over the years. If he *was* blackmailing someone, there'd be regular payments into his bank account too.'

'Unless they slipped him bundles of cash.'

'But he'd still have needed to *communicate* with them in some way.'

'Perhaps you were right, Jenny. They messaged each other through crossword clues!'

Jenny grinned. 'That would be a first, wouldn't it? Anyway, I think I'll wander home now. Marek said he'd call round later, and I'll text and tell you all the latest. Thanks for the coffee. And the cake.'

'Well, thanks to you for taking Maisie seriously. And for the apples. I'm doing another library round on Monday afternoon—would you like to come? It'll only be Mrs Pycroft and Ruby; the others haven't finished their books yet.'

'Mm, yes,' Jenny said, hoping that Neeta wasn't planning another raid on Avery's house. 'I'll be in the library, so we can go from there. Should we tell Ruby who Skye Savory really was, do you think?'

'Why not? I want to see her face!'

'And did Mrs Pycroft like her books?'

'She did not. She rang me to say that talking kittens was a stupid idea, and someone in the other book—the murderer, I think—called Adolphus a stump-legged little bastard. Really, there is no pleasing some people!'

It was late afternoon and the light was starting to fade when Marek's car drew up outside Jenny's house.

'Tea? Coffee?' she offered. 'Or something stronger?'

He blinked, undecided. He looked tired, she thought.

'I have a nice whisky. Speyside.'

'Will you have one too?'

'Of course!'

'In that case, yes please. I'll leave the car here and walk home afterwards, if that's OK.'

'Well,' he said, when they were both settled, 'the bones have been dug out and taken to the lab. A complete skeleton, but no clues about how old it is. Nothing handy like a wristwatch. And no clothes—or remnants of clothes—either. The pathologist is pretty sure it's a man, about average height. He should be able to give us an approximate age.'

'Will he be able to tell you how he died? I suppose that might not be possible if all the soft tissue has gone.'

'Our one piece of luck! The back of the skull had a depressed fracture. He was hit—probably hard enough to cause his death.'

'Definitely murder then?'

'Looks that way, unless a ton of bricks fell on him. But, of course, we'll only get involved if the body is relatively recent. A hundred years old and we can all go home.'

'More whisky?'

'Oh, go on then.' He grinned at her as she topped up his glass. 'I take it you found your books OK? I got my sergeant, Ceri, to play postperson.'

'Marek, you're not really expecting me to read every single one of them, are you?'

Marek laughed. 'Of course not! I just couldn't resist pulling

Neeta's leg. Sorry, Jenny! I'm sure you have far better things to do with your time.'

'Yes, I do!' she said, with mock severity.

'Although ... suppose you just read *bits* of them? Books usually have acknowledgements, don't they? Where the author thanks everyone, including his—or her—cat, for their help and inspiration. And *dedications*—it would be interesting to see what names crop up there. Because we're finding it very hard to discover any details of Avery's past life. He didn't use social media —he left it up to his agent to maintain a website for him—and his emails and texts are nearly all to a small group of friends: men of about his own age. We'll be talking to them of course, but at first glance they seem eminently respectable—teachers, university lecturers, even a High Court judge. Not a conviction between them—apart from a handful of speeding fines.'

'I'll take a look,' Jenny said. 'But not having a criminal record might not be significant. This was a very unusual killing, wasn't it? I got the feeling someone really *hated* Avery. The way they drove the needle into him.'

'Yes,' Marek said, putting his glass down. 'Are you OK? I don't want you to go on thinking about that.'

'I'm all right. And doing something positive—like checking the acknowledgements and so on—will help. Dora Wedderdale mentioned that Avery did some private tutoring after he left the school—it might have been through an agency. There aren't so many of those, especially locally—it might give you a lead or two. And there's the crossword community, of course.' She smiled at him.

'The *crossword community*? Heaven help us! Do they all sit round filling in their little black and white squares and swapping anagrams?'

'They post online. And they use pseudonyms. It's hard to see crosswords as a motive for murder, though. Have you found out any more about the man seen speaking to Avery in the library?'

'That's another weird thing. He's picked up by the cameras

leaving the mall at about three o'clock. That would fit with Avery being killed about two hours before you found him. He goes into Lattimer's. And then that's the last we see of him.'

'You mean you don't see him come *out*?'

'I mean exactly that.'

Jenny had been in Lattimer's herself. It was the nearest thing in Kerston to a department store, stocking cookware, ornaments, gifts, stationery, and, on the first floor, a decorous array of men's and women's fashions. There was a good food hall, with a café attached.

'He might have gone out the back way. Through a fire door, or something.'

'If he had, an alarm would have sounded. There's also a side exit, for the staff, but you need to enter a code on a keypad for that.'

'Do they have CCTV of him inside the store?'

'They're rather behind the times. Electronic keypads are as far as they go—they don't have CCTV at all. Our crime prevention officer did suggest they install it, especially as they're always complaining to us about shoplifting, but they didn't take the hint.'

'Perhaps he was an employee then? Or perhaps he *knew* an employee, who gave him the exit code.'

'Yes, that's possible.' Marek sighed. 'We're interviewing all the staff who were at work that afternoon, to see if anyone spotted him. And we'll need to talk to *all* the staff full stop—if this guy knew about codes, he might be an employee who'd come in on his off day. Or, as you said, he—or she, for that matter— could have passed the info on to someone else—although they're hardly likely to admit that to us.'

'Did you contact Pat's friend Zara about Mr Sykes touching her inappropriately?'

'Yes, had a video conversation with her yesterday. She wasn't keen, tried to wriggle out of it, but I told her the alternative was the police turning up at her place of work—she runs a hairdressing salon in Glasgow—and taking her down to the station for questioning.'

'And she confirmed what Pat said?'

'Not initially. I didn't mention that Pat had rubbished her story, just told her we were investigating the death of Avery Sykes, who'd been her teacher at Kerston Comprehensive about twenty years ago. And that I understood she had made a complaint about his behaviour towards her. She came out with the same accusation —that he'd put his hand up her skirt—and then I played the Pat card. I told her that misleading the police in a potential murder investigation was a very serious offence and could result in a custodial sentence. I can do scary. She went to pieces after that, just kept saying what a horrible man he was, and that they were all terrified of him.'

'So, at least that's out of the way.'

'Yes. It removes one lead, but at the moment we're hard-pressed to find anything to replace it. Anyway, I must be off. Thanks so much for the whisky!'

'I hope you can relax a bit tomorrow.'

'I'm not on duty. Which is good, as I need to do some relationship repair.' He smiled ruefully. 'You would know all about that, Jenny. Pressures of the job.'

'Yes,' Jenny said. 'It *was* hard sometimes. But not being with Alan—*that* would have been unbearable.'

Marek had been pulling his raincoat on, but he stopped and looked at her.

'Yes,' he said. 'Yes.' He laid his hand on hers for a moment, and then he was quickly out of the front door.

When Jenny woke the next morning, his car had disappeared. She decided to spend the day going through the Skye Savory books, as he'd suggested. First, though, she pottered in the garden, cutting dead stems back, raking leaves from the grass, and filling a bag with more apples. The more she worked, the more she felt at home—that this was a place she would shape and, in time, come to love.

She stopped at midday, to make herself a sandwich, and to text Neeta:

> Bones are a complete skeleton! Marek says skull is fractured, but can't tell age yet. See you tomorrow!

After lunch, she settled down with a coffee and rearranged the books in order of publication. The earliest had come out ten years ago, so, since Avery had been an author for about twenty years, she guessed Neeta's books covered the first half of his career. She started to read the Acknowledgements, which typically thanked Skye's agent, Catherine Esson, copyeditors, proofreaders, and the publisher's marketing team. Also, *My lovely readers, without whom* ... There was an offer of 'special content' for those who followed Skye, and a request to post reviews on Amazon and Good Reads, 'so that more and more people can share the unique Skye Savory experience'. All pretty run-of-the-mill stuff.

Many of the books had no dedications, but a few names cropped up, all of them men. *For Gerald. For Peter.* Jenny copied them down, wondering if they would tally with Marek's list of Avery's contacts. The last three books all had the same dedication: *For C. He really loved him*, Jenny thought to herself, sadly.

At four o'clock, she rang Melanie, as she did every Sunday. She had been undecided about how much to tell her daughter. Mostly, she didn't want her to worry. But there was the off-chance that Melanie would get to hear of the incident some other way— if it made the national news, for instance.

'Mum!' Melanie said. 'I guessed it would be you. What have you been up to?'

'Actually,' Jenny said, resolving to jump straight in, 'I found a body. In the library here. And some bones. On a piece of ground called the common.'

There was silence on the other end of the line. Then, '*Mum! Are you having me on?*'

'No, I'm afraid not,' Jenny said, and she went on to describe both discoveries.

'But that must have been awful for you. Especially the first one, the stabbing. Why didn't you tell me straightaway? I could have come down.'

Why didn't I? Jenny had already asked herself that question. Part of the answer was that things had moved so fast—Neeta had stepped in to help her, and then they'd begun their *investigation*. Over the past few days, she'd met more new people than she had in the whole three months since she'd moved to Kerston—Neeta, Jonty, and Maisie, Dani and Marek, Ruby and Dora, Colin—and something inside her had started to flourish, to bloom again in their company. Melanie had been a wonderful support after Alan died, comforting her, helping her to simply carry on. And she still needed that support—she looked forward to their weekly chats on the phone, and to Melanie's visits. *But whatever it is that I'm part of now,* Jenny thought—*this adventure, perhaps—is just for me. I'm going to use my own skills, my own initiative to see me through it.*

'I'm sorry, darling,' she said. 'I didn't want you to worry. And I'm fine, I really am. I've actually made some new friends because of all this.'

'Well, that's good,' Melanie said. 'Anyway Mum, take care. I'm away next weekend, at a conference, but I'll be up to see you soon after that.'

'That will be lovely!'

On Monday morning, Jenny arrived at the library shortly after it opened at nine.

'Not so many nosy people,' Valerie said, with a sigh of relief. 'Do you know if the police are any further forward, Jenny?'

Jenny shook her head. 'I think they're trying to trace all the people Avery knew, but it's a slow process.'

'And what about this *man*—the one in the identikit?'

'They haven't had any luck with him either. They can see him on CCTV leaving the library, and going into Lattimer's, but they lose him after that.' Jenny decided not to say anything about the body on the common. If it *did* turn out to be recent, and the focus of a new investigation, the news would get round soon enough.

'Dear me. Of course, that face mask is no help at all, and I really don't see why he should have worn it. Most of the germs in libraries are probably in the books themselves.'

Jenny nodded, thinking of the bacon rasher.

'I suppose it *must* have been a disguise,' Valerie continued, and Jenny agreed that was the most likely explanation.

'And how is that poor man—the fiancé?'

'Well, very upset, obviously. He identified Mr Sykes's body, but he's gone back to London now.'

Valerie gave another of her world-weary sighs.

'Still, life goes on, Jenny. Oh, before you do the shelving, could you tidy the Recommended Reads stand? I thought I'd decorate it with a spray of blackberries, to underline the nature theme, but the students ate them.'

In between shelving the returned books and answering a few queries, Jenny noted down the titles of a few classic murder mysteries that the demanding Mrs Pycroft might enjoy. Roy Vickers, Fredric Brown, Josephine Tey ... Surely there'd be *something* there to take her fancy! She shared the list with Neeta, who arrived at about half-past one. No shopper, just a carrier bag, as there weren't that many books to deliver.

'Good, good,' Neeta said. 'Ruby isn't a problem—just more Skye Savorys. I wonder what she'll do when she's read them all.'

'She's got some way to go yet,' Jenny said, thinking of the pile on her desk. They wouldn't all be stocked by the library, of course, but they could be ordered in. 'Are we *really* going to tell her who her favourite author was?'

'Aren't we just!'

First, they had to present Mrs Pycroft with her new selection, remove the soppy kittens and the unfortunate Adolphus, and listen to a lecture on the deplorable state of publishing today.

'Why they can't tell a good, simple story without all this bad language, I will never know. It's just showing off—it's not true to life.'

She's never been in Kerston at chucking-out time, Neeta whispered, as they made their escape. *It's funny—she doesn't mind gallons of blood and people having their heads bashed in, but just one bugger and she's up the wall.*

Ruby, however, hailed them enthusiastically. 'Ah! Come in, me dears, come in! You tell me what's been happening. Last week, I see somebody try to burgle Mr Sykes's house. Then, Saturday, Sunday, police arrive again, park a big van over the road, go and put a tent up on the common. I try to see what they up to, but I can't walk that far. Mrs Wedderdale nosing around, but I think they tell her to go away.'

'Well, Ruby,' Neeta said, crossing her fingers behind her back, 'we can't tell you anything about burglars, but the tent on the common is so the police can dig up some bones and take them back to the lab to see how old they are. My daughter uncovered them on Saturday when she was looking for a lost puppy. Jenny was there too.'

'My eyes!' Ruby's own eyes opened wide. 'We are all going to be murdered in our beds. Perhaps I better take the egg sign down. Stop *advertising* meself.'

'I don't think you have anything to worry about, Ruby. The bones *could* be very old ones. Anyway, here are some more Skye Savory books. *And* we have some news for you about your favourite author. We know who she is.'

'Well, of course. I know that too.'

'Not yet you don't! Skye Savory was really Avery Sykes. Your neighbour across the road.'

Ruby stared at them, speechless. Then, 'You mean old Mr Sour-Puss wrote me books? *All* of them?'

'Uh-huh.'

Ruby looked up at the ceiling, then all around her, in utter bemusement. 'How come he know all about sex, then?'

'He used his imagination, Ruby,' Jenny said.

'Well, I got imagination too, but it is not a patch on the real thing. I suppose he practise it all on Mrs Wedderdale. No wonder she look so happy when she come out of his house some days. She never look like that when her husband was living with her, that's for sure.'

'How long ago did he die?'

'*Pah!*' Ruby snorted. 'He ain't *dead*. He *left* her. Walked out while he still had his dick. Before she could polish it off.'

Neeta and Jenny exchanged glances. That would explain why Dora had no photos of the much-lamented Frank on display.

'How long ago was that, Ruby?' Neeta asked.

'Oh, few years after the fireworks.'

'You mean the Millennium fireworks?'

'Yes, they's the ones. Two thousand five, two thousand six?'

Sixteen, seventeen years ago then.

Jenny felt a spurt of pity for Dora Wedderdale. Appearances were so important to her—no wonder she kept quiet about her husband's desertion.

'So, Skye Savory won't be writing no more books?' The thought seemed to have suddenly struck Ruby.

'Well, no,' Neeta said. 'But she—*he* wrote ever so many, so you still have a lot of good reading in front of you. And then'—as Ruby looked glum—'I'm sure we can find you another author you like just as much.'

'Won't be the same. No one shake the booty like Skye Savory.'

'I wonder what will happen to Mr Sykes's book collection,' Neeta said, as they walked back towards the town centre.

'It'll go to whoever he left his property to in his will. I wonder if Marek's found that out yet. Oh,' Jenny said, 'that reminds me. Marek doesn't expect us to read all the Skye Savorys, but he thought it might be useful if we just looked at the acknowledgements and dedications and made a note of the names that appear there. He's trying to find out more about the people that Avery knew.'

Neeta growled. It was clear she hadn't forgiven Marek yet.

'I can do yours,' Jenny offered. 'It won't take me long because I've already checked mine and made a list. I'd just add the names in your books to it.'

'Well, that would be very kind, Jenny. I have to admit it makes me cross just looking at the wretched things. I'll bring them round to yours.'

'Marek's also been looking at the CCTV around the library. He can see the man who was talking to Avery come out of the mall, walk down the High Street, and go into Lattimer's. But he vanishes after that. He doesn't appear to come *out*.'

'Aha! Perhaps he's still in there!'

'After a week?' Jenny toyed with the idea of a feral individual lurking in some forgotten corner and emerging every now and then to filch food from the café.

'OK, perhaps not. But, actually, he wouldn't have had to stay more than a night—they'd only have been trying to pick him up on CCTV on the day of the murder. Why don't we go and have a poke around? See if anything occurs to us. We could have a cup of tea and a bun, too,' Neeta added, when Jenny looked doubtful.

They stopped off at the library to unload the returns from Mrs Pycroft and Ruby before making their way to Lattimer's.

'That reminds me,' Neeta said. 'Jonty needs some new socks. Do you mind if we just pop upstairs for a mo?'

Jenny didn't mind at all. She browsed among the ladies' fashions while Neeta selected socks for her husband. When Neeta rejoined her, her eyes were shining with excitement.

'*Jenny!* I've worked it out! How that man disappeared. He came up here, and bought a change of clothes, so when he left the store, he looked like somebody completely different!'

Jenny considered this. 'You mean he got changed, then came out and told the assistant he'd keep everything on? People do that with *shoes* sometimes, but not with entire outfits. And surely the assistant would remember such odd behaviour and mention it to the police. Marek thinks someone might have let him out the staff exit, so they're questioning all the employees.'

'*H'm ...*'

'Also,' Jenny went on, 'he'd have used a credit card to pay with, and that could easily be traced back to him.'

'Unless the card was stolen. Or he paid cash. Wait a minute—perhaps he *didn't* pay for the clothes. Perhaps he shoplifted them. And, thinking about it, he wouldn't need a *complete* change, just a cover-up. An anorak or a puffa jacket instead of his duffel coat. Plus, er—a Panama or a tweed cap instead of a beanie.'

Jenny thought that a man with such a peculiar fashion sense would surely have stood out.

'He couldn't have put them on *over* his duffel coat—he'd have had to take that off. So, what did he do with his coat?' Into her mind popped a line from one of G. K. Chesterton's *Father Brown* stories: *Where would a wise man hide a leaf? In the forest.* The detecting priest was investigating a murder, of course, not a disappearing duffel coat—but the principle still applied. 'Perhaps we should check the coats here ...'

They worked their way through the racks, and there certainly were navy blue duffel coats on offer; however, they were all equipped with tags—security tags, in fact, expressly to deter shoplifting.

'Let's go and have that cup of tea,' Jenny sighed.

THE KNITTING NEEDLE MURDER

'I wonder if the police checked *all* the exits,' Neeta said, lifting the teapot lid and mashing the teabags inside, out of habit.

'Surely they'd have done that. What are you thinking?'

'What about the loos? If the officers were all men, they might not have gone into the Ladies. Especially if there were ladies in there at the time.'

'Can you get out of the Ladies?'

'Well, I seem to remember there are windows. On the wall above the basins. I can't picture quite how big they are, though. We'll take a look afterwards.'

Which they did, after two cups of tea and a slice of caramel shortcake each. Neeta and Jenny eyed the windows critically. They *were* big enough to allow an athletic person to climb through.

'Let me see,' Neeta said. 'If you put one foot in the basin and the other on the sill, you could wiggle the catch open.'

'I hope you don't mean *me* by *you*,' Jenny said. 'We don't know what's the other side of the windows anyway.' Predictably, the glass was frosted, impossible to see through.

'It must be somewhere *outside*. I think loos have to have a fresh-air outlet, for hygiene reasons. And we're on the ground floor; a person wouldn't have to jump very far.'

'Well, that person is not going to be *me*.'

'I'll at least see if they *can* be opened.' With Jenny's help, Neeta scrambled up into one of the basins, lifted the window latch, and pushed at the frame. There was a horrible cracking sound, and the basin started to part company with the wall. Neeta hastily jumped to the floor.

'Oops! That window can't be budged—somebody's painted all round the frame and sealed it shut.'

Jenny was more worried about the drunkenly tilting basin. Together they shoved it back in place—it went nearly all the way. There was a telltale gap, though, and shards of broken plaster round the plughole. Neeta quickly swept these up with a hand

and dropped them in the waste bin. Then she fetched a loo roll from one of the cubicles, tore off strips of paper and wodged them into the crack.

'There!' she said, slightly breathlessly. 'You'd never know, would you?'

Jenny hoped very much that the basin didn't suddenly collapse on to the feet of some poor person innocently washing their hands. *Wanton destruction of property. Resulting in serious injury.* She could just imagine Marek's face.

'Perhaps we should take a look in the Gents,' Neeta said. 'After all, we don't *know* that the police checked in there.'

'*No, Neeta!* We are *not* going into any more loos. I don't think a man would have risked going into the Ladies anyway. Someone might have spotted him.'

'He could have waited until they were empty. *We* haven't been disturbed, have we? And this man—the murderer—is a risk taker. Just think about how he killed Mr Sykes. I'll just pop in— you can guard the door.'

As Neeta 'popped in', an alarmed-looking man popped out, hastily zipping up his flies. Jenny shifted to and fro uneasily, scanning customers for men who looked like they might need a pee. To her relief, Neeta quickly reappeared.

'There *are* windows, but they're small, high up. Yuk! Why do men's loos always smell so bad?'

They walked back to Neeta's house. Neeta loaded her box of Skye Savory novels into her car and drove Jenny home.

'Thanks again for doing these!'

'That's OK. It won't take me long. Do you think we should tell Marek about our theory? That the man changed his appearance in some way and came out looking different?'

'We should, I guess. He'll probably just laugh, though.'

'*Neeta!*' Jenny said. 'I've just had a thought. The man was carrying a rucksack, wasn't he? That's what the witnesses said. Suppose he already had his change of clothes *in the rucksack*? Then he wouldn't have had to bother about climbing through windows or disposing of his duffel coat. He could have got changed in one of the cubicles and walked out of the main exit just like a normal customer. That would mean he'd *planned* on killing Avery when he entered the library—it wasn't a spur-of-the-moment thing. But we believed that was the case all along.'

'You're right, Jenny!' Neeta beamed. 'You're absolutely right. So, to quote our revered Sherlock, the game is now most definitely afoot!'

CHAPTER 9

After some hesitation, Jenny emailed Marek with their latest theory.

Dear Marek

Neeta and I wondered whether the man shown going into Lattimer's on the CCTV might have had a change of clothes in his rucksack, so when he exited he would look quite different. But this is just a theory, and we don't want to interfere in your investigation!

Best wishes,
Jenny

She wasn't at all sure how he would respond, especially as the first word he'd read would be *Neeta*; however, after a few minutes, his reply appeared in her inbox:

Thanks v much Jenny. A good thought! I'll ask my sergeant to trawl through the footage again.

Another email arrived, this one from Colin Ingram:

Dear Jenny

Thank you again for your wonderful support. The police are releasing Avery's body to me, and I have been speaking to the funeral director in Kerston. The funeral service will be at the crem in Syrenham this Thursday at 12.30 pm, and afterwards his friends will get together for drinks and refreshments at the Kerston White Rabbit. I do hope you are able to join us! And if you know of any more of Avery's acquaintances — even just people who enjoyed reading his books! — who would like to come along, please invite them too.

Kind regards,

Colin

PS. I took the liberty of taking a few photos of your garden, and have worked out a design for it. Of course, you are at liberty to ignore it!

Jenny opened the attachment. It showed a garden plan, expertly drawn, with beautifully lettered suggestions for planting in the now remodelled flowerbeds. How wonderful! Jenny thought she might employ someone to do the heavy digging—there must be gardeners for hire in Kerston!—but she would enjoy sourcing the plants herself and arranging them in a pleasing scheme. Perhaps if she made a start now, she could bed in some bare-root perennials, ready to shoot up in the spring. Colin had even suggested creating a miniature pond, and had added a widely grinning frog on top of a lily pad.

Dear Colin

Thank you SO MUCH for the plan! It's fantastic, and I'll do my best to follow it. Of course I will come to Avery's funeral, and to the reception afterwards. There are a few people who might also like to come, including Inspector O'Keeffe and my friend Neeta, who was with me in the library. I will ask them and let you know numbers.

With best wishes and thanks again,

Jenny

Jenny emailed Neeta and Marek—separately—about the funeral arrangements. The crematorium was on the outskirts of Syrenham, while the White Rabbit was a classy gastropub in Kerston—it was a place she and Alan had had lunch in years ago, and it still seemed to be going strong. A few minutes later, Neeta rang her on her mobile.

'Are you going, Jenny? Yes, of course you are. I'm free that afternoon; it should be interesting. What I was wondering is whether we should tell Dora and Ruby—and offer to take them too.'

'I think we should offer Dora a lift—she was an old friend of Avery's. And Ruby qualifies because she was such a great fan. But would you mind having both of them in your car?'

'As long as they don't fight! One of them can sit in the front—Ruby, her legs are longer. And you can entertain Dora on the back seat... It won't be a very long drive,' she added, as she heard a stifled groan.

'I'll go round and tell them,' Jenny said. She fancied some fresh air.

Ruby flung open her door as soon as Jenny set foot on her drive. She happily agreed to come to Avery Sykes's funeral, but it was the prospect of the reception afterwards that really sparked her enthusiasm.

'*Refreshments.* That is a *lovely* word, don't you think, Jenny?'

'Well, yes, I suppose it is. I'm going to ask Mrs Wedderdale too,' Jenny added, uncertain of what Ruby's reaction would be.

'Ahh!' Ruby gave a magnanimous sigh. 'That is right, you know. Cannot put into words what she has lost. I wonder if she wear a veil.'

Jenny wondered what *Ruby* was planning to wear. Hopefully not the Yeti slippers.

Across the road, Dora Wedderdale was equally keen to attend, and Jenny was unable to avoid being ushered into the room she and Neeta had sat in just a week ago. This time she needed no prompting to remove her shoes and station them in the hallway. She did manage to refuse tea, pleading 'a work date' at the library.

Dora padded to and fro, her hands to her cheeks. 'But what shall I *wear*, Jenny? I have some nice black courts, but I don't think I have a complete black outfit. It's never been one of my colours—it's so *draining*, isn't it?'

'I'm sure that doesn't matter,' Jenny said. 'People are far more relaxed about what they wear to funerals nowadays. A spot of colour would cheer everyone up, after all.'

'Yes, you're right. And no one could object to *lavender*, could they?'

As Jenny walked back home, her phone pinged with a text from Marek. Yes, he would be at the funeral and at the reception afterwards, together with his sergeant, Ceri. The police *did* attend the funerals of murder victims, she thought to herself—as much to scrutinize the attendees as to pay their respects. Sombre figures, parked a few steps back from the open grave into which the deceased's coffin was being lowered. That was a remembered image from some TV programme, though—it would be different at the crem.

The next couple of days passed without incident. Jenny continued with her editing work and finished checking the pile of Skye Savory books for dedicatees. She emailed a list of names to Marek, and he replied promptly:

> Many thanks Jenny. Will cross-reference these against guests at the funeral. A pity there are so many Johns and Peters. A Zebedee would be much more helpful!

On Thursday, Neeta picked her up at the agreed time, looking effortlessly elegant in a long black pleated skirt and purple velvet jacket. Jenny had chosen a dove-grey suit with a turquoise scarf—to add a touch of colour, and to reassure Dora if necessary. Dora came tripping out to meet them in a pale mauve wool coat, her bouffant topped with a tiny black hat wound round with black netting. However, they were all eclipsed by Ruby, who shuffled down her path in moon boots and an extraordinary feathered cloak—*like a monochrome Big Bird*, Jenny thought. The cloak shed a few feathers in her progress, and filled Neeta's car with a strange, fusty smell. Dora rummaged in her handbag for a bottle of cologne, dabbed a few spots on a hanky and held it to her nose. She and Ruby studiously ignored one another, but both talked non-stop throughout the mercifully short journey—Ruby to Neeta and Dora to Jenny.

At the crematorium, Neeta stopped in front of the chapel and let her three passengers out before driving to the car park. Jenny saw a gathering of a few elderly men, one or two of them leaning on sticks and all of them, she guessed, anxious to go inside and sit down. Colin, the youngest by at least three decades, left his post on the fringes of the group and came forward to embrace her.

'Jenny! So glad you're here!'

He was bright and positive, and Jenny guessed he was buoyed up by the occasion of the funeral, and the practical demands it made on him. Afterwards, she feared, it might be a different story. She introduced Dora and Ruby to him as Avery's near neighbours. Dora proffered a limp hand, with a simpering smile, and murmured something about being *So sorry for your loss*, while Ruby announced loudly, 'Skye Savory! She was the best writer ever! No one like her to get the juices flowing!'

Marek had appeared and was making conversation with the mourners. With him was a short, squarely built woman in her twenties with wine-red spiky hair—his sergeant, presumably. When he saw Jenny, he broke away from the group and came over to her.

'Jenny, Ms Scrivens, Ms Wedderdale. It's good to see you. This is Detective Sergeant Ceri Beynon.'

Ceri, who had followed him, grinned, and held out her hand. 'General dogsbody, me!'

The ushers were now guiding people into the chapel. As Jenny hung back, waiting for Neeta, a chauffeur-driven black saloon rolled up, and a man and a woman alighted. He was in his forties, broad-shouldered, with severely brushed-back hair that did nothing to hide his rather prominent ears; she was younger—mid-thirties, perhaps? Ash-blonde hair swung in an elegant bob, and she wore a belted black coat brightened with what Jenny was pretty sure was a Hermès printed scarf. Knee-length tan leather boots completed her outfit.

'Andrew Quigley,' Neeta hissed in her ear. 'Leader of the council. And his wife—she's called Helena. I wonder if he knew Avery or if he's just here in his official capacity. Like Marek. He hates Marek, by the way.'

'*Why?*' Jenny hissed back.

'I think we can guess.'

Anger? Disappointment? Jenny felt them both. She'd started to look on Marek as a friend, had trusted him with feelings close to her heart. And now, he was revealed as someone fully deserving of his reputation. *Lock-up O'Keeffe*. It didn't seem to bother Neeta, who had known him far longer than she had—but it bothered *her*.

Inside the chapel, she and Neeta sat together, keeping Dora and Ruby apart. A couple of late-comers hurried in—both were smartly dressed middle-aged women. Recorded music played softly—Schubert's 'Serenade in D Minor', arranged for cello and piano. It was one of Jenny's favourite pieces too, and once again she felt herself in sympathy with the enigmatic Avery Sykes. The framed photograph that she had seen in his house stood in front of a woven willow coffin. The celebrant, a middle-aged bearded man who could easily have been taken for a vicar, led the small congregation through the various parts of the service. Colin made a short speech, laced with humour about Avery's 'double-life' as the author of the Skye Savory 'romances'. Several of the elderly mourners grinned—they were evidently in on his secret—and Ruby grunted approvingly. Then Andrew Quigley was introduced and rose to address his audience.

'I am afraid I did not have the privilege of being acquainted with Mr Sykes,' he began. His voice was measured, carefully modulated—he was clearly well used to public speaking. 'However, his tragic passing is a loss that the whole of Kerston will feel—and, as leader of the town council, I wish to convey my most sincere sympathies to all his friends who are gathered here. Avery Sykes was a man of many parts, of many talents, a most valued member of our community. It is to be regretted, of course, that the police have made no progress whatsoever in investigating his untimely death, but our *hope* is that that will soon be remedied.' (*Miaow*, Neeta muttered in Jenny's ear.)

More Schubert—this time his song, 'An die Musik'—accompanied the mourners as they processed out of the chapel. Andrew Quigley stalked off to his waiting car, followed by his wife. Jenny saw Marek and Ceri Beynon raise their eyebrows at each other. Neeta went to fetch her car from the car park, followed by the fitter of the elderlies, who would be giving the others a lift.

The sun, which had been hidden behind clouds, came out as they drew up outside the White Rabbit. The pub's frontage was cheerful, with tubs full of late-blooming violas, and a hanging sign depicting Tenniel's White Rabbit from *Alice in Wonderland*—a Victorian gentleman rabbit consulting his pocket watch. Jenny thought he would have fitted right in with Avery's friends at the crematorium.

In a room leading off the main bar, a tempting display of sandwiches and wraps, fruit tarts and cheeses had been laid out, and waiting staff carried in trays of hot food: mini-quiches and burgers, sausage rolls, prawn and veggie skewers. Wine was also on offer, and Ruby headed for the table of gleaming glasses like a parched horse to water. The elderly mourners filled their plates and settled down on chairs around a table. They all seemed to know one another, and raised a quiet buzz of conversation, like bees in a hive. The two women who had come in late introduced themselves to Jenny and Neeta as Catherine Esson, Avery's agent, and Delia Tate, his regular editor. They were both friendly and easy to speak to, and Delia questioned Jenny about her freelance editing experience, explaining that she was always on the lookout for skilled copyeditors and handing her her card.

Marek and his sergeant circulated unobtrusively, and Jenny realized that Ceri was noting down information—names and contact details probably. After a while, she came over to join them.

'Well, this is all very nice, isn't it? A shame we can't stuff ourselves, but we *are* on duty.' She raised her glass of tonic water.

'Have you found out anything interesting?' Jenny asked.

Ceri shook her head. 'No such luck. The most noteworthy happening so far is that one of the old gents propositioned the DI.'

Neeta snorted with laughter, and Ceri joined in.

'He is something of a babe magnet, but it appears he is also an elderly gentleman magnet.'

'Talking about me?' Marek said, appearing at her shoulder.

'Just about your not-so-secret admirer.'

'Oh, come on! All that happened was I felt a hand travelling where it shouldn't have been travelling. I gave a reproachful sort of *look*, but no words were exchanged at all.' He grinned and moved away from them again.

'He's actually great to work with,' Ceri said. 'We have a lot of laughs.'

Jenny saw that Colin had brought the picture of Avery with him and set it up on one of the tables. It was the same photo, but the frame was different from the one in the house. *That knitted pullover, though* ... She had to say *something* to Marek about it, even though she now felt awkward about approaching him. She moved away from Neeta and Ceri and stood by the table, half willing him to come and talk to *her*.

And he did come. 'Are you OK, Jenny? Can I get you anything?'

She didn't turn round to look at him.

'No thanks, I'm fine. Have you found out any more about the bones?'

He drew a long breath and let it out in a sigh. 'Well, they're those of a middle-aged man, probably fifty to sixty years old. Average height. Fractured skull—which I mentioned to you before. The blow was apparently serious enough to have killed him. Our pathologist thought he'd been in the ground for fifteen to sixteen years. But we're no further forward in finding out who he is—we've gone through missing persons' files, but there are no local matches. Of course, he might *not* have been local; he could have been visiting the area or his body could have been transported to the common.'

'But it's more likely that he *was* a local person,' Jenny said. 'You can't see the common from the road—you'd have to *know* it was there. And it's not a specially sensible place to bury a body—there are houses all around.'

'That's very true. Buried in haste, perhaps. Apart from the skull damage, he hadn't suffered any other visible injuries—no broken bones, no telltale metal plates. His dental profile has gone round to local dentists but no luck so far. It's a long shot. He had a couple of missing teeth but no fillings, and, as I'm sure you know, a lot of people—men especially—avoid visiting a dentist.'

'So—no progress?'

'*No*,' he said, and there was a questioning lilt to his voice.

Jenny blushed—she hadn't *meant* to repeat Councillor Quigley's exact words.

'You wanted to talk to me about something else?' Marek continued. 'Something to do with Avery's death?'

'It's to do with this photo. It was in Avery's house; I remember seeing it there.' Jenny scrambled to marshal her thoughts, re-set her concentration. 'Avery was wearing the same pullover when he died. The point is, I'm sure it was hand-knitted —the pattern is so unusual. And Neeta and I wondered who knitted it for him. And whether it could be connected with the knitting needle that was used to stab him.'

Marek picked up the framed photo and peered at it closely. He set it down and took a snapshot on his mobile. Then he turned and walked away. When he returned, Colin was with him.

'We were wondering, Colin, whether you could tell us anything about the occasion when this photograph was taken. Avery had a copy on display too—it was obviously important to him.'

'Oh yes,' Colin said happily. His cheeks were flushed and Jenny guessed he wasn't entirely sober. 'Avery's receiving an award from Romantika—it's an American organization that gives prizes to the best romantic novels published every year. This would have been about twelve years ago, before I got to know him. Of course, he didn't let on *he* was Skye Savory. Everyone was told she had a phobia about flying—the ceremony was in New Jersey—and he accepted the award on her behalf. As A. Arden Sykes. It was for the best romance novel with a historical setting.'

'He's wearing a very snazzy pullover. One of his favourites, I'm guessing.'

'Oh yes! Not to my taste, I have to say—all those funny little figures—but he loved wearing it.'

'Did someone knit it for him? A fan, perhaps?'

'I don't *think* so—I mean, I'm pretty sure it wasn't some random fan. Although they did send him all sorts of strange stuff by way of his publisher—little lacy whatsits and so on. Knickers with no—well, you get the idea.'

'We do indeed.'

'I *think* he said it was a friend. Someone he knew quite a long time ago. He didn't tell me their name.'

'So, you're not sure if it was a man or a woman?'

'No, 'fraid not. I suppose more women knit than men, but men knit too, of course. Fishermen's jerseys—although I suppose those might not be made by your actual *fishermen*.' Colin frowned and swayed on his feet.

'Thanks very much, Colin,' Marek said. 'You've been very helpful.'

'*Have* I?' Colin blinked. 'Is this to do with what happened—to Avery?'

'We're not sure yet. Still collecting evidence. As soon as we have anything concrete, I'll be certain to let you know.'

Colin nodded and wandered off, back to the party at the table —which, Jenny noticed, Ruby had now joined.

'Interesting,' Marek said, 'although I'm not sure how we can take this forward. Give all our suspects a knitting test? Not that we *have* any suspects, as the good Councillor was quick to point out.'

'Why doesn't Councillor Quigley like you?' The words were out before she could stop them. Jenny saw expressions flit across Marek's face: surprise, puzzlement, then—unbelievably—a dash of humour, of suppressed laughter. What she *didn't* see was anger —and he'd have been well within his rights to tell her it was none of her business. But how could he find his actions *funny*?

'It's to do with something that happened a long time ago,' he said, after a pause. 'I behaved extremely badly. I'll tell you about it sometime, Jenny—but not right now.'

Jenny turned, and walked away. She heard Marek call after her, but she ignored him. She was angry with herself for being taken in by his charm. When he was quite obviously someone who toyed with people's feelings and had no conscience whatsoever about the hurt he caused.

The quiet murmurings of conversation from the oldies' table had morphed into roars of laughter, and Jenny saw that Ruby was holding court with what sounded like a series of best-of-Skye-

Savory extracts. *The one where she sit down and she forget the duke left his signet ring in her knickers ... The one where he stick his bottom out of the window, and the gamekeeper ...*

In another part of the room, Catherine Esson and Delia Tate were chatting with Dora. Jenny had noticed that Dora had been ill at ease, looking around her anxiously, too nervous to approach anyone, and she'd made a mental note to go over and talk to her—and then forgotten about it after the business with Marek. She was glad that Catherine and Delia had kindly filled the gap. Dora's tiny black hat jiggled, and the netting threatened to unwind as she waved her hands to and fro. *Such a dear, dear friend*, Jenny heard. *He was a real tower of strength when my husband passed. I don't know what I'd have done without his help. 'No, Dora,' he said to me, 'Let me take care of all of that for you' ...*

H'm, Jenny thought. *She's being a bit economical with the truth.* However, she understood Dora's reluctance to confess what really happened. If she wanted to paint a picture that showed her —and Frank—in a rosier light, who could blame her? Her motive was simply to praise Avery as a caring, considerate neighbour, and she could see her story went down well with Catherine and Delia, who both nodded and smiled.

When Dora saw Jenny approaching, she backed away, clutching the glass of fruit juice she had parked on a table and murmuring something about *not wishing to intrude*. The two women assured her she wasn't doing that at all but failed to stop her retreat. Once she had gone, they welcomed Jenny in her place.

'This is all very jolly,' Delia said. 'Well, one shouldn't use the word *jolly* at a funeral, I suppose, but I do get the impression folk are glad to come together and share their memories of Avery—or, strictly speaking, of Skye Savory.'

'He certainly made a lot of people very happy,' Jenny said, and they both grinned at her, and raised their glasses in a mock salute. Jenny liked them both, but she was also aware that they had made a lot of money out of the Skye Savory name.

'So,' she said, 'No more Skye Savory novels. I know at least one person who'll be sad about that.'

Catherine and Delia looked at one another, and then Catherine said, 'We were just talking about that, Jenny. Skye Savory was *big*, you know. A really stellar brand. Delia and I have been discussing ways in which she—*he*, whatever—might live on.'

In what way? Jenny wondered. She found herself picturing a Skye Savory theme park. Adults only, of course, featuring … She slapped down her wayward imagination and listened more attentively to the conversation.

'To be perfectly brutal,' Delia said, 'there *was* no Skye Savory. She was a *construct*. So there's no reason why she shouldn't have an after-life. We'd have to find a suitable ghost-writer—if that's the word—but I have one or two names in mind.'

'I think Colin said that Avery might have made a few notes about the plot of his next novel,' Jenny said.

'Ah yes, *Colin*. He's Avery's heir, you know—even before they planned to get married, Avery rewrote his will, leaving him all his property—including his *intellectual* property. We'd have to get his consent, in writing. But, from a brief conversation I had just now, I think he'd be very much on board.'

Jenny wondered whether Colin, who was strolling around laughing merrily, glass of wine in an unsteady hand, had been able to give properly informed consent. Still, he'd have sobered up by the time any paperwork was presented to him. She also wondered who Avery's heir had previously been. Who had been displaced in favour of Colin?

Delia and Catherine were discussing the new life of Skye Savory. 'I'd suggest a *slight* restyling of the covers,' Delia said. 'So the books are recognizably from the same stable, but a touch more up-to-date. Gold-blocking of the author's name, perhaps? And photographs rather than artwork.' Her gaze roved round the room, and lighted on Marek, who was standing in a corner talking to Ceri.

'Isn't he absolutely your idea of the Duke of Enfield? I

suppose your dreamboat Inspector hasn't ever done any *modelling*, Jenny?'

He's not MY Inspector, Jenny thought to herself, but she answered politely that, as far as she knew, he hadn't.

'I wonder if he could be persuaded ...' Delia mused.

'Would it involve getting his kit off?' Jenny asked, naughtily.

'Ideally, yes. We could always do a spot of photoshopping, but that probably wouldn't be necessary.' She eyed Marek appraisingly.

Why don't you ask him? were the words on Jenny's lips, but she decided she'd misbehaved enough. 'I don't think he'd be allowed to,' she said. 'He is a senior police officer, and it might be seen as bringing the service into disrepute.'

'Yes, I suppose there's that,' Delia said regretfully.

'What was Avery like?' Jenny asked. She was genuinely curious. The people she'd spoken to so far—Neeta, Ruby, Dora, Colin—had given such different accounts of him that she found it hard to combine those impressions into a coherent whole.

Catherine lowered her eyes for a moment, evidently considering what to say. 'He was quite a complex character, Jenny.' Delia nodded in agreement, as she continued. 'I always got on well with him, but he could be quite sharp, quite cutting if he thought someone wasn't pulling their weight—not doing what they were supposed to be doing. He had a few run-ins with his publicity team, didn't he, Delia?'

'He did indeed.'

'*But* he could be very thoughtful. He was sweet to me when my cat died. He was basically a kind person, I think. With this amazing imagination.'

'And, of course, you have absolutely no idea who might have wished to harm him?'

They both shook their heads. 'It's baffling,' Catherine said. 'Utterly inexplicable.'

The party was breaking up; the waiting staff were discreetly removing empty plates and glasses. Ruby rose from the table, waving and blowing kisses to her new friends, and leaving the odd feather or two spinning in her wake. *Should I say goodbye to Marek?* Jenny asked herself. She didn't want to—she always found it hard to conceal her feelings, and she was sure that he was sensitive enough to have picked up on her coldness. Ruby solved the problem by lurching into a table and having to be guided, gently but firmly, to Neeta's waiting car. She seemed somehow *wider* than before—as if Big Bird had spread its wings. Could she really have eaten so much in such a short space of time?

'That was the best party ever!' she announced between hiccups as she settled herself in her seat, while Dora sniffed fastidiously behind her.

'Off we go, then!' Neeta said, and all her passengers were quieter on the journey home. Once they'd arrived, Dora hopped out of the car with profuse thanks, while Neeta took Ruby's arm to escort her to her bungalow. Jenny spotted a cupcake in the footwell, while a mini pork pie or two dropped from the lining of Ruby's cloak as she staggered up the path. She hadn't put on weight in record time; she'd filled her pockets with goodies, to be enjoyed later.

'Well, Jenny,' Neeta said, buckling her seatbelt and starting the engine, 'what have we learned from all *that*? Apart from Ruby being a human dustbin?'

Jenny, who had moved to the front seat, told her about the plans for more Skye Savory books, but not about Delia's interest in Marek as a cover model. It didn't seem quite right to her to raise a laugh while she was still angry with him—and with herself.

'Colin said that a friend of Avery's knitted that pullover for him,' she went on. 'Quite a long time ago, before they got together. He didn't know if it was a man or a woman, just that it was one of Avery's favourites. In the photo where he's wearing it, he's receiving an award for his novels, in America. Oh, and Colin is Avery's heir—his agent and editor were talking about getting his permission to continue the Skye Savory series.'

'*Interesting*,' Neeta said. 'It does look as though the reason for

Avery's murder lies way back in his past. Has Marek turned up anything? I saw him talking to you, and he's been going through all of Avery's correspondence. I expect they've managed to get into his phone and computer by now, too.'

'He didn't say.'

'What about the bones?'

'They're fifteen or sixteen years old, apparently. And the victim—a middle-aged man—had been hit on the head: his skull was smashed. But there aren't any clues about who he was, and he doesn't match the profile of anyone who's been reported missing locally.'

Neeta pulled up outside Jenny's house. She turned and looked at her.

'*What if it was Avery?*'

'You mean the skeleton? But how could it have been? And if it *was*, who was the person killed in the library? Wait—that *was* Avery: Colin identified him.'

'You told me yourself, Jenny—Colin hasn't known Avery very long. Just a few years.' (*Five years*, Jenny recollected.) 'And Avery had no close family.'

'He did have friends, though.'

'Yes, but not a lot. Perhaps the impostor engineered a sort of turnover in his friendship circle—dumped the old lot and brought in some new ones.'

'But why would this person *pretend* to be Avery? And why would they kill him?'

'Well now, let me think. Avery was a superstar writer. Perhaps he was killed by a jealous rival, who simply stepped in and filled his place.'

'They'd have had to go on writing the Skye Savory books.'

'True. But they could have been a *good* writer themselves, just not a very successful one. They wouldn't have had to be Jane Austen to churn out all those bosoms and stuff.'

'So, if it was the fake Avery who was stabbed in the library, who killed *him* and why?'

'Oh, I don't know, Jenny. Someone who found out his secret? Who wanted to avenge the real Avery?'

'Dora Wedderdale would have had to be in on it,' Jenny said. '*She* wouldn't have been fooled by a new Avery moving in next door to her.'

'Then the two of them must have been in cahoots. That's not impossible, is it? Perhaps she really hated the original Avery and was glad to see the back of him.'

Jenny took a deep breath. 'This is actually all completely daft, Neeta. You've forgotten that *you* recognized Avery's body in the library. And I'm guessing Marek did too, at the postmortem, because Avery also taught *him*.'

'Ah yes, that would seem to put the lid on *that* particular theory. Unless Avery had an evil twin, of course ... Well, it's just out-of-the-sky blue-box thinking—the kind Sherlock is always doing. And it's fun! Oh, while we're on the subject of detectives, Figaro's family sent Maisie a really nice present—a set of notebooks and different coloured pens. And a card, *To the Pet Detective, with love and gratitude from Figaro*. She was over the moon. Of course, it does mean she's on the lookout for more cases now. She's even bought a fishing net with her pocket money in case she has to chase down an escaped budgie.'

Jenny laughed. 'Did she tell you about using your special knife to cut a tree root? I was rather worried we'd ruin it, but we did have to get Figaro out.'

'She mentioned it. The knife's OK, just needed resharpening. She also said Figaro was sick in a soup bowl.'

'Er, yes—I was going to tell you.'

'Not to worry. Quick whizz through on the dishwasher's hot cycle. We have to be broad-minded, being pet owners. Ben once did a wee in a casserole. Anyway, why don't you come to lunch on Saturday? It'll just be sandwiches and fruit, but we can put our heads together about all the info we have so far. It's OK,' she added, as she saw Jenny wince, 'the casserole is a plant pot now.'

'That would be lovely! And thanks for the lift.'

THE KNITTING NEEDLE MURDER

Once indoors, Jenny found she was restless, unable to settle. She liked to process events carefully, one by one, and the day's happenings were still a whirligig in her brain. The two central puzzles—Who killed Avery? Whose were the bones on the common?—were still unsolved, and a resolution seemed as far away as ever. And even if Neeta's suggestion was completely fanciful, it still drew attention to the fact that Avery Sykes's true nature remained elusive. Delia had described Skye Savory as a *construct*, and there was something of that tacked-together quality about Skye's creator. Impressions that didn't meld into a whole. *But*, Jenny told herself, *Colin knew Avery. Loved him. That person—someone who could inspire love—was real all right.*

She'd have said she enjoyed mysteries, but she was starting to realize that the ones that had taxed her brain so far had always offered at least an initial clue, a way in. Here, there seemed to be no entry point: all the possible leads that had emerged—the accusations by the girls at school, the crosswords, the masked attacker, the knitted pullover—had come to nothing. It was like rotating a ball of wool or string, trying—and failing—to find the thread that would unravel the whole.

Jenny found herself walking down through the garden, going over Colin's plans for it. It was soothing to picture the re-shaped flowerbeds, the little pond with floating lily pads. Probably too small for fish, but it might attract frogs and toads. But something uncomfortable was still lodged in her mind, like a stone in a shoe. It took a moment for her to realize what that was.

Marek! She'd ruined their friendship, just as it was starting to develop. *And*, thought Jenny, *I was too hard on him. Up on my high horse, as though I was a guardian of morals.* She'd assumed he'd made a play for Councillor Quigley's wife, but he'd said that whatever happened had been a long time ago, quite possibly before their marriage. He'd done *something* wrong, something he was ashamed of, but it needn't have been what she first thought of. She'd been too quick to believe the worst of him.

As she made her way back to the house, through the fading late-afternoon light, Jenny pulled leaves from the lemon balm bush, rubbed them between her fingers. That sharp, insistent scent ... *I'll make myself remember it before I jump to any more conclusions*, she promised herself.

CHAPTER 10

On Saturday, Jenny walked to Neeta's, carrying an apple pie she'd baked the previous day.

'Oh, lovely!' Neeta welcomed her. 'The apples from your trees are absolutely delicious—much tastier than the ones in the shops.'

They sat down to a pile of sandwiches, and then progressed to slices of the pie with cream.

'How is your detecting going?' Jenny asked Maisie.

Maisie wrinkled her nose. 'I haven't had any new cases recently.'

'That's a good thing in a way, isn't it? It means there aren't any animals in trouble.'

Maisie looked unconvinced.

'Is Jonty working?'

'Yes,' Neeta said. 'He's making a few home visits, but he should be here soon. He said he had a surprise for us, didn't he, Maisie?'

Maisie brightened up. 'It might be another rat. I found Ben in a litter bin—did I tell you, Jenny? Someone had just thrown him away—which was very cruel. He was only a baby. I think that's why he's a bit dopey even now: he had such a bad start in life.

Anyway, Mummy, can I get down? I need to run through some more exercises with him.'

Neeta nodded, and Maisie ran up to her room, reappearing with a small apricot-coloured rat—very pretty, Jenny thought. She had been half-expecting an actual wild rat, like Manuel's 'hamster' in *Fawlty Towers*. Maisie had also brought a towel with her, and she spread this over a low coffee table. She plonked Ben in Jenny's lap and collected a wide cardboard tube from one of the bookshelves.

'Now, Ben, do you remember what you have to do?'

She placed Ben at one end of the tube and an apple core at the other. Ben ran round the outside of the tube and was about to grab the apple core when Maisie whisked it away from him.

'*No* Ben—you need to go *through* the tube. Like Bill does.'

The exercise was repeated a few more times, with the same result, and Jenny felt sorry for Ben, who perhaps was claustrophobic as a result of his litter-bin experience.

'Maybe he doesn't like squeezing into narrow spaces, Maisie.'

'No Jenny, rats *love* being in tunnels. I'm afraid he's just not terribly bright.'

However, while they were discussing him, Ben had managed to tip the apple core on to the floor, had hopped down after it and was busily nibbling. Perhaps *not* so dopey after all.

There was the sound of a key turning in the door, and Maisie ran to welcome her father.

'Daddy! Is the surprise another rat?'

'No Maisie,' Jonty Biddle said, handing her a parcel wrapped in brown paper. 'Two rats are quite enough. This arrived at the surgery for your mum—from a grateful patient, I'm guessing. Don't know *who*, though—unless there's a card inside.'

'Can I open it, Mummy?'

Neeta nodded.

Maisie ripped off the sticky tape and tore the paper apart to reveal a box of chocolates.

'Mmm! Can we have one now?'

'Just one, and offer them round first.'

Maisie wrestled with the close-fitting lid, the box flew from her hands, and the contents scattered over the floor.

'Oh *Maisie*! Pick them up—quickly.'

Jenny knelt to help Maisie rescue the chocolates and replace them in their paper cases.

'There, that's all of them. Oh, there's one still missing.'

Maisie crawled under the table, brushing the carpet with her fingers.

'It must have *rolled* somewhere.'

Jenny stood up and scanned the room. Over by the door, a small mound of orange fur lay unmoving. *Oh no!* Her heart stabbed painfully. But Maisie had spotted Ben too and was kneeling beside him. Jenny saw the rat's paws clench and unclench while tremors shook his body; beside his nose was the missing chocolate.

'*Mummy!* Ben's ill! He must have nibbled the chocolate.'

'Oh dear—poor Ben! I didn't know it was bad for rats—it can poison dogs if they eat a large amount. Jonty, what should we do?'

Jenny picked up the chocolate, grooved with tiny teeth marks. Now she saw there was a minute hole in the top.

'Neeta, look at this! I think something's been injected into it.'

'Oh my God! It must be some kind of *poison*. Quick—let's look at the rest.'

Jonty lifted the tray and peered at it closely. 'Yes,' he said. 'Two or three of them have holes in. What on *earth* does this mean?'

'Daddy! Help Ben! You're a doctor! *Please!*'

'Maisie, sweetheart, we don't know what the poison is. The best thing would be to take Ben to the vet straightaway. With the chocolate. Mummy will drive you; I'll phone ahead to say you're coming.' Jonty reached into his pocket for a grip-seal plastic bag and dropped the chocolate inside. 'But first, wash your hands with soap. You and Jenny. We don't know how toxic this stuff might be.'

The journey to the vet's took about five minutes—but they were very long minutes. Jenny prayed for all the traffic lights to stay green. She and Maisie sat on the back seat, with Ben in a towel-padded shoebox on Maisie's lap. He had stopped convulsing and lay still, only the faint fluttering of his fur showing he was alive. Maisie stared ahead, eyes tearless, stroking Ben with one finger.

'It was my fault. I shouldn't have dropped the box.'

'*No*, Maisie,' Jenny said, sliding her arm round her shoulder. 'That was an accident. The person to blame is whoever's done this.' *And who had? And why?* Jenny knew that Neeta too was thinking it had been pure chance that it was Ben who'd eaten the poison. Otherwise, it would have been one of the adults, or—far worse—Maisie.

The vet's surgery was a brick bungalow—luckily, the car park was only half full. Jenny and Maisie ran in, to be met by the vet herself, Alison Stayt, who had already been briefed by Jonty.

'Poor little fellow,' Alison said, taking the shoebox from Maisie. '*Poison*, your dad thought.' They followed her into an examination room. She lifted Ben out of the box and placed him on the table. Jenny handed her the see-through bag, and Alison pulled on a pair of surgical gloves, opened the bag, took out the chocolate and sniffed it.

'It doesn't smell of anything, apart from chocolate. Some poisons have quite distinctive odours.'

By this time, Neeta had joined them. 'Jonty was given the box at the surgery. It was addressed to me, and it came in the morning's post—there were stamps on the wrapper.'

Alison frowned. 'So, it was meant for *you*! This isn't good at all—you need to notify the police. No one else ate a chocolate, I'm hoping?'

They shook their heads.

'Right. As we have no idea what the poison was, the best thing I can do is give Ben a dose of activated charcoal. That should help to absorb it, before it travels all the way through his system. How long is it since he ate the choc?'

'Only about fifteen, twenty minutes ago,' Neeta said.

'That's good. And he's still alive—also good. Rats are tough little characters, you know. They're also very curious about new sources of food, but they've learnt to be cautious. He probably took only the tiniest of nibbles.'

'And the chocolate by itself wouldn't have poisoned him?'

'No—chocolate contains a substance called theobromine that's toxic to dogs in particular. Not to rats though. And Dr Biddle said there was a hole in the choc where someone seemed to have injected a liquid.'

Ben had now received his treatment, and they watched him anxiously. For what seemed like ages, nothing changed, and then he stirred and waved his paws in the air—not in spasms but as though he was trying to get on to his feet.

'I think we were in time,' Alison said, smiling. 'Keep an eye on him, ring me if he becomes ill again, and let him have water but no food for the rest of the day.'

'*Thank you,*' Maisie whispered. Then she burst into tears.

As Neeta drew up outside her house, she and Jenny noticed Marek's car parked a short way down the road, and when they followed Maisie inside, they found Marek, DS Ceri Beynon, and Jonty standing next to the dining table.

'The hero returns!' Marek said, smiling at Maisie.

'Ben was very brave.' Maisie had lifted him out of his shoebox and was cuddling him.

'He saved you, Maisie. He warned you that those chocolates weren't good to eat. I think that deserves some kind of commendation, don't you, sergeant?'

'Certainly,' Ceri said. 'A medal?'

'I'm not sure where we'd pin it. Perhaps a scroll with his name on it? And a peanut biscuit just for him.'

Maisie beamed. 'I think he'd like the biscuit better. But he isn't allowed any food today.'

'No, of course not. Just leave it with us—we'll sort something out.'

'Take Ben upstairs now, Maisie,' Neeta said. 'You'd better not put him in with Bill—there's food in their cage that he'd try to eat. He can have a rest in your toybox, with a towel and a dish of water.'

Maisie and Ben disappeared to her room, and the two detectives turned back to the table. Lying on it, side by side, were *two* boxes of chocolates.

'Gracious heavens!' Neeta exclaimed. 'Don't tell me we've been sent *another* one!'

'No,' Marek said. 'This one arrived at the police station this morning. Addressed to me.'

'You didn't eat ...?'

'I did not. For one thing, we're not supposed to accept gifts from the public. And for another, when we do get sent things, they quite often have nasty surprises hidden inside.'

Ceri nodded vigorously.

'Without going into any details,' Marek added hastily.

'The boxes aren't quite the same,' Jenny said.

'No, these are a different brand. But they're both ones you can easily buy in any supermarket. The wrapping, the stamps, the lettering are pretty much identical.'

He was wearing a pair of disposable gloves, and now he spread the two brown-paper sheets out on the table.

'You shouldn't touch either the paper or the boxes. We're not going to get any useful fingerprints—the boxes have been through the postal system, so any number of people will have handled them—but it's conceivable there's still some poison adhering to the wrapping.'

The sheets were hand-lettered, in an awkward, laboured hand.

Marek's was addressed to 'Detective Inspector Marek O'Keeffe', Neeta's to 'Neeta Biddle Practice Nurse'. The addresses, postcodes included, were accurate.

'It looks as if the sender had difficulty writing,' Jenny said. 'They might have had some disability, like arthritis.'

'That's possible,' Marek said. 'Or they could be disguising their natural style. Using their non-dominant hand, for instance.'

'The writing is a bit like Ruby's,' Neeta commented. 'On her eggs sign.'

They all laughed. 'We'll keep Ruby in mind,' Marek said. 'She could probably do the writing and wrapping and posting, but she'd be hard-pressed to go out and buy the chocolates. And she was very friendly when I talked to her about Mr Sykes—I can't see she has a motive for wanting me poisoned.'

'Well, that's the question, isn't it?' Neeta said. '*Why* is someone doing this? Is it connected to Avery's murder?'

'A warning? But that's not going to work, is it? We're already deep into our investigation. Which *you're* not part of,' Marek added.

'Excuse me a moment,' Jenny said. A disturbing thought had struck her. The parcels, although addressed to individuals, hadn't been sent to private addresses. She moved away from the table, took out her mobile, and keyed in Val's number.

'Val, hi! This is an odd one, but you don't happen to have received a box of chocolates in the post this morning?'

'Well now, Jenny, you must have second sight! We *did* get a box—addressed to me, in funny squiggly writing. I was going to save it for when you and Neeta are both in.'

'Val, don't touch it! Neeta's also been sent a box, and it turned out to be poisoned!'

'Heavens above! Is Neeta all right? I thought it was a bit odd —there wasn't a card or anything—but people do express their gratitude sometimes.'

'Neeta's fine—her daughter's rat ate a choc, but he's going to be OK. Is the box on your desk?'

'It's on a shelf in the office.'

'I'll tell the police—they'll want to collect it. You just need to make sure no one else touches it.'

Jenny turned to the others, who had caught the gist of the conversation.

'That's *three* boxes. Could there be others?'

Marek and Ceri stared at each other.

'Police station, health centre, library,' Ceri said. 'Is someone trying to disrupt civil society in Kerston? An anarchist cell, or a terrorist group—something like that?'

'But the library is also connected to Avery Sykes,' Jenny said. 'It's where he was murdered.'

Marek paced up and down. 'OK. OK. We need to get these boxes to the lab as quickly as possible. I'll get someone from the station to pick ours up and also the one at the library. Let's think —what other *institutions* might be targeted?'

'The hospital?' Neeta suggested. Kerston had a small cottage hospital. 'The council offices?'

'Right. I'll ring the hospital now, before I ring the station. Ceri, can you do the council? Most likely a parcel would be addressed to Councillor Quigley, but if I rang him, he'd think it was a piss-take. Just ask them if they've received anything at all apart from letters in the post this morning. And if something *does* show up, tell them not to touch it but to let us know at once.'

'Will do.' The two detectives retreated to the other end of the room to make their calls. Ceri quickly returned, shaking her head. 'Nothing at the council offices.' But Marek was still talking, and they watched the expression on his face turn to shock and concern.

'Marek—what is it?' Neeta stepped forward and touched his arm.

'The hospital hasn't received a parcel. But they *have* had an emergency admission—a case of poisoning. It's Pat Brudenell, the manager of the pharmacy on the High Street. She's critically ill.'

'Oh no! Poor Pat! Marek, this *has* to be connected to the

murder investigation. Pat was one of the girls who accused Avery of assault all those years ago.'

'Yes, I talked to her. Strictly, the pharmacy is still an institution—a business—but it's looking as if the Avery connection is the one to follow up. Oh God, the other girl—Zara. Ceri, can you ring her? Use my phone; it's got the number.' Marek handed his mobile to Ceri. 'The hospital ran urgent tests on the poison—again, it was in a box of chocolates. It's arsenic.'

'*Arsenic?*' Jonty said. 'No pharmacist, or doctor, would stock that now.'

'No, but it used to be quite commonly available. It was an ingredient in rat poisons, for example.'

'So, someone might have hoarded a supply.'

Marek nodded.

'But how far does this go?' Jenny said. 'Is somebody targeting *everyone* involved with Avery? And what are they trying to achieve? It can't be revenge, because the police are *trying* to solve his murder. And Val and Neeta and Jonty are blameless, and so, really, is poor Pat—although I can see a person with a disturbed mind might not think so.'

'Zara hasn't received a parcel,' Ceri said, rejoining the circle. 'I've told her what to do if she does.'

'Good,' Marek said. 'Our two deliveries have a Kerston postmark, so it might take longer for a package to reach Glasgow. Monday, perhaps.'

'What's our next step, guv? A public appeal?'

Marek frowned. They could all sense the pressure on him—the need to act quickly and effectively in a desperate situation where there were so many unknowns.

'We won't spook the public just yet. We're bound to get a massive response, and it'll divert resources. Let's go for broke on the Avery connection—contact all the people at the funeral, for a start. We'll do that at the station—we can spread the load. I'll take these boxes with me—we'll get them independently tested, but it's probable the same poison's been used. I'll get someone else to pick up the library one. We'll keep you posted—and take care. All of you!'

Once the detectives had left, Jenny, Neeta, and Jonty stood quite still for a few moments, needing time to absorb what had just happened. Then Neeta said, 'I think we ought to go round and see Ruby and Dora. Check that they're all right.'

'They'll be on the funeral list for the police to contact.'

'Yes, Jenny, but I know Ruby doesn't always hear her phone. And I'm not even sure Dora's *got* one—I didn't see one when we were there. The police will no doubt send officers round, but that'll take time. We can be there quicker. And I do feel kind of responsible for them, since we invited them to come to the funeral.'

'You know what I feel, Jenny?' Neeta said, as she drew up outside Ruby's bungalow.

'*Angry*,' Jenny said, with confidence. She felt the same. Poisoning was such an underhand attack, with the perpetrator safely at a distance. And whoever had been their target, they'd been quite prepared to harm innocent people too.

'*Yes*,' Neeta said, gripping the steering-wheel hard. 'We're going to solve this one. Bring that person to justice.'

'Ruby's OK, anyway.' Jenny could see the binoculars swivelling in her window.

'Well, me dears,' Ruby said as she opened the door to them. 'It is always good to see you. But I am still reading me library books. You would not *believe* what the duke and Lady Thingamy get up to! When they think no one watching them.'

'We need to come in and have a chat, Ruby,' Neeta said. 'Some people have been receiving boxes of chocolates that have made them sick. We just wanted to check *you* hadn't been sent one.'

Ruby led the way into her front room. 'It is funny you should say that. Chocolates came this morning. I think they are from the Judge—at the funeral, you know. He was very admiring. I understand why he didn't put a card in—wanted to keep me guessing. And, as well, there might be a Mrs Judge.'

The box, opened, lay on the table next to Ruby's observation post.

'So, you haven't eaten any yet, Ruby?' Jenny said. The rows were all complete.

'Not yet. Think I have one with me afternoon tea. With cupcake from—um, um ...'

'*Ruby*,' Neeta said, 'you mustn't eat the chocs. Other people have received boxes, and one of them has become very ill. If you look closely, you can see there are tiny holes where a syringe has been used to inject poison.'

'*Poison?* My eyes! That is a sneaky thing for the Judge to do. Perhaps he seeing off his rivals.' Ruby picked up the box and peered closely at it. 'Yes, I see those little holes. But they are not in all the chocs. Not in this Turkish Delight, fr'instance.' Before they could stop her, she had popped the chocolate into her mouth.

'Ruby!' Neeta wrestled the box away from her. 'You mustn't eat *any* of the chocolates. Even the ones without holes—some of the poison could have transferred to them. We're going to take this box away with us—the police will want to examine it. And they'll ring you soon or come and visit, to ask you about it—you can tell them that we've got it.'

'I don't understand this at all,' Jenny said as they walked back down the path to the car, leaving a disgruntled Ruby on her doorstep. 'Why would anyone want to harm *Ruby*? Does she *know* something—without knowing that she knows it?'

Neeta shrugged. 'Quite beyond me, Jenny.' She unlocked the car and put the chocolate box on the back seat. 'Now for Dora.'

There was no answer when they rang Dora's bell.

'I suppose she might have gone out—shopping or something?' Neeta peeked through the windows. 'She's not in her sitting room.'

Jenny pushed at the front door, fully expecting it to be locked, but it swung open into the hallway. She and Neeta looked at one another.

'That's odd, isn't it?' Neeta said. 'I'd have expected her to be very security conscious.'

They entered, cautiously.

'Dora, hello!' Neeta called. 'It's me, Neeta, and Jenny. We've just come to see if you're OK... What was that noise?'

They had both heard it, a faint groaning sound.

'It's coming from upstairs!' Jenny followed Neeta as she homed in on a closed door at the end of the top landing. Without bothering to knock, they entered. Dora was slumped on the floor next to the toilet, vomit staining the front of her dress.

'Jenny! Ring for an ambulance!' Neeta wetted a flannel with water, knelt by Dora, and gently wiped her mouth. Dora's eyelashes fluttered and she moaned again. 'There, there, Dora, it's going to be all right. A doctor is on his way. I guess you've eaten something bad, something that's made you sick?'

Jenny, who had now made the 999 call, thought she saw Dora nod. 'I'll stay with her,' Neeta said. 'Have a look; see if you can find the chocolates.'

The box was on the coffee table in the sitting room, where Dora had served them the Earl Grey tea and the malted-milk biscuits. There were several empty paper cases. Jenny stood by the window, listening for the ambulance's siren. Her anger at whoever had done this dreadful thing mingled with complete puzzlement. Ruby and Dora—two elderly ladies who certainly had their eccentricities but were basically harmless. They couldn't have done anything to deserve this, or to pose a threat of any kind. Their only connection with Avery was that he was their near neighbour —and also, of course, that Dora was his cleaner. Cleaners saw a lot of what was going on in a person's life—could Dora unwittingly be holding some vital piece of information? And Ruby, with her spyglass scrutiny of everything that was happening in the neighbourhood—could she have *noticed* something? Something she had probably barely registered at the time, but that Avery's killer realized would incriminate him? Were these two the key to the mystery, with the other poisonings merely an attempt to cloud the issue?

Jenny's musings were cut short by the approaching whoop of an ambulance siren. She opened the door to two green-suited paramedics, who ran up the stairs. *Ah, Neeta!* she heard one of them say. One of them returned, to collect a folding stretcher, and shortly afterwards Dora was carried out to the ambulance, which took off down the road, siren blaring. Its blue lights crossed with those of an approaching police car.

'They're taking her to the cottage hospital,' Neeta said, coming down the stairs slowly, holding on to the banisters. No matter her profession, finding Dora had been a shock to her too. 'I told the medics we think she ingested arsenic—that will mean they can start treatment straightaway.'

'Do you think she'll be OK?' Jenny asked. 'I've looked at the box, and she ate quite a few chocolates.'

'Oh dear, let's hope so. This is *awful*. And we're not even sure if this is the end of it.'

There was a rap at the door, which was still standing open. Two uniformed police officers entered—Constable Hollis and Sergeant McBride, who had been first on the scene at the library. To Jenny they almost felt like old friends, although they both eyed her with suspicion and the sergeant said, 'In the thick of it again I see, Neeta.'

Neeta was too shattered to be cross. Jenny quickly explained that DI O'Keeffe knew about the poisonings—Neeta herself had been one of the targets—and they'd come here to check on their friends, Ruby and Dora.

'The poisoned chocolates are in the sitting room,' she finished. 'And the box sent to Ruby is in Neeta's car.'

Sergeant McBride appeared to soften. 'Right then. We'll take these back to the station with us. Jack, you go and talk to the lady opposite—get a statement from her. Looks like she had a narrow escape.'

Jack Hollis looked reluctant—perhaps Ruby's reputation was general knowledge—but he crossed the road and disappeared into the bungalow. Neeta and Jenny gave their own statements to the sergeant.

'Have you found any more of these boxes?' Jenny asked, but Sergeant McBride pursed his lips and frowned. She thought, though, that he shook his head ever so slightly. 'And do you know how Pat is? Pat Brudenell?'

'All I can tell you is that she's currently undergoing treatment. I don't know any more than that.'

The sergeant bagged Dora's chocs, and Neeta fetched Ruby's box for him.

'Can we go now?' Jenny asked.

'Yes. We know where to find you if we need you again. Now, what can be keeping that lad?' He drummed his fingers impatiently on the roof of the police car, and stared across the road, to where the curtains had been pulled across Ruby's window.

Neeta sat upright in her driving seat, closed her eyes, and took a few deep breaths.

'Why don't you go straight home, Neeta,' Jenny said, laying a hand on hers. 'You don't need to give me a lift—I can easily walk from here.'

'No!' Neeta was awake, alert, focused again. 'If it's OK with you, we'll go to the pharmacy and see if there's any news of Pat. It's only just gone five—they don't shut till six.'

Jenny agreed, inwardly fearing the news would be the worst.

Mandeep was making up a prescription for a young mother with a baby in a buggy, so they waited until she had left.

'Oh Mandeep,' Neeta said. 'Such a terrible thing, this poisoning. There've been quite a few cases, you know. We were just wondering if you knew how Pat was getting on.'

'I have just spoken to the hospital,' Mandeep said. 'Pat is still seriously ill, but she is off the critical list.'

'Oh, thank goodness for that! I suppose it was chocolates. In a box, with no card?'

'Yes, they came this morning. I thought it was strange that we didn't know who sent them, but Pat said some people were embarrassed about the conditions they suffered from—they were grateful we'd been able to help, but they didn't want us to contact them to say thank you.'

'And you didn't eat one yourself?'

'Well, yes—I did.' Mandeep smiled shyly. 'Just one. Pat had two or three, and she collapsed almost immediately. If I may tell you in confidence, her health is quite compromised: she is asthmatic, and she is still suffering from long Covid, after being infected during the pandemic.'

'Poor Pat! No wonder she became so ill. I think you were just lucky, Mandeep. Your choc must have been OK.'

'Yes,' he said. 'I don't think I will eat one ever again, though.'

'And does Pat have any relatives?'

'Yes, she has two sisters, and they have visited her and will look after her when she leaves hospital. Also, a friend of mine from college is coming to help me run the pharmacy while she is convalescing.'

As they left, after asking Mandeep to give Pat their best wishes, both Jenny and Neeta saw they had a text from Marek:

briefing tomorrow café 3pm

CHAPTER 11

Dani's café was shut on Sundays, but Neeta and Jenny turned up on time, rang the bell and were promptly admitted by Marek.

'Table over there?' He pointed to a corner. 'Tea, coffee?'

'Coffee, please,' Jenny said, wondering if he'd make it as expertly as his mother.

He did.

Neeta opted for tea.

Marek also produced a plate of honey biscuits. 'I thought it would be good to share our ideas,' he said, pulling up his chair. He smiled at them both—a little tentatively and questioningly at Jenny, she imagined. She smiled back, aware she was once again succumbing to his charm, but also convinced that the new, distressing developments in the case meant they needed to work together, with any irrelevant misgivings set aside. Marek was casually dressed in a faded green sweatshirt and jeans, but he looked fresh and well rested, ready to take on the challenges ahead. This was probably the biggest case he'd worked on so far, Jenny thought, and how he handled it would have a bearing on his future promotion prospects. That was the cold way of looking at it, but it didn't preclude his genuine sympathy for the victims, and desire to get justice for them. Also, of course, he had to do all he could to ensure there were no further attacks—*for this wasn't over yet.*

'Right,' Marek said, 'I'll tell you what we've discovered about the poisonings. I got the lab to rush through an analysis, and it was arsenic, in every case. Injected into the chocolates, with a syringe. But not all the chocolates were treated—so it was a matter of chance whether or not you'd be affected. Unless you ate the whole box, of course—which I suppose you might do, in theory, but even a chocoholic would start feeling ill before they got that far.'

'So, it was like a lottery,' Jenny said. 'It just feels so callous—as if the poisoner was playing a game with us.'

Marek nodded. 'I suppose it would have taken too much work—and too much arsenic—to doctor every single choc. But it's still interesting that the *number* of poisoned chocolates varied from box to box.'

'How many were in our box?' Neeta asked.

'Only four. Poor Ben was very unlucky. If you or Jonty or Maisie had eaten one, you'd certainly have felt unwell, but you wouldn't have needed emergency treatment—as Pat Brudenell and Dora Wedderdale did.'

'What about the other boxes?' Jenny asked.

'The library one and the police station one each had five poisoned chocs. Ruby's had six but Dora's only had three—so, again, she was unlucky to pick those. She's doing well, though; the hospital will probably discharge her before too long. It was good you got to her so quickly. How did you get in, by the way?'

'Her front door was open,' Neeta said. 'I thought that was a bit strange at the time. Perhaps she started to feel ill, opened the door to go out and get help—I'm not sure she has a phone—and then had to rush upstairs to the toilet.'

'H'm. The person worst affected was Pat Brudenell. More of her chocolates were doctored than Dora's or Ruby's—ten—and they contained a higher dose of poison. It wasn't by any means a lethal dose—although if you ate a couple, you'd quickly feel awful. Pat, however, had underlying health issues, which made her particularly vulnerable. It was touch and go, but her assistant acted fast, and she was rushed to the hospital in time. She'll be there a few more days, though.'

'It's all absolutely horrible,' Neeta said. 'Six boxes. Did anyone else get sent one? You were going to contact everyone who'd been at the funeral.'

'We've done that, and no, no more boxes have turned up. But there are no deliveries today, of course—it's possible some will arrive on Monday. We've alerted people about what to do in that case.'

'And all the choc boxes were just ordinary ones? Like ours?'

'Yes. Nothing fancy—though obviously quite a nice present. We've questioned local supermarkets about anyone buying a large number of chocolate boxes, but no luck so far. It's more likely the poisoner spread their purchases over time, and over several different outlets. Corner shops, petrol stations, and so on. As for the poison, it seems to have been rat poison. Arsenic isn't used on rats anymore, but anyone could have hoarded their supply. I'm sure there's lots still lying around in garden sheds.'

'But I don't understand what they were trying to achieve,' Jenny said. 'There's an obvious connection with Avery Sykes's murder—but what is it? Were they trying to hamper the investigation? Punish the person they thought was responsible? Or simply mess everything up?'

'There *is* an element of mess-up,' Marek said. 'I don't believe for one moment that this is a motiveless crime. But I think we can discount three of the cases—the boxes delivered to you at the health centre, Neeta—and so, unfortunately, to your family and pets as well—the police station, and the library. They were sent to distract us from the other three. Which are the ones we need to focus on. What are your thoughts?'

'Well,' Neeta said, 'Jenny and I think that Dora and Ruby were the real targets. We agree that the others were just a distraction—although I'm not so sure about Pat. It's possible she had some kind of exchange with the poisoner in the pharmacy—he might have enquired about some toxic preparation that made her suspicious. Dora and Ruby, though, are both near neighbours of Avery. Dora went into his house regularly, cleaning for him, and she might have spotted some compromising document or object. Without realizing what its significance was—otherwise she'd have mentioned it to you. And Ruby spends hours at her window, watching the world go by. She could have seen a person acting suspiciously—although I can't think why she'd keep quiet about it.'

'OK, let's run with that for a moment. The difficulty is, if either of those two had important information, surely the poisoner would want to silence them permanently, not just make them ill. Now our focus is squarely on them, and we're going to ask them to reconsider everything they've told us so far. That's hardly what the poisoner would want. No—I think the real outlier is Pat Brudenell.'

'Why Pat?' Jenny asked.

'Well, we agree the poisoning is somehow connected with Avery's murder? At the very least, it's a strong working hypothesis.'

Jenny and Neeta nodded.

'The connections between the murder and five of the recipients are fairly obvious—they don't require any special knowledge. Dora and Ruby were Avery's neighbours, and his body was found in the library. I'm the investigating officer—I did the TV appeal, for instance. As for you, Neeta, news about you being in the library when the body was discovered could simply have got around—probably by way of Valerie Raeburn, who didn't strike me as the most discreet of individuals. Or the poisoner might have decided to make up a suite of institutions—library, police station, health centre, possibly the pharmacy—to distract us from the fact that their targets were particular people.'

'I was in the library too,' Jenny said. 'In fact, I found Avery.'

'Yes, and you *haven't* been sent a box. That's ... interesting.'

Jenny wasn't sure whether to be relieved or disappointed that she'd been overlooked. *Relieved, surely!*

'The only recipient who doesn't have an *obvious* connection with the murder is Pat. That is, once we discount Neeta's suggestion about prior contact with the poisoner—and we can check on that by talking to her once she's feeling better. Pat *does* have a link with Avery, though—she was instrumental in getting him fired from his teaching post twenty years ago. But—who would remember that? And want to act upon it?'

'So,' Jenny said, 'someone was punishing her for what she did to Avery?'

'It sounds flimsy, doesn't it? And why would they wait such a long time? I'm just putting it forward as a suggestion. After all, Pat was the person most harmed, and that does look deliberate, although it's doubtful that the poisoner knew about her pre-existing conditions that made her specially vulnerable. They probably just wanted her to have a very nasty experience. If that theory has any traction at all, it means we have to go back and look more closely at Avery's teaching career.'

'He did some private tutoring after he left the school. Dora mentioned that to me.'

'We followed that up. Talked to most of the kids he tutored. They didn't all particularly like him, but they agreed he was a good teacher. No complaints at all about inappropriate behaviour.'

'But who would want to *avenge* Avery? He didn't have any close relatives. There's Colin, but he's only known Avery for a few years. Avery was going to *confess* something to him, and I suppose it could be connected with whatever happened at the school—but he never got round to it. And you said Colin has an alibi for the time of the murder.'

'Yes, solid as the rockery he was building that afternoon.'

'If Pat was poisoned because she accused Avery and got him dismissed,' Jenny continued, 'Zara must be at risk too.'

'You're right, and Ceri told her not to open any parcel she received but to contact us immediately. Zara was quite hard to track down, though: she'd moved to Scotland, and she changed her name when she got married. We could do it because the police are good at such things, but it would be more of a challenge for someone who didn't have our resources. Not *impossible*, however.'

'I've had a thought about why I didn't receive a chocolate box,' Jenny said. 'Maybe the poisoner didn't know my full name, or even that I was in the library at the time of the murder—I don't think it was mentioned in any of the reports. And if they *did*, they might not have been able to find out my address—it's not very long since I moved to Kerston, and I'm probably not on the electoral roll yet, or any other records.'

'That's entirely plausible,' Marek said. 'The virtues of keeping a low profile.' He winked at Neeta.

'Or perhaps he'd set up enough distractions already. Six boxes are a lot of work.'

'Also true.'

'And nothing came from your examination of the boxes?'

'No. No fingerprints—or, rather, too many. Brown paper wrapping—you can get that anywhere. Handwriting—obviously disguised. Enough stamps on each parcel to cover the postage, and the boxes themselves were slim enough to slip through a letterbox.'

'So, where are we now?' Neeta said. 'And where do we go from here?'

'I wish I knew. We *are* going to focus on Avery's teaching career—see if he was especially friendly with anyone he worked with. For a start, it cuts down the number of people we need to speak to: his colleagues, in other words. And it's likely some of them will have moved away—it was such a long time ago. Because we are looking for a *local* person—I'm absolutely convinced of that.'

'Yes, I'm sure that's right,' Neeta said. 'I suppose you're under a lot of pressure to make an arrest.'

'Mm. And, to cap it all, we have a missing person case—although Ceri's handling that.'

'Is it connected with the murder?'

'No. It's a young lad called Tommy Petty, who hasn't been seen for about a week. His girlfriend made the report—his parents don't seem that bothered. He's known to the police as a persistent joy-rider—although I'd prefer to call him a car thief. Anyway, it looks like Tommy may have come to a sticky end—a car's been found submerged in the old quarry. Ceri's there now, for the retrieval.'

'That quarry is incredibly deep,' Neeta said. 'And not fenced or anything. People do swim there—although I wouldn't: it's so dangerous.'

'I wouldn't either. The report about the car came from some people calling themselves free divers—which strikes me as an even weirder thing to do. I really don't get this wild swimming craze. Give me a pool with a hefty slug of chlorine any day. I had to wade into a lake once, to rescue a dog that had got itself caught in some reeds. It was bloody horrible. There was about a foot of mud at the bottom. *And* the dog bit me.'

Jenny wondered why he had to do that—it sounded rather beneath the dignity of a detective inspector. Perhaps he'd been on his own.

Marek must have picked up on her quizzical look, because he grinned and continued, 'It was years ago, I was still a probationer. There was a sergeant with me, but he just stood on the bank and laughed. When I got home, my mother shoved me straight into the shower, clothes and all. Anyway, I'd better go and see how Ceri's getting on. Thanks for talking to me—it's kind of sorted things out in my mind.'

'And you haven't found out anything more about the bones on the common?' Neeta asked.

'No—we've drawn an absolute blank so far. Which is strange.

Unless this person had dropped out of society altogether—a vagrant, for instance—you'd think *someone* would have missed him.'

'And what can we do to help?'

'You can go on producing theories, Neeta. Even if they're off-beam, they keep my brain cells active. Just don't take any action on your own. We know so little about this case, we can't predict where there may be dangers.'

'I thought I'd go and visit Dora in hospital,' Jenny said. 'Pat has her sisters to help her, but as far as we know, Dora doesn't have anybody. That would be OK, wouldn't it?'

'Of course. That would be very kind of you, Jenny. The police ought to do more to help the victims of crime—it's something that gets lost in the everyday rush of events.'

'I was going to bring your mother some apples too,' Jenny said, smiling. 'I forgot them today, but I'll drop them in during the week.'

'Terrific! I'll let her know. Oh, nearly forgot.' Marek walked over to the counter and collected a rolled-up sheet of paper tied with a pink ribbon. He presented it to Neeta, who opened it up. Under a picture of a rat, she read:

Ben Biddle
Commendation for BRAVERY
First class
Signed
Marek O'Keeffe   Ceri Beynon
Detective Inspector   Detective Sergeant

'I drew Ben from memory,' Marek said. 'I hope I've done him justice—Ceri said I made him look like a satsuma with ears and a tail. And here are his biscuits too.'

'So—theory time,' Neeta said as they walked off together. 'I'm at the health centre all day tomorrow—I don't have a library round—but meet you here Tuesday, about three?'

Jenny nodded, thinking there was plenty of editing she should be getting on with.

'I'm going to say it,' Neeta went on. 'I'm glad it's not going to be me visiting Dora. I *know* she's had a horrible experience, but, but—ever since that business with the shoes, and having to hide the wheely bug behind a bush, I just want to giggle every time I see her. Obviously *not* when we found her and she was so distressed, but now she's getting better I can just imagine her polishing ... polishing ...' She grabbed a tissue from her sleeve to muffle her snorts. 'I'm a dreadful person, aren't I, Jenny!'

'If *you* are, then I am too!'

The next day, Jenny spent the morning on her editing work, then walked into the town centre after lunch. She wanted to take something to Dora—not chocolates, obviously. And many hospitals didn't allow flowers anymore—something about pollen allergies, or bacteria in the water. She chose a large bunch of sweet seedless grapes from Waitrose and stood contemplating the racks of newspapers and magazines. Dora, she thought, wasn't much of a reader, but she might enjoy something light, like *Hello!* or *OK!*—time in hospital could drag, so any distraction would be welcome. In the end, she picked several magazines, hoping that at least one would prove acceptable. And then she thought she'd better wash the grapes, as it said on the packet, so she sluiced them under the tap in the Ladies. Goodness—so much to think about!

Dora was in a four-bedded ward, with the curtains drawn around her bed. Jenny parted them cautiously, in case she was sleeping. But she was awake; she turned her head slowly on her pillow and tried to smile.

'Hello, Dora,' Jenny said, pulling up a chair. 'How are you

THE KNITTING NEEDLE MURDER

feeling? It was such a horrible thing to happen to you—Neeta and I are both so sorry.'

'Thank you, Jenny,' Dora said. 'It is very good of you to visit.' Her voice was croaky, her lips chapped, and Jenny poured a glass of water from the covered jug on her bedside cabinet. Dora took it and sipped slowly. Her hair, combed straight back, had lost all of its volume, and her face, dry and lined, looked so much older. Jenny felt nothing but pity—and anger, again, at whoever it was who had caused so much suffering.

'I brought you some grapes. Just in case the hospital food isn't very nice.' Jenny retrieved them from her bag and placed them on the cabinet. She also spread the magazines on Dora's bed. 'And these are to stop you getting bored.'

Dora stared at the magazines as though she wasn't quite sure what they were.

'They're a bit light and silly,' Jenny said apologetically. 'Let me know if you'd like something different.'

'Oh no,' Dora said, reaching out and touching a gaudy cover with a finger. 'These are very nice. I will enjoy looking at them.'

'Are they keeping you in another day? I wondered if there was anyone you'd like me to ... give your news to.'

'The doctor says I can go home tomorrow. They will arrange a lift for me. And no, Jenny, there is no one to tell.'

Jenny thought she saw tears swell in the corner of Dora's eyes. 'I'll come and visit you,' she said. 'That is, if you'd like me to. I can help with shopping, do any little jobs that need doing.' *To have no one close to you—how lonely that must be!*

'Oh, would you, Jenny?' Dora brightened and clutched Jenny's hand. 'That would be so kind. I must admit I'm nervous about going back into my house again.'

'That's perfectly understandable,' Jenny said. 'But I'm sure you'll be quite safe. You can lock the door after you.' She remembered that she and Neeta had found Dora's front door unlocked. 'I suppose,' she went on, 'you left your door open when you started to feel ill. It was just as well you did, because it meant we could get in and help you.'

'Of course,' Dora said, 'normally it is bolted. There are so many dreadful people about. But, yes, I felt unwell and thought I would leave the door unlocked so the ambulance people could get in. Then I was going to telephone them, but I just felt so ill ...'

'So, you do have a phone?'

'Oh yes, I will give you the number.'

She recited it, and Jenny took a notebook from her handbag and wrote it down. She tore a spare page out, wrote her own number on it, and handed it to Dora. 'And this is mine. You can leave me a message if I don't pick up.'

Dora took the page and glanced at it. Jenny hadn't the heart to tell her she was looking at it upside-down.

'I don't understand, Jenny. Who would want to poison me? I don't have any enemies.'

'We don't know yet, Dora. The police are working on it. They think it's probable you were just an accidental victim and the poisoner's real target was someone else. They poisoned more people just to confuse the issue.'

'But they might *really* have wanted to harm me. They might come back and try again.' Dora's gaze flickered to and fro, as though danger might be lurking outside her curtained sanctuary.

'I don't think that's likely. It's not as if you *know* anything about Avery's murder.'

'You mean—the poisoner was the same person who killed Avery?' Dora gasped in horror and clutched her sheet with both hands.

'It's looking that way. All the other chocolates boxes were sent to people with some connection to the murder.'

Dora's clenched hands relaxed a little, but she continued to breathe heavily. 'Perhaps I *do* know something.'

'But what would that be? Was it something you saw in Avery's house? Something he said to you? If you remember, you must talk to the police again.'

'But I *don't* remember, Jenny.' Dora turned sad eyes towards her. 'There were just his books, his crosswords, his computer, his papers. And I never touched any of those—he asked me not to, not even to dust them.'

'Then it's most likely you *don't* have any relevant information,' Jenny said in what she hoped was a brisk, reassuring tone. 'That you were just tremendously unlucky. Try not to brood on it, anyway. I have to be off now but give me a ring once you're back home and I'll come round.' Jenny had started to feel drained. She reasoned with herself that it wasn't helping Dora to keep circling round and round the same subjects, replaying what had happened and conjuring up future threats, but she felt guilty nevertheless as she said her goodbyes. She pressed Dora's hand, which now lay limp on the sheet. Dora nodded, resignedly.

The following day she packed apples into a bag, and overtook Neeta as they both headed towards Dani's café.

'How was Dora?' Neeta asked.

'She's getting better. But she's frightened that someone's still trying to harm her. She's such a nervous person, and I'm worried about how she's going to cope.'

'So, you offered to go and visit her?'

Jenny nodded ruefully. 'Only for a few days after she's been discharged.'

'You are a saint, Jenny!'

The café was shut. A blind had been drawn down over the window in the front door, and a CLOSED notice dangled in front of it.

'This isn't right,' Neeta said. 'Dani must be unwell.' She peered through one of the side windows, where red-checked curtains hadn't quite been pulled together. 'There's someone inside.' She tapped on the pane. 'Oh—it's Hanna.'

The door was unlocked, opened, and a woman of about

Neeta's age beckoned them inside. Hanna was small, round-faced, with fair hair gathered in a ponytail. She and Neeta hugged. She was like her mother, Jenny thought. Unlike Marek, who must take after his father.

'*Hanna!* It's lovely to see you. This is my friend Jenny.' Hanna turned, and hugged Jenny too. 'But—is your mum ill?'

'She's OK,' Hanna said. 'She's upstairs, with Marek. We've had a shock, Neeta—the police have found the car that killed Dad.'

'Oh Hanna, *no*! Was it the car in the flooded quarry? Marek told us it was being retrieved, but he thought some joyrider had driven it in.'

'Yes, that's right. It had been down there all this time. The police still had pieces of the broken headlight, and they matched flakes of paint too. Look—I'll tell Marek you're here.'

Hanna disappeared through the door behind the counter, and they heard her climbing the stairs. Shortly afterwards, Marek appeared.

Neeta dashed forward and flung her arms round him. 'Oh Marek, I'm *so* sorry!'

'Thanks, Neeta.' He released her, brushed his thumbs quickly under his eyes, blinked, tried to smile at Jenny. 'Come up to the flat.'

Marek's flat was on the top floor. He showed them into a large sitting room lined with bookshelves. Jenny glimpsed novels, history, poetry. She and Neeta sat together on a sofa, while Marek stood facing them with his back to the window.

'Your poor mother—all of you,' Neeta said. 'It must have been such a shock.'

'Yes. It's taken Mum back to that day when we found him.'

And taken you too, Jenny said to herself. She pictured the twelve-year-old boy running out into the frosty morning, ready to tease his father about falling asleep in the pub. Looking forward to walking back home with him. And Marek was that boy today. Detective Inspector or not, he was still so *young*—younger than her daughter by a couple of years. That tragedy had shadowed his teens, his twenties ...

'Are they really *sure*?' Neeta was saying. 'About the car? Hanna said they'd matched the glass from the broken headlight, and the paint, but I suppose there isn't a chance ...?'

'It was definitely the car that hit Dad,' Marek said.

'And do they know any more about it? Who it belonged to?'

'Yes,' Marek said. 'They do. It was registered to Avery Sykes.'

CHAPTER 12

Neeta and Jenny both stared at Marek, open-mouthed.
'To *Avery*?' Neeta said. '*Avery* was the driver who ran down your dad?'

'He may have been. All we know is that his car was used.'

'But surely the odds are that *he* was driving it? Wasn't it noticed afterwards that it had that damage? I suppose he must have dumped it in the quarry almost immediately.'

'He reported it stolen,' Marek said. 'But not until a week after the accident. According to his statement, it disappeared from a supermarket car park. Of course, with hindsight, that could have been checked—CCTV would have shown if it really was there at the time. But no one bothered. It was a run-of-the-mill crime, and the police were under pressure, not only investigating my dad's death but dealing with a series of sex attacks—some of them on the common, as it happens.'

Jenny thought back to the buried bones. 'And did they find the attacker?'

'Yes, he was convicted and served a sentence.'

'But he's been released now?'

'He has—I don't know what's happened to him or where he is. You're thinking he might be connected with the skeleton, but that killing happened when he was safely locked up. No connection. Anyway, Jenny, Neeta—would you like a drink? Coffee, tea—or something stronger? I'm going to have a whisky.'

'Whisky for us too, please,' Neeta said, glancing at Jenny, who nodded.

Marek crossed to a cupboard and took out three glasses and a bottle of Lagavulin. He poured three generous measures. 'Hope you like this. It's one of the smoky ones.'

Salt air and seaweed. Campfires. Jenny remembered driving round Islay with Alan. He'd wanted to visit all the distilleries, and they'd just about managed it ...

'So—what happens now?' Neeta asked.

Marek shrugged. 'It's not up to me anymore. I'm no longer on the case. The Superintendent's brought in a DCI from Syrenham to replace me—I briefed her this morning. I've been told to take a couple of days off, and when I go back, I'll be working on something different.'

'At least they can't think *you* had anything to do with Avery's death.'

'I'm sure that did occur to the Super. After all, I'm the only person so far who appears to have a motive for killing him. It clearly wasn't me in the library—and I was at the station all that afternoon—but, in theory, I could have arranged the murder. Organized a hit.' He grinned, and for a moment they saw a flash of the old Marek.

'But they'd have had to prove you *knew* Avery was guilty,' Jenny said. 'And there wasn't even a hint of that before they found his car.'

'True. Although the police have so many devious ways of finding things out, I could have been tipped off. Colin might have known, for example, and I could have put the screws on him.'

'But Colin didn't come into the picture until *after* Avery's murder. And he didn't know about the hit-and-run—he just knew Avery had *something* on his conscience.'

'Also true. In any case, I'm not being treated as a suspect—

which, unfortunately for the new investigators, wipes the list totally clean again.'

'But let's go back to Colin,' Neeta said. 'He told us Avery wanted to confess two things to him. And that they both involved another person. Jenny and I thought one must be the murder of the person found on the common—Avery either killed him, or he knew who the murderer was but kept quiet about it, for whatever reason. Now it looks like the second was the death of your father —but, again, someone else was involved. That person could have been driving Avery's car but, once more, Avery covered up for them.'

'Why would he do that?'

'Colin was sure it wasn't an ex-lover—which would be the obvious deduction. Avery could have decided to blackmail the person—and eventually they got tired of being blackmailed, or they ran out of money, and so they killed him.'

'H'm. My father's death wasn't the *second* in time—it was the first. He died twenty years ago, but the bones on the common are about sixteen years old—eighteen max, according to our pathologist. And the two deaths are very different—whoever knocked Dad down almost certainly didn't do so deliberately. Dad had no enemies—everyone liked him. There was nothing about his job to make him a target, either—he ran the local taxi firm. The driver of the car that hit him is to blame for his death because they failed to get help for him—and quite possibly also because they were unfit to drive because of drink or drugs.'

'But someone *did* mean to kill Common Man,' Jenny said. 'They smashed his skull. It's hard to see how *that* could have been an accident.'

'So—two killers, or one? And was Avery involved in one killing—or both of them—or neither?'

'I think we can say for sure that he *was* involved in some way,' Neeta said. 'Are they letting you carry on with your investigation into the body on the common?'

'Yes, they are—for now. I have to report all my findings to the

DCI, and if I turn up anything that confirms a link with Avery's murder I'll be off that case too.'

'So, you're left with the missing joyrider?'

'No—he's turned up. He was staying with another woman in Syrenham, and his girlfriend caught him when he came back to their house to collect some of his stuff. Not drowned at all—he just has a thick ear from where she whacked him with the TV control.'

They all sat in silence for a while. Jenny thought she could almost see the wheels in Neeta's brain spinning as she pondered their next move. Then, 'Let's go downstairs,' Neeta said as she tipped back the last of her whisky. 'I can catch up with Hanna's news, and Marek, I'm sure your mum would like you to be with her. Jenny—you too?'

'I think I'll head home,' Jenny said. She didn't wish to intrude on Neeta's reunion with her friend. 'Give Dani and Hanna my love. Oh—I brought some of my apples.' She handed the bag over.

'Will do.' Neeta took the bag from her. 'I'll pop round this evening after supper, if that's OK. *New theory*,' she whispered in her ear.

Marek accompanied Jenny down the stairs to the front door. 'Thanks so much for coming,' he said, one hand on the latch.

'How are you feeling? Really?'

He rubbed his hands over his face. 'I don't know. I've always thought I *hated* the person who killed my father—if you *can* hate somebody totally unknown. But I don't hate Avery Sykes. For a start, I don't know for sure he was driving the car—and it's more than likely I'll never know. But even if he was ... From what he said to Colin, my dad's death preyed on his mind, and he was going to speak up about it, even if it was twenty years too late.'

'He would have been charged, wouldn't he, if he'd confessed? With failing to report an accident, at the very least?'

'Yes, and he might have faced a custodial sentence. But that's all academic now. Anyway, Jenny—thanks again. And—take care!'

He put his arm round her and kissed her lightly on the cheek before opening the door for her.

Neeta appeared at Jenny's cottage at about eight o'clock.

'Coffee? Tea? Whisky?'

'Oh, not more whisky, Jenny. Jonty made a remark or two when he sniffed it on my breath. I told him it was an emergency whisky, but I probably couldn't pass another one off like that. Also, I'll be driving. Do you have decaf?'

'I do.' Jenny spooned grounds into a cafetière, filled her kettle, and switched it on. 'How are Dani and Hannah? And Marek?'

'Well, devastated, obviously. But they'll be OK—they'll support each other. Hanna is staying over tonight, and she'll help Dani open the café tomorrow. But *knowing* who was driving the car—that would help, of course.'

'And is that part of your new theory?'

Neeta settled herself at the table. 'What I've realized, Jenny, is there's one person we've completely overlooked in our investigation into the murders.' She grinned. '*Pregnant pause!*'

'Well, then?'

'It's Frank Wedderdale—Dora's husband.'

'*Frank?* But he disappeared ages ago.' *When had Ruby said it was? A few years after the Millennium fireworks.*

'Yes, he *disappeared*. He might have had good reason to, quite apart from the stress of living with a compulsive polisher. Perhaps *he* killed the person buried on the common. Perhaps, also, he was the driver who ran down Marek's dad.'

'You mean—he borrowed Avery's car? Why wouldn't he have used his own?'

'Oh, any number of reasons. It might have been in the garage for repairs, he couldn't get it to start ... he might not even have *had* a car.'

'Why didn't Avery report him to the police? I can't believe they were great buddies.'

'Maybe ... maybe he didn't fess up. Told Avery the car had been stolen, and that he could claim for it on his insurance.'

'While actually Frank had driven it into the quarry. Avery *did* report it stolen, but not until a week after the accident. Why wouldn't he have done that straightaway?' Jenny got up to pour the coffee.

'No idea ... There's so much we *don't* know about Avery ... If he *did* find out about the crash, Dora might have pleaded with him not to inform on Frank. Frank could have been charged with dangerous driving, even if they couldn't get a blood sample off him in time to show he was under the influence. He might have been uninsured. He might have been banned from driving ... He could have faced a prison sentence.'

'Frank could have denied that Avery had lent him the car. Then Dora's testimony would have been crucial. I wonder which way she'd have gone?'

'Yes, it was such a strange relationship, wasn't it? Living in each other's pockets but not being romantically involved—since Avery was gay.'

'Perhaps Frank and Dora didn't *know* he was gay—he was quite secretive about it. Travelling down to London to meet Colin —and his other friends.'

'Aha, Jenny! If they *didn't*, this leads us nicely on to my *second* theory—that Frank murdered Avery in the library out of jealousy!'

'But it was Frank who left Dora, not the other way round.'

'True, but he could still have felt that he possessed her and hated the idea of another man stepping into his shoes. There are some characters like that, you know.'

'But where has he been all this time, and why murder Avery *now*?'

'He could have gone anywhere, even abroad. If my *third* theory is right, a few years later he'd have wanted to get as far away from Kerston as possible.'

'Neeta—how many theories are there?'

'Oh, this is the last. Three deaths, three theories. Frank also killed the man on the common. Again, it was out of jealousy—probably of someone who was making a play for Dora.'

'But why was that person never missed by his own family? Marek thought he must have lived outside society in some way—a vagrant, or someone who was sleeping rough. I can't see Dora falling for a person like that.'

'She might not have fallen for him; it could all have been in Frank's twisted, suspicious mind. And he could have been an itinerant or a seasonal worker, travelling the country between one job and the next. He could even have come from abroad, and his family there still don't know what happened to him.'

Does all this fit together? Jenny asked herself. *Dora as femme fatale? Frank as implacable, vengeful killer?* Somehow, she couldn't quite believe it. It was more like a film than real life. *Film noir*, at that. Wasn't it equally probable that Frank—about whom, she recollected, they knew absolutely nothing—was a timid, inoffensive person who found he could no longer live with his wife's obsessive cleanliness, and quietly made his escape one day?

'So, are you saying it was Frank who sent the poisoned chocolates to everyone?'

'Yes! Most of the boxes were dummies, as we thought, but he really meant Dora to eat some. It must have been his way of warning her to stay quiet about what she knew.'

'But there were only three poisoned chocs in *her* box—there were more in Ruby's, and in Pat's.'

'H'm—shelve that for now. Perhaps he accidentally mixed up the boxes.'

That didn't compute for Jenny. A person capable of such

fastidious work with a syringe would surely not make such an elementary mistake.

'He disguised his handwriting on the parcels,' Neeta went on. 'Perhaps Ruby's funny egg sign gave him that idea.'

'Where do you think Frank is now? Is he still hanging around? Surely he's done what he wanted to do—killed Avery and sent a warning to Dora. You don't think he's after anyone else—do you?'

'Well, if he is, it would be Dora, wouldn't it? Are you still planning to go and visit her?'

'Yes, I said I would. She was due to be discharged today—I'll give her a call tomorrow.'

'So, she *does* have a phone?'

'Yes, a landline. She said she was going to ring for an ambulance, and she'd opened the front door ready for it, when she felt sick and had to rush upstairs.'

'You'd think she'd ring *first*,' Neeta said. 'But I suppose she was feeling dreadful and wasn't thinking clearly. When you're at her house, Jenny, see if you can find any evidence of *knitting*. Because I think *she* knitted Avery's pullover for him.'

'I suppose that's possible,' Jenny said. 'I could just ask her.'

'OK, but if she says "no", you could still look for the evidence.'

'Balls of wool lying around? I don't think Dora leaves *anything* out of place.'

'No ... I've got it! She's sure to be wearing a woolly something or other and you can admire it and ask her if she made it herself.'

'You don't think *Dora* stabbed Avery, do you?'

'No, but I think Frank used a knitting needle to send her a very clear message. Jenny, I'm not happy about you going to see her on your own. Couldn't you leave it till Thursday? Then I can come with you.'

'That's kind, but I'll be perfectly all right,' Jenny said. She was very far from believing Neeta's story about a murderous ex-husband lurking in the background. 'I'll have my phone with me—if anything looks remotely dodgy, I can ring the police.'

Something was needling its way into Jenny's dream. Surely the sound—an annoying, trilling insect—would stop soon? But it didn't, and now she was properly awake, groping under her pillow for her watch. *Half-past seven!* Whoever rings that early? It must be bad news, and it must be about Melanie—nothing else would make her heart thump in her chest, her mouth dry up.

However, when she answered the call on her mobile, it was Dora's voice she heard—high, panicking, incoherent. Something about a *man*? In the *garden*?

'*Dora!*' Jenny sat up and shoved the pillows behind her back. 'I can't understand what you're saying. Take some deep breaths, and then speak more slowly.'

She could hear Dora puffing obediently. And then, 'Oh Jenny, I didn't know who else to ring.' (*The police?* Jenny thought, with a touch of resentment.) 'I was woken up—well, no—I was already awake—I sleep so badly after ... after ... Anyway, there was a noise outside my window. Like hailstones—as if someone was throwing *stones* at it. And I got up and I pulled back the curtains—and he was *there*. In the garden. Just standing there. Looking at me.'

'*Who* was there?'

There was a pause and more laboured huffing at the other end of the line. 'It was Avery, Jenny. Avery Sykes.'

'*No*, Dora. It wasn't Avery. It couldn't possibly have been.' Jenny was about to remind Dora that she'd seen his body when she remembered that she *hadn't*; she'd refused to make the identification when Marek had asked her. Perhaps that was the problem. All the same, how could she possibly believe ...

'It was *him*, Jenny. Oh please, please, can you come round?'

'Is he still there?'

'I don't know. I'm too frightened to look out again.'

'Dora, you can call the police. Just dial 999 and say you have an intruder.'

'Oh Jenny, I can't do that. I can't breathe properly. My fingers won't grip. My chest hurts ...'

'All right,' Jenny said, trying to mask a resigned sigh. 'I'll be with you in a few minutes. Try not to worry—all your doors are locked, so no one can get in.'

She wondered whether to call for a taxi—there weren't many buses running so early—but decided a brisk walk would be almost as quick. Fifteen minutes at the outside. Good exercise—although the thought didn't quite blot out her annoyance. *Was Dora going completely round the bend?* And, if she *was*, how should she handle it?

At Dora's house, she paused at the front door. If she knocked, would Dora think it was a spectral Avery Sykes, determined to gain admittance? Well, so be it, Jenny said to herself, banging with her fist and then lifting the letter flap and shouting through, 'Dora! It's me!'

Cautious steps approached, and there was the sound of bolts being drawn. The door opened, to reveal Dora dressed in a nightgown and her fleecy bedjacket. She laid a hand dramatically to her heart. 'Oh Jenny—thank heavens! Do come in.'

She was far more composed than she'd been over the phone. No evidence of a tight chest, breathlessness, sweaty fingers ...

'Show me where you saw the man,' Jenny said, stepping into the hallway. She decided *not* to take her shoes off. Dora led the way upstairs to her bedroom, which was wallpapered with roses winding through a trellis. A flouncy pink duvet had been flung back from the bed, and vases of dried flowers and bowls of seashells clustered on a mahogany chest-of-drawers. *No photos, no bedside reading*, Jenny observed to herself.

Dora swished back the curtains with a dramatic gesture, more confident now she was no longer alone. They both stared down into the garden, which was empty.

'Dora,' Jenny said, 'could you have had a nightmare? Avery's death must have upset you greatly, and these feelings—these *fears*, perhaps—do tend to surface in dreams.'

Dora turned towards her, hurt, reproachful. 'I can see you don't believe me, Jenny. But there really *was* someone there.'

'Well, maybe there was, but don't you see that it couldn't possibly have been Avery?'

Dora shook her head. 'He's not dead,' she persisted.

'But why would he come back to scare *you*? You were friends.'

'I know things, Jenny. He wants to make sure I keep quiet about them.'

'What things? You told me you *didn't* remember anything.'

Dora's lips tightened. 'I know. But I can't break the promises I made, Jenny. It's more than my life's worth.'

Jenny was starting to feel exasperated. It was pointless trying to reason with Dora. 'I'm going to go into the garden,' she said. 'See if there's anything there that might give us a clue.'

She descended the stairs and walked into the spotless kitchen. The door that led into the garden had bolts fitted top and bottom as well as a key in its lock. *Was Dora just paranoid about security?* Jenny wondered. Her fears must pre-date Avery's death.

The garden was neat, *regimented*. A paved patio area, and below it a rectangular lawn, mowed in stripes and bordered with flowerbeds. No trees for an intruder to lurk behind. *All that leaf-fall would be too messy*, Jenny said to herself. She wondered if Dora had considered laying down an artificial lawn—which she could happily hoover. And then she caught her breath in a gasp. For there were footprints—clearly imprinted on the dew-wet grass. A man's—they were large—coming from the gate at the garden's end.

Jenny's brain clicked into gear. By the time anyone else came to look at them, the prints might have disappeared, so she took her phone out of her coat pocket and snapped them from varying distances. Then she crossed the lawn, taking care where she placed her feet. She noted that the prints led from the garden gate to a spot below Dora's window and returned, partly overlaying the first set but, at one point, veering off into the earth of the flowerbed. She glanced quickly up and there was Dora, framed between the curtains, hands pressed to her mouth. Jenny gave her a quick wave.

The wooden garden gate was bolted, but it was only about five feet high. A person could quite easily reach over from the other side, the alley side, and let themselves in. Jenny shot the bolt, opened the gate, and stepped out into the alley. Too late she wondered if she should have been more careful, in case there'd been fingerprints on the lock. The alley, with its bins and weed-strewn gravel, brought back the evening when she and Neeta had broken into Avery Sykes's house next door. She could hardly believe that was only two weeks ago—so much had happened since then.

The gravel had been trodden by many passing feet, so it was impossible to track any individual prints in it. Jenny wandered to the end of the alley and peered to and fro. When she'd been here before, it had been dark, but now she could see the bushes and grasses of the common at the end of the road. Even the oak tree where she and Maisie had uncovered the skeleton. She shivered. What did all this *mean*? *There's a connection*, she said to herself, *between the buried body, Avery's murder, and Dora's terror. I just can't see what it is.*

And who was the intruder? Not Avery, of course, but could it have been Neeta's mystery man, the murderous ex-husband? Surely not—Dora would have recognized him and would have no reason not to call him out. Unless she really *was* terrified of him, and substituted Avery to hide that fact? But, *why Avery*? She could just have said there was a strange man in her garden.

Perhaps, though, Jenny thought, there's no mystery here. Someone might have entered the wrong house by mistake—because they were drunk possibly. Or they were looking for somewhere to pee—although they could have done that in the alley.

But why would they have walked through the garden, stood under Dora's window, even thrown a handful of stones to wake her up. That fitted if—in their sozzled state—they really did think they were in the right place and wanted to be let in. And if they were woozy, that would explain why they wandered off into the flowerbed. But it was still extremely improbable. And the *time* too —so early! Drunk people spilled out of the pubs at midnight or thereabouts, not at seven in the morning.

Jenny walked back up the garden towards the house, thoughtful. On the patio she noticed a spatter of gravel that had been scooped from a terracotta pot containing a trimmed lavender bush. So, Dora was right—the intruder *had* wanted her to notice him.

When she re-entered the kitchen, she found Dora waiting for her, eyes wide with fright, hands clutching woolly scrunches of bedjacket.

'Someone *was* in the garden,' Jenny said. 'I don't know what they were doing there, but I'm going to ring the police.'

'Oh no, Jenny—*please* don't ...'

But Jenny had had enough. 'Dora—someone broke into your property. Of *course* it wasn't Avery, but it was still an intrusion.'

'But then he'll *know* it was me ...'

Shut up about bloody Avery! Jenny felt like screaming—but she didn't. Instead, she mustered all her self-control and said, 'Dora, if you're frightened of someone, the police will protect you. You just need to give them all the information you can.'

'I can't, Jenny—I *can't*.' Dora gulped out a sob.

'Is it your husband? Is it Frank that you're scared of?'

Dora's mouth fell open, her hands dropped to her sides, and she stared at Jenny, angrily, unbelievingly. 'What are you saying, Jenny? Frank is *dead*. I buried my own dear husband, and you come to me with this? I thought that you, of all people, would understand. Well, I was wrong, wasn't I? Sadly wrong.'

'I'm sorry,' Jenny said, although she did not feel particularly remorseful. Evidently, Frank lacked Avery's special gift of being able to return from the dead. What she *did* feel was stifled. It was as if listening to Dora's fantasies used up all the available, breathable air. She opened the kitchen door and went out on to the patio. What she really wanted was to talk to Marek, but she remembered he was still off-duty. But there was his sergeant ...

CHAPTER 13

When Jenny rang the police station, she had only the faintest hope she'd be able to speak to Ceri Beynon. It was still early—not nine o'clock yet—and if she *was* in, it was likely she'd be busy on some other task. But the desk officer, after asking her name, quickly put her through to her.

'Well, good morning to you, Jenny. How are you doing?' Ceri's warm Welsh tones were immediately consoling.

'Ceri, I'm sorry to bother you so early, but something very odd has happened. At Dora Wedderdale's house. She seems to have had an intruder. They got in through the back gate and stood in her garden and threw gravel at her window to wake her up. She's in a state—keeps saying it was Avery Sykes—which it wasn't, obviously. I wondered whether to phone her doctor, but she wasn't imagining the man who broke in—he left footprints on her lawn.'

There was a pause, and then Ceri said, 'OK, Jenny, thanks for that. I'll come straight round. You're there now, I'm guessing?'

Jenny re-joined Dora in the kitchen. 'Sergeant Beynon will be here soon, Dora. You need to tell her everything you know—it's the only way she can help you.'

Dora said nothing but looked sulky. Jenny had missed her

breakfast cup of coffee and was dying for something now. *If only Dora had proper teabags. Not bloody camomile*, she thought to herself, noticing at the same time that she was doing a lot of silent swearing.

A few minutes later, they heard Ceri's car draw up outside. Jenny opened the door to her.

'Thanks so much for coming. I was worried it'd be too early.'

'Well, crime doesn't sleep, as they say. Although in my experience it *does*, just at different times from everyone else.'

Jenny led the way into the kitchen, where Dora hovered anxiously, clasping her hands together, over and over.

'This is Detective Sergeant Ceri Beynon, Dora. I expect you remember her from the funeral. Now, you need to tell her everything you told me.'

Ceri advanced, holding out her hand, and Dora had to free one of hers to grasp it. 'Now Dora—is it all right if I call you that? —I understand you've had a most unpleasant experience. I will go out and have a look at the garden, but in the meantime, what about putting the kettle on and making us all a nice cuppa?'

Dora nodded and moved to fill the kettle from the tap while Jenny followed Ceri out through the kitchen door.

'I'm afraid she only has herb teas. They're not very nice.'

'Oh—*blah*! But they're probably an improvement on station coffee.'

The prints on the lawn had started to fade, but they were still —just—visible. The ones in the flowerbed were much clearer. Jenny showed Ceri the photos she had taken.

'Ah—well, there's no quarrelling with these. Either a man or a woman with unusually large feet. I'm putting my money on the former. Wearing boots rather than shoes, I'd say. And here's some gravel, which bears out Dora's story of the intruder peppering her window. You would only do that if you wanted to wake someone up.'

Ceri stood still, looking around her, gathering her thoughts.

'So, they came in from the alley ...'

'Yes,' Jenny said. 'The gate's easy to open from the outside.'

'Funny she hasn't clocked that. Her front door has bolts like Fort Knox. You told me she thought the intruder was *Avery Sykes*?'

'Yes, she did say that. But it was on the phone and she was very shocked—probably not thinking clearly.'

'All the same, it's a strange assumption to make ... Let's go inside and have a word with her. And brave this herbal concoction.'

'I thought you might prefer coffee,' Dora said, indicating cups filled with a greyish liquid. *Half a teaspoon of instant*, Jenny thought, as she sipped warily.

'That's very kind—thank you,' Ceri said, settling herself on a chair at the table. 'Now, Dora, I can see that *someone* has been into your garden. And having an intruder on your property is always upsetting. Especially with all that has been happening recently. But it's possible this person simply made a mistake—thought they were at a different address. Alcohol may have had something to do with that—although, of course, we have no way of telling. Were they *familiar* to you at all?'

Dora blinked and shot a quick glance at Jenny. 'I—I'm not sure. It was only just getting light. I did think it was Avery—but it can't have been, can it?'

'No—we can definitely rule *him* out. Possibly it was someone who *resembled* Avery. There is no one like that among your acquaintance?'

Dora shook her head miserably.

'I'm afraid we don't have enough evidence to hunt for a suspect—and trespass, in itself, is not a criminal offence. Although, should we happen to identify your intruder—if we discovered, say, that he was making it a habit of this elsewhere— we would naturally have strong words with him. In the meantime, if you are disturbed by any other occurrences, no matter how trivial, you can contact me directly—here's my card.'

'But I don't feel *safe*,' Dora pleaded. 'That man wanted to send me a message. And he might come back.'

'What message might that be?'

Dora shook her head and closed her eyes, fending off further questions.

'You are perfectly safe, Dora. All your doors are lockable—no one can get in without your say so. The one weak point of access is your garden gate, and you might consider a padlock there. If it helps, I will arrange for one of our patrols to drive past during the night, just to make sure that all is well.'

'Thank you.' Dora nodded, but kept her eyes closed.

'I'll say goodbye for now,' Ceri said, extending her hand to grasp Dora's limp one. 'Try not to worry. It's most unlikely this person will ever come back.'

Jenny followed Ceri out to her car. 'A puzzle, isn't it?' Ceri said. 'I must say, if you hadn't found the footprints, I'd be tempted to put the whole thing down to a bad dream. Well, that's all I can do, I'm afraid. Let's hope there are no more alarms and excursions.'

'Thanks for coming,' Jenny said. 'I'm sure she feels better for having talked to you. How is the Inspector, by the way?'

'I called on him yesterday evening, just to bring him up to date. He was rather low—not only this business with the car in the quarry, but—in confidence, mind you—his girlfriend has given him the push.'

'That was unkind—when he was troubled anyway.'

'Oh, it was a couple of days ago, before we identified the car. I could see it coming—she was getting fed up with him breaking appointments and just generally refusing to commit. The usual story, I'm afraid. He has no trouble getting dates; it's further down the line that things tend to go wrong.'

'It sounds all too familiar,' Jenny said. 'I was married to a detective and, yes, you do need a lot of forbearance.'

'Very true! Without wishing to gloat, I'm exceptionally lucky in my bloke. Stonemason. Biker. And a flaming good cook! Plus, the kids are old enough to be left on their own ... *Stepkids*,' Ceri added when she saw Jenny's querying gaze. 'Steve's first wife died from leukaemia when they were very small. Well, time to be getting back to the station. Don't forget, Jenny: give me a ring if you have any more concerns. And the DI is back in harness tomorrow—it'll do him good to have other things to think about.'

Dora was still in the kitchen when Jenny returned to the house.

'I have to be going, Dora,' she said, glancing not-at-all-guiltily at her undrunk coffee. 'Will you be all right now? Sergeant Beynon gave you some very good advice about not worrying anymore. And seeing to the gate.'

Dora looked up. 'Yes, Jenny, of course. You were so kind to come round. I wonder—could I ask you for one last little favour?'

'Er—what is it?' (*Does she want me to fit the padlock for her?*)

'I've been so ... nervous since I came out of hospital. It's all very well for the sergeant to tell me that man won't bother me again, but he's out there somewhere, and I'm so afraid he's going to attack me if I leave the house.'

'Oh *Dora*,' Jenny said with a touch of irritation, 'that isn't going to happen. I can understand you need some time to get your confidence back, but the only way to do it is to take small steps. Down to the corner shop, perhaps?'

'I might be able to do that if you came with me, but their food isn't very well kept—their bananas are so brown they've split, and I saw *flies* round them. No, I'd go to the supermarket if I felt up to it ... Jenny, would you mind doing a spot of shopping for me tomorrow? There's just a few things I need.'

They do deliver, Jenny thought to herself, and then she remembered that Dora didn't seem to have a smartphone. Or a computer. 'If you can wait,' she said, 'Neeta and I could bring your groceries round when we next do the library run. Can you hang on for a few days?'

'Well, I did want some perishables. Milk and butter. And please, Jenny, I'd much rather you did it than the Indian lady. When she came with you the first time, I couldn't help feeling that she was laughing at me behind my back. When I asked her to leave her shopper outside.'

'Oh, I'm sure she *wasn't*,' Jenny lied. Dora seemed to have forgotten Neeta's kindness and prompt action after she'd been poisoned. 'Well—all right. If it's just a few things.'

'*Thank you*, Jenny! Let me see: milk—semi-skimmed, butter—unsalted, yoghurts—blackcurrant flavour, or peach if they don't have that—no *pips*—a tin of tuna—not the oily sort ...'

'Hold on!' Jenny said. 'I'll have to make a list.' She drew her notebook out of her shoulder bag and started writing, at Dora's dictation. *Rather more than a 'few' items*, she thought, as she filled one page and continued on to another.

'... jam—has to be seedless, Cheddar—mild, not *tasty*—a soft brioche loaf, and *teabags*.'

'Earl Grey or camomile?'

'Oh, what you would call *proper* teabags, Jenny. Because of course I will make you a nice cup when you return from your expedition.'

Dora is more observant than I gave her credit for, Jenny said to herself. She was wondering how to broach the subject of payment when Dora got to her feet, crossed to the kitchen dresser, and pulled open a drawer. She withdrew a fat bundle of notes, freed them from an elastic band, peeled several off, and laid them on the table in front of Jenny.

'There, that should cover it.'

There were at least ten twenties there. 'Dora—this is far too much. I won't be spending more than about fifty.'

'That's quite all right,' Dora said gaily. 'Just bring me back the notes you haven't used.'

'And don't you have a bank account? That's where you

should be keeping such large sums. It's rather risky having all this cash in the house.'

'Oh, I can't be bothered with banks. I much prefer actual money—and it's perfectly safe here, hidden away from spying eyes.'

Jenny thought that the dresser would be a burglar's first port of call, but she didn't want to prolong the conversation. She said goodbye and walked back to her cottage. Her steps were slow, and energy seemed to have drained from her. 'That's the last favour I'm doing for Dora,' she said to herself. Surely there were other organizations who could help her. Age Concern? Victim Support? She'd do a bit of research when she felt more alert.

Once through her front door, she was very tempted to crawl back into bed. Instead she made a pot of coffee and a round of toast and ate her breakfast in front of the TV. And then—despite the coffee—she did doze for an hour for so. She woke up with a dry mouth and a disorienting conviction that she hadn't come home at all but was still at Dora's. What she wanted to do now was speak to Neeta, but she remembered it was one of her workdays—she'd have to leave it until the evening. Jenny heaved herself off the sofa, had a revivifying shower, and settled down to an afternoon of editing work.

She rang Neeta after supper.

'Oh *hello*, Mrs Saintly!' Neeta giggled. 'How did your visit to Dora go?'

Jenny told her about her early-morning phone call, and Dora's panic when she thought she'd seen Avery in her back garden. 'She's still nervous about leaving the house,' she finished, 'so I said I'd go to Waitrose and buy some things for her tomorrow. I wondered if I could borrow your shopper-on-wheels.'

'The wheely bug? Yes, of course. Although you are just too nice, Jenny. Surely she could get stuff delivered?'

'Well, I'm only going to do it the once. I'll come round and pick the bug up, if that's OK.'

'No—I'll bring it to you. It's about time we had a confab, anyway.'

Neeta was sure to have plenty of ideas about what had happened, Jenny thought. And she had her own theory about Dora to bounce off her.

'Avery's *evil twin*! Didn't I say it earlier? That's who Dora must have seen!' Jenny and Neeta were drinking white wine —*Just one glass, then!*—and nibbling crisps. 'He murdered Avery and took over his life. And no one realized, because they were identical!'

'I can't believe a twin would have stayed hidden for so long,' Jenny said. 'Why wasn't he found when Marek was looking for Avery's relatives?'

'I don't think Marek would have gone all the way back to look at birth records. Colin said Avery was an only child with only a few distant cousins, and there was no reason for the police not to believe him.'

'So, when do you think this twin took Avery's place?'

'Well, if the skeleton you found is the *real* Avery, it must have been sixteen, seventeen, eighteen years ago. After he'd stopped teaching, but when he'd started to have success with the Skye Savory books. Which provide a motive, of course.'

'Wait a minute, Neeta. I'm not saying you're *wrong*, but whose was the body in the library? Are there *three* Avery Sykeses?'

'H'm. I can see that *is* something of a stumbling block. Triplets? Not impossible. Or perhaps the man Dora saw was another brother, or even a cousin, who looked enough like Avery for her to think it was him. She's perhaps a bit shortsighted and doesn't wear glasses out of vanity.'

'A cousin who came over from Canada?'

'Avery *told* Colin his cousins were there, but he might not have been telling the truth. They could have been much closer to hand, and he wanted to distance himself from them. Socially.'

Jenny could feel her head starting to spin. Avery's connections seemed to be mushrooming, with a band of rogue cousins now entering the mix.

'But what did this *cousin* want from Dora?'

'I don't know. Possibly just some information. They could have got to hear of Avery's death—or, at least, the death of the person who was *identified* as Avery—and they might have hoped he'd left them something in his will.'

'But to go round to his neighbour's house at seven in the morning and throw stones at her window—that's not normal behaviour.'

'Perhaps all the cousins are unhinged. Inbred, or something. That could be why Avery didn't want to acknowledge them. It *could* have been a cousin in the library with the knitting needle—after all, that *is* a pretty crazy murder weapon.'

How many cousins does she think there are? Jenny wondered. 'So, you're not saying the killer was Frank Wedderdale anymore?'

'Well, I'm not exactly *dismissing* him ... Goodness, Jenny, this is a real bag of worms!'

'I think I've found out something about Dora—though I don't know how relevant it is.'

'What's that then?'

'That she's functionally illiterate—she can't read or write, or, at least, she has very great difficulty doing either.'

'Well, she told us she'd never been to the library, and she didn't seem to have any books lying around, but it's a big jump from that to say that she *can't* read.'

'Yes, and I'm not absolutely certain, but a lot of things point that way. Like you say, she doesn't seem to have any books at all—or magazines. And when she asked me to buy the Waitrose groceries for her, she didn't write down what she wanted; she reeled off a list. I could hardly keep up with her!'

'A *list*? I can see why you'd need the wheely bug. It would also explain why she doesn't own a computer.'

'Yes.' Jenny was retrieving more memories. 'When I visited her in hospital, I gave her some magazines to read, and she said thank you, but she didn't show any interest in them at all. She just said, "I will enjoy looking at them." And when I wrote down my phone number on a piece of paper and handed it to her, I happened to notice that she held it upside down. She also keeps a lot of money in the house, as if she doesn't want the bother of dealing with bank transactions—which she'd need to do online, anyway.'

'So, as well as being illiterate, Dora is—what's the word?—*un-numerate*? It must make life very hard for her.'

'It must do.' Jenny tried to imagine a world in which words and numbers were just a mystifying code. How much pleasure Dora was missing out on! Even simply coping in today's hyper-textual world must pose a constant challenge for her. The wonder was, really, that she'd managed to hide her handicap so well, and for so long.

'You'd think Avery would have tried to help her,' Neeta said. 'They were friends, even if we haven't *quite* got the measure of their relationship. And he was an experienced teacher.'

'Perhaps he did try. Perhaps she has—I don't know, some kind of mental block about reading and writing. Almost like a phobia.'

'*Interesting* ... But, like you say, I'm not sure it takes us any further forward in our search for the murderer. Or *murderers*.'

'No, it doesn't. It means she couldn't have read any of the Skye Savory books, though.'

'She must have *known* about them. Seen them on the shelves when she went in to clean. And she didn't faint with shock when Colin mentioned them at the funeral.'

'She might not have realized quite how risqué they were.'

'Only if she didn't look at the covers. Well, Jenny, this is *interesting*, but I can't see how it fits in with any of our murder theories. We gave up on the idea that Avery was killed because of his naughty books.'

'Back to the drawing board, then?'

'I suppose so ... Oh, you could find out about Avery's pullover when you bring Dora the shopping. Perhaps a gentle little enquiry about hobbies, and such?'

The next morning, Jenny dutifully pulled Neeta's bug to Waitrose and loaded it with all the items on Dora's list. She played her usual game of deducing what people were like from the contents of their trolleys. Determined veggie, fastidious foodie? Harassed mum—all those sacks of Monster Munch? Looking at her own haul, she thought she'd come across as a conventional, elderly shopper. Nothing too taxing on the teeth or the digestion.

She could have got the bus to Dora's house, but it was a fine day, so she decided to walk. When she rang Dora's bell, the chiming tones echoed into silence, and there was a wait of about a minute before she heard bolts being drawn back. *Why is she so afraid of everything?* Jenny asked herself. Because Dora's obsession with security—not to mention cleanliness—must long pre-date Avery's murder.

'Oh Jenny! Bless you!' Dora seemed to be her old self again, hair backcombed, cheeks discreetly rouged. She was carrying a pair of capacious carrier bags, and she and Jenny transferred the shopping into them before Jenny wheeled the bug away to its designated hiding place behind the bush.

'Do come in!' Dora's hand fluttered in welcome.

Jenny crossed the threshold and slipped off her shoes (*Don't smile!*). She followed Dora into the kitchen, and watched her stow away the various items, disposing them neatly on the shelves or in the fridge.

'You gave me far too much money,' Jenny said, delving in her pocket for notes and loose change and placing them on a countertop.

Dora smiled. 'Well, I didn't want you to be *caught short*.'

Which reminded Jenny. 'Oh Dora, could I use your, er—

bathroom?' (*Lavatory, loo, ladies*—none of those sounded quite right.)

'Up the stairs and turn left.' Dora's voice was abrupt, and Jenny wondered if her visit would be followed by manic applications of bleach.

'I won't be a moment.'

The last time Jenny had been in Dora's bathroom had been when she and Neeta had helped her after the poisoning. Now, she took in more details. The bath and washbasin were a shade of green she hadn't seen in a long time. *Avocado?* There was a curly mint green bathmat, and an array of tins of talcum powder (*Freesia, Attar of Roses*) on the windowsill. Dora's bedjacket hung on a peg on the door. After Jenny had washed her hands with scented soap and dried them on a fluffy white towel, she ran her hands over it. Its fleeciness was somehow inviting. But there was something else on the peg, behind the jacket. A fabric face mask, hanging by its strap. A *black* mask. *'It's never been one of my colours—it's so draining, isn't it?'* Dora's words before the funeral echoed in Jenny's head.

Before she knew quite what she was doing, she had lifted the bedjacket off its peg and freed the mask. Her fingers moved over it, slowly, consideringly. This was important—she was certain of that. Still holding it, she opened the bathroom door. Dora stood outside on the landing. She glanced at the mask Jenny was holding, and then directly up, at Jenny.

'You *know*, don't you?'

'Yes,' Jenny said. 'I know.'

CHAPTER 14

Jenny followed Dora downstairs, the mask still dangling from her hand. In the lounge, they seated themselves opposite one another, Jenny on the sofa, Dora in an armchair. Dora shifted to get comfortable and joined her hands on her lap, pleating her fingers. She smiled at Jenny.

'They all thought I was stupid at school, you know. *Dora the moron*—that's what the other children called me. I did try, I truly did. But the letters and the numbers wouldn't make sense for me, the way they did for other people. After a while, the teachers stopped caring. Sat me in the corner with a big sheet of sugar paper and a box of crayons and told me to draw houses and gardens, that sort of thing. Well, I could do that. *More* than that, in fact. While they were wittering on at all the clever children, I was making up stories about the houses, and the people who lived in them. They weren't always very nice stories, either. Once I drew a baby falling out of a window, and Miss Herring—she was a horrible old bat—came up behind me and said, "Oh, Dora, whatever is happening here?" "The mother left the window open," I said, "and the baby fell out." Miss Herring was just squeezing her lips together to make a *tut-tut* sound when I quickly drew a man underneath holding up his arms. "But the baby's daddy is going to catch her," I said. She sniffed and went away. Of course, I only drew the man because *she* was there. It would have been a much better story without him.'

Dora sat back and smiled at Jenny. Jenny found she was breathing shallowly, all her senses honed for whatever was coming next. 'It's not too late, Dora,' she heard herself say. 'You can still learn to read—and count.'

'Oh, I can count all right. *One potater, two potater, three potater, four. Five potater, six potater, seven potater, more* ... That's what we used to sing in the playground. But I can't understand how a little mark made in ink can mean the same as *seven potaters*.'

'It's only a sign,' Jenny said. 'Just something you have to learn —like you learned that song.'

'That's what Avery said. He tried to teach me. He was very patient, but in the end even he gave up.'

'You were very close to him, weren't you?'

'I *loved* him, Jenny. And he loved me. Not in a horrible, bothering way, like my husband, but—yes—we loved one another.'

'And you didn't love Frank?'

'No, Jenny, I did not. I lied to you, I'm afraid. He was so *coarse*. And demanding. Dirty too—he made a mess everywhere and expected me to clean up after him. Luckily, he was often away: he was a sales representative for an animal feed company, and he had to do a lot of travelling. That meant I could be there for Avery when he most needed me.'

'And when was that?'

'It all started when those horrible girls told their teacher he'd *interfered* with them. As if he would do anything like that! It meant he had to leave his job—which he loved. And he was so good at it! Anyway, he was *very* upset, and—Frank being away—I tried to cheer him up. "Let's go out somewhere," I said. "Just for a drive in the country." And we did, and we ended up in a pub in a little village, and he bought me a drink—he was always generous like that—and he bought himself one, and then another ... and another. "Avery," I said, "I think perhaps you've had enough", but he said—excuse the language, Jenny!—"I don't care, Dora, I don't *effing* care!" Well, when we left the pub, he was a little unsteady on his feet, but we were in the middle of nowhere and driving was our only way of getting back to Kerston. I've never learned myself, you see. I could never have done *the test*.

'We were nearly home, and we were going down a country lane. The car was wandering a bit, swiping the brambles either side, and I was worried we were going to end up in a ditch. Then, suddenly, there was a *thud*. We'd hit something. Avery said some bad words again and his hands went haywire, and the car skidded and hit another something. This time there was a cracking, scraping noise. Avery pulled on the handbrake and got out of the car. He said he'd run into a metal post at the entrance to a field. Then he walked back down the lane to see what the other thing he'd hit was.

'He was gone quite a long time, and I started to feel anxious and wondered if I should go and find him. Then, suddenly, his hands slapped on my window and made me jump. He disappeared, I wound the window down and saw that he'd moved to the back of the car and was leaning against it, gasping for breath.

'"What is it, Avery?" I asked him. "Did you hit a deer?" Because it had sounded like something quite big.

'"I've killed a man," he said. "I didn't see him—there was no light. But he's dead." Then he began to cry.

'I slipped my arm through his. "Are you *sure* he's dead?" I asked him.

'He nodded. And I didn't want to go and look for myself—I can't bear anything like that.

'"We must telephone the police," I said. "And for an ambulance." I was thinking we didn't have proper lights anymore, so we'd have to walk somewhere—but not past the *body*. Find a phone box. But Avery shook off my arm and then he gripped me by the shoulders.

'"*No!*" he said. "Don't you understand, Dora? The police will breathalyse me, and they'll find out I've been drinking. I'll be charged with dangerous driving—causing *death* by dangerous driving—and I'll probably go to prison."

'His face started to tremble, and I knew he was going to cry again. It was up to me to take charge.

'"*Avery*," I said, "no one has seen what happened. There are no witnesses. All we have to do now is get rid of your car."

'He stared at me. "But how can we do that?" He was completely at a loss. Truthfully, Jenny, men—even the best of them—are so helpless, aren't they? I was thinking fast—it was like the accident had speeded up my brain.

'"Do you know the old quarry, about a mile outside Kerston, on the Syrenham road?"

'He nodded.

'"We'll get rid of your car in it. It's very deep, it'll never be found."

'So that's what we did. We drove there, very carefully because we only had the one headlight working. Luckily, we didn't see another soul, and no cars passed us. At the quarry, Avery drove the car as close to the edge as he dared and then we got out and we both set our hands to it and shoved. The quarry made a sort of swallowing sound, and the car was gone. Avery was trembling—that final push seemed to have taken all his strength. He stood and stared at the black water for a long time, like he was expecting the car to rise up again. But of course, it didn't.

'We walked back to Kerston together. It was cold, and I didn't have the shoes on for a long walk. Avery kept stopping and rubbing his hands over his face, as though he was in a nightmare and wanted to wake himself up. When we got to the gates of our houses, he turned to me and said, "Dora—you won't ever tell anyone, will you?" And I promised that I wouldn't. "*Thank you*," he said, and he kissed me on the cheek, and I could smell the whisky on his breath, but it didn't matter because I loved him. And I'm only telling you this now, Jenny, because no one can hurt him anymore.'

Dora smiled at Jenny, and laid her arms on the arms of her

chair as though there was nothing more to be said about the matter. It was as if, for her, the story ended with Avery's death. Jenny felt chills spread up her spine. It wasn't just the horror of what Avery had done, it was the apparent nonchalance with which Dora had recounted it all.

'*Dora*,' she said after a few seconds' silence, 'Avery's car has been found. In the quarry.'

Dora shrugged. 'Well, Jenny, like I said, they can't do anything to him now.'

'But you need to speak to the police. Tell them exactly what happened.' As she spoke, Jenny wondered whether Dora herself might have committed an offence. She'd known about the accident, but, like Avery, she'd failed to report it. And it was *Dora* who'd suggested pushing the car into the quarry, destroying evidence, concealing Avery's guilt, and condemning Shaun O'Keeffe's family to years of painful uncertainty.

'What good would that do, Jenny? It's not as if *I* knocked the man down. It was his fault anyway, walking in the road in the dark like that.'

'He was called Shaun O'Keeffe, and he was Marek's father—you remember Marek, the detective who talked to you after you found Neeta and me in Avery's house?'

'Maybe I do, maybe I don't. I'm not going to say *anything* to the police, Jenny, and if you talk to them, I'm going to deny we had this conversation.' Dora sat up straight and moved her hands to her lap.

'It was *you*, wasn't it?' The words were out of Jenny's mouth before she had time to second-think. '*You* sent those boxes of chocolates round. To Neeta, Pat, Val—even to yourself.'

'Well, of course I did, Jenny. It was a good *diversion*, wasn't it? Frank used to kill rats with the poison, and it was still in the shed. *And* he was a diabetic and used a syringe to inject himself with insulin. It was all there for me.'

'You could have killed someone, Dora. Pat nearly died.'

'She must have eaten the whole box then. The greedy pig! I

wanted *her* to suffer, because of what she did to Avery. It was a long time ago, but I have *never* forgotten. You could say it was Pat's fault that the accident happened in the first place.'

'But why everyone else? And how did you find the addresses?' Jenny remembered the awkwardly stilted lettering.

'Oh Jenny, Jenny! I wanted to keep people *confused*. If I'd just sent Pat the chocolates, it would have pointed straight back to what she and that other bitch did. Eating a chocolate myself was a price I had to pay, to make sure *I* would never be suspected. As for the addresses, I found them easily enough. You all gave them to me. Look!'

Dora raised herself from her chair and walked to the sideboard. She gathered a handful of cards and leaflets together and dropped them into Jenny's lap. *Neeta Biddle, Practice Nurse, Kerston Health Centre ... Valerie Raeburn, Manager, Kerston Library ... Detective Inspector Marek O'Keeffe ...*

'I just copied what was on the cards.' Dora beamed at Jenny, a self-satisfied smile on her face. 'I can *copy*, you know. I had a bottle of pills from the pharmacy, so there was Pat's address too. And I worked out how many stamps I had to put on, and what colours, from parcels that were sent to me in the past. I always keep books of stamps in the house.'

'And you'd know Ruby's address,' Jenny said to herself, 'as she's just across the road.'

'You didn't send *me* a box,' she said out loud, wondering if her tone sounded disappointed, rather than curious, as she'd intended.

Dora fixed her with a reproachful stare. 'Oh Jenny, how can you even *think* I'd do such a thing? You're my *friend*. I wouldn't have wanted to hurt *you*.'

'You didn't know my address either,' Jenny added to herself. This was turning into a battle of wits, and she wasn't at all sure who was winning. But she had another card to play.

'And there was no intruder in your garden, was there, Dora?'

'Of course not.' Dora smirked, as though it was she who had

solved the puzzle. 'I put on a pair of Frank's old boots after I'd stuffed sheets of kitchen towel into the toes to make them fit. Then I tramped down the garden to the gate and back again and scattered a handful of gravel on the patio. I wasn't sure you'd be able to see the prints on the lawn, so I walked on the flowerbed too. Although, as it turned out, I needn't have bothered.'

'But *why* did you do it, Dora?' *Was she addicted to being centre-stage, frustrated when the searchlight turned elsewhere?*

'You're not as clever as I thought you were, Jenny. Didn't you understand when I said I wanted to keep people *confused*, and make sure *I* was never suspected?'

Jenny shook her head slowly. Something awful was about to happen, and she had no power to stop it.

'It was because of Frank, Jenny. So people didn't find out that I killed him.'

Jenny felt as if ice was creeping all the way down her arms. In the street outside, a mother pushed a squeaky buggy past, chattering to her baby, and a woodpigeon cooed in one of the trees. Normal life was going on, but she and Dora were islanded, isolated. Time itself seemed to have halted in this spotless, airless room.

'You'll be wanting to know *how*,' Dora continued, almost cheerily. 'I don't really need to tell you *why*, but I will. As I said, Frank was a horrible man. Always *pestering* me. *Forcing* himself on me, even though I told him I didn't want it. And his *habits*! He left his dirty clothes on the floor, he trod cigarette ash into the carpet, he never put the seat down when he'd been to the toilet—sometimes, he didn't even flush it properly. But I put up with it all because I had Avery to console me. He was so different, a true gentleman. Frank knew about our friendship, and he kept teasing me about it, but I paid no attention to him. Then, one evening I was making supper, and he came into the kitchen and just *hovered*, not saying anything. I had hot pans to carry, and he was distracting me, so I said, "Frank, stop *bothering* me!"

'I think he'd had a few to drink, because he started laughing, in a sneery sort of way, and he said, "Oh, heaven forbid that anyone should *bother* you, Dora. I suppose him over the fence, he doesn't *bother* you."

'"No, he does not," I said. "Not like *you* do. Now, get out of my way, please."

'But he staggered over to me and shoved his bristly chin against my neck and hissed in my ear, "He's never going to be bothering *you*, Dora. *Effing* nancy boy like him!"

'Well, he startled me with his horrible words. I was carrying a saucepan to the sink to drain the carrots, and some of the boiled water slopped on to his arm. He shouted, and then he hit me, swiped me across the cheek. I dropped the saucepan, and the carrots scattered all over the floor. And I was bending to pick them up to throw them away, thinking I would have to cook a whole lot more, when my arms were filled with a sort of power, and I gripped the pan by its handle and swung it at Frank. I don't think it really hit him *hard*, because he saw it coming and dodged, but he slipped on the wet floor and as he fell, he cracked his head on the kitchen worktop. Then he was lying on his back, not moving, and a pool of dark blood was spreading, mixing with the spilled water and the carrots.

'I just stood and stared at him. His chest wasn't going up and down, so I knew he was dead. And my first thought, Jenny, was, "*At last I'm free!*" But, of course, I had to get rid of his body. I couldn't just *leave* him where he was. So, I went next door and told Avery what had happened. He was very shocked, and I don't think he believed me at first. But he followed me into my house and into the kitchen, and when he saw Frank lying there, his face went very pale and had to lean against the door. He said I should phone the police and explain what had happened—that it had been an accident. Frank had slipped on the wet floor. That there was no need to say I'd hit him with the saucepan.

'But I wasn't having the police involved. They might find out Frank had a saucepan-shaped dent in his head as well as his other injury. Avery tried to argue with me—he said I could plead self-defence as Frank had hit me first—but I just couldn't take that risk. "We'll have to bury him," I said.

'Avery stared at me, because he knew I was expecting him to do the burying. But I reminded him that I had kept *his* secret, so it was only right that he should do the same for me. And I knew where we could dig a grave—in the common at the end of the road.

'So, that night I undressed Frank—because people can be identified from their clothes—and at about three in the morning, when no one was likely to be stirring, we loaded his body into a wheelbarrow and draped a groundsheet over it and wheeled it to a spot near some brambles. Avery dug a hole with his spade, but he was very slow, and I was anxious he wouldn't be finished before daylight. He said the grass was tussocky and the roots were tangled together at quite a depth—I think also he wasn't very fit, because he kept stopping to pant and wipe his forehead. But at last, we had the grave prepared, and we lifted Frank in, and Avery spaded the earth back on top of him. Then he spent a long time ramming the clumps of grasses back into place, checking with his torch that it didn't look as though someone had been digging there.

'We walked back to our homes with the wheelbarrow and the spade and the torch. Avery disappeared at once—he really didn't look well at all—but I mopped up the blood and the mess in the kitchen, and then I got down on my hands and knees and scrubbed very inch of the floor. And the worktop.'

'And you've been madly cleaning ever since,' Jenny said to herself.

'Next time I saw Avery,' Dora continued, 'I reminded him that *he* should give the wheelbarrow and the spade a thorough scrubbing. Because they were both his.'

Dora settled herself more comfortably in her chair and smiled at Jenny. Jenny's whole body had tensed. She tried to relax her muscles, but they wouldn't obey her. How was it possible that this had happened *here*, in this fussy little house, amid cushions and curtains, and soft upholstery? That Dora, whom she'd labelled as mildly neurotic—but no more than that—had committed such a terrible crime? Because it *was* a crime ...

'They found the body,' she said, lips uncomfortably dry.

'I know that,' Dora said. 'I saw them digging.'

'You have to talk to the police, Dora.' *Because if you don't, I will.*

'Talk to the *police*, Jenny? Why should I? Frank is dead and buried. No one is missing him.'

'And why is that? Didn't he have any family?'

'Well, a sister or two. But he didn't get on with them. Not even a card at Christmas.'

'It doesn't matter whether or not anyone *missed* Frank, Dora. He was killed—even if it was by accident—and his body was secretly buried. I'm sure there were ... mitigating circumstances, but the police still need to be told. I can talk to them with you, if you like.' *Would Dora be charged with murder? That seemed unlikely—manslaughter, perhaps. A good lawyer, drawing on what was in all likelihood a history of abuse—perhaps even marital rape—might be able to persuade a jury that she'd acted in self-defence ...*

But Dora was shaking her head. And fluttering her hands and arms too, as though she was brushing away all this unpleasantness.

'*No*, Jenny. My mind is made up.' She suddenly relaxed and smiled. 'I expect you would like to know the rest of the story. About me and Avery.'

Taken aback, Jenny nodded. *What more could she possibly have to say?*

'Well, after those bitches got him dismissed from his teaching post, Avery had to find some other way of making money. He did some private tutoring, but that didn't pay an awful lot. Not as much as he *deserved*. He had the idea that he would write a book —a novel—and he made a start on that. This was while Frank was still alive. But he found it very difficult. "The trouble is, Dora," he said to me, "I can't really *see* my characters. And I can't hear them speak. Also, I think I've written myself into a corner—I can't find a way out."

'Of course, I wanted to help, so I asked him to read me what he'd written so far. It was all in beautiful English, but somehow it didn't grip you, didn't make you want to go on listening. I thought I could help, because I've always been good at making up stories, so I suggested a few changes he could make. He brightened up at once. "You're a genius, Dora!" he said. Well, I wasn't *that*, was I? But I was pleased *he* was pleased, and his praise gave me a lovely warm feeling. Well, Avery finished his book, and it sold lots of copies. He was asked to write more, and of course he did. With my help. I worked out the plots for him, and I told him about the different characters.'

'But Dora,' Jenny said, amused in spite of herself, 'those books were quite—how shall I put it?—quite *spicy*. Lords and ladies getting up to, er ...'

'Oh, making love, you mean? I'm not an *innocent*, Jenny. I knew very well what they were about. It didn't bother me. It wasn't *real life*. Avery used to call me his *muse*—whatever that meant—and he wanted to thank me, in a note at the end of the books. But I said no—I didn't want people finding out what I'd done. Specially not Frank. And after Frank died, I didn't want any attention at all.'

'Oh, well, that's understandable,' Jenny said. She was still getting her head round Dora's newly revealed talents.

'And we were getting along so beautifully,' Dora continued. 'Avery said that people *loved* the books—he had quite a fan club. They didn't know *he'd* written them, of course—he disguised his real name. And then ... and then ...' She faltered, for the first time in her story. 'I went round to his house one day, as usual. I was pleased, because I had thought of a really good plot twist, all about babies being swapped at birth. Avery greeted me, and then he said he had something to tell me. He sat me down in a chair, and made me a cup of tea, which was quite unusual for him— usually I made it.

'"Dora," he said, with a little smile on his face, "I have some very special news for you. I'm getting married."

'Well, you could have knocked me down with a feather! I knew he had friends in London—he went up to visit them on the train—but there'd never been any hint of a *lady*. I wondered if it was an old, rich person and he was marrying them for their money. That happened in one of his books, after all.

'"I can see you're surprised," he said, because my mouth had dropped open. "You haven't met him yet, but his name is Colin. He lives in North London, and he works as a garden designer."

'"He's a *man*," I blurted out, before I could stop myself.

'"Well, yes, of course he is," Avery said. He looked at me curiously, and not in a very friendly way. Then he went on, in a hurry, "I want to make a new start with Colin—I don't want to keep any secrets from him. So, I'm going to tell him about the accident. And about the way you've helped me with the Skye Savory books —because I've allowed him to think that they're all my own work."

'"You're going to tell him that you knocked down and killed that man in the lane?" I couldn't believe what I was hearing, Jenny. Didn't he realize that this Colin could tell the police, and he could be arrested and sent to prison? That *I* could too? He seemed to guess what I was thinking, because he went on, "There's nothing *you* need to worry about, Dora. If Colin wants me to talk to the police—and I'll be guided by whatever he decides—I'll say I was alone in the car, and that it was my idea to push it into the quarry. And, of course, I would never reveal what happened to Frank. Not to Colin, not to anyone. You have my word on that."

'His *word*? What was *that* worth, after he'd been tricking me for so many years? Allowed me to think we were *partners*, when all the time … all the time … How could he marry a *man*, anyway?'

'Well, you can,' Jenny said. 'A marriage between two men—or two women, for that matter—is just as proper and lawful as one between a man and a woman. And I've met Colin. He really loved Avery. They would have been very happy together.'

Dora snorted, and her face crinkled in disgust. 'Avery was *mine*, Jenny. And there he was, sitting there, in the pullover I'd knitted specially for him, telling me he was going to desert me and marry this—this *Colin*.'

'I thought you might have knitted his pullover,' Jenny said. 'It was very ... smart.'

Dora nodded. 'He adored it. Wore it whenever he went to one of his events. I couldn't read a knitting pattern, so I made up the design. It came easily to me—it was like my fingers were telling me what to do.'

'Avery was wearing it when he died.'

'Of course he was.' Dora's expression was strange, almost triumphant.

'Dora ...' Jenny couldn't bring herself to ask the question.

'Did I kill him? I did, Jenny. I loved him, but I couldn't allow him to live. The betrayal was a bad thing—very bad—but there was also what he knew about Frank. I couldn't take the risk that he'd tell Colin everything. I know he'd given me his word, but I could no longer trust him.'

Jenny drew in each breath slowly and deliberately. There was a pain behind her eyes. How could she be hearing this? And yet, she'd *known*, the instant she'd picked up the black mask in the bathroom.

'*Why the library?*'

'Oh, it was the right place, Jenny. Among all his beloved books. Including the ones *I'd* helped him write. I filed the knitting needle sharp, and I dressed myself in some of Frank's old clothes. I had to turn up the trouser cuffs but otherwise they fitted quite well. And I found a pair of his spectacles—although they made things look a bit blurry. The mask—well, you know about the mask. I'd never been in the library before, so I wandered round a bit at first to get my bearings, pretending to look at the books on the shelves. Then I saw him, in a corner. He was filling in one of his crosswords, resting the page on a book on his knee. And smiling to himself, like he was pleased about something. I checked there was no one nearby, and I pulled on a pair of plastic gloves so I wouldn't leave any fingerprints. Then I went up to him. "Avery," I said, and he looked up, with an annoyed face because I was interrupting him. Then I think he recognized me, despite the disguise, because he opened his mouth to say something. But I couldn't have him calling out, so I plunged the needle into his heart. He didn't make a sound. Then I left the library and walked to the department store on the High Street, and I went into the lavatory—the Ladies—and I changed into my own clothes, which I'd brought with me in a rucksack—again, that had belonged to Frank. And then I went home.'

Dora eased herself in her chair, smiled at Jenny, and pleated her fingers in her lap. Jenny was speechless.

'I know you understand, Jenny,' Dora continued. 'But it's a lot to take in. Time for a tea break. I have the teabags you like—I won't be a minute.' She got up and moved off into the kitchen.

Jenny closed her eyes. Her heart's pulses seemed to be sounding in her ears. She would *have* to tell somebody—Marek? Neeta? She had no choice. Her coat lay next to her on the sofa, and she delved into its pockets for her mobile. But it wasn't there. In her shoulder bag? A quick rummage failed to find it, so she tipped all the contents out on to her lap. Notebook, diary, pen, tissues, comb, purse—but no phone. As she puzzled over this, Dora's voice sang out from the kitchen: '*Sugar*, Jenny?'

'No thanks.' Jenny stuffed everything back into her bag. Perhaps she hadn't brought it with her. But she *had*—she'd shown her app to the Waitrose cashier. Had she left it at the checkout? She'd have to go back there and see if it had been handed in.

Dora appeared with a tray loaded with two mugs of tea, two plates, two paper napkins, and a dish of chocolate chip cookies.

'There you are, Jenny. I'll give you the kittens.' Her own mug was patterned with blue and yellow budgies, and Jenny thought of Maisie, the Pet Detective. She needed that kind of lifeline, to the everyday world outside.

'I'll put a cookie on a plate for you,' Dora said, posing one on a napkin. 'Now, these really are my own bakes. I hope you like them. It's quite hard to time them so they don't dry out in the middle.'

Jenny obediently took the plate, but she knew she couldn't bear to take a bite. The crumbs would lodge in her throat. Imagining the scrape of them, she took a few sips of tea.

'What ... what are you going to do now, Dora?'

Dora bit into her cookie. 'Oh, they've turned out all right. What a relief! Well, Jenny, I don't see that *I* need to do anything. No one suspects *me*—they suspect that little old man in the cords and the duffel coat. Good luck to them, I say, trying to find *him*. More tea? I'll top yours up from the pot.' She took Jenny's mug from her hand and retreated with it into the kitchen.

Jenny tried to marshal her scattered thoughts. The best thing would be to humour Dora—drink some more tea—and then leave as quickly as she could. Walk to Neeta's. She'd need her shoes. And what about the bug? Her mouth was uncomfortably dry—nerves, she supposed—and when Dora reappeared with the refill, she drank gratefully.

When her mug was half empty, she replaced it on the table next to her and started to get to her feet. But the room and its patterns were swirling around her, and a rhythm was thrumming in her ears. She fell back on to the sofa, tried to push herself up again. But her arms had no strength in them. She lay back, panting. *This was ridiculous*. She made a final effort to stand, but her legs folded, and she fell, knocking over the table with her half-drunk mug of tea. And now she was lying face-down on the carpet, and Dora was speaking to her, her voice gentle, controlled.

'Don't try to fight it, Jenny. Just—go to sleep. Join your dear husband. Because that's what you really want to do, isn't it?'

Sleep! She was halfway down that path already. But something in Jenny rebelled. *I don't want to die ... I want sunshine, I want my apple trees, I want my friends. I want my darling Melanie ...* She breathed deeply, deliberately, treasuring every breath. Then hands gripped her shoulder, and she was turned over on to her back. Dora's face hovered above her. She was holding a cushion and was smiling down at her benignly. The cushion was embroidered in bright colours and showed a lady in a hooped petticoat standing in a garden. Hollyhocks, roses ... Little stabbing stitches ...

'I'm so sorry, Jenny. You must believe me—I don't want to do this. You're my friend. But I can't let you tell other people about me and Frank. Or me and Avery. I'm sure you understand that.'

Then the cushion descended.

Dora was strong. And although Jenny tried to kick and struggle, to fling her head from side to side, her body wasn't obeying her. Her body was giving in ... *Melanie!*

Suddenly, there was a smashing, shattering noise. Then another, and another. The pressure eased as Dora rose from her knees to investigate. Jenny batted the cushion off, gulped in air. Trails bright as sunlight were streaking down the windowpane. With the last of her strength, she rolled on to her front and tried to crawl away, fingernails scrabbling for purchase on the soft carpet. But Dora had flung the curtains together and was coming for her again. Once more on her back, Jenny heaved her arms up, crossed them in front of her face. It was the last thing, the only thing, she could do. Dora whipped them away roughly, and pressed the cushion down ...

Everything was fading ... She heard an explosion, but it seemed to be a long way away. Wood splintering, bodies colliding, shrieks of fury and frustration. A hand patting her cheek, and Marek's voice saying, 'Jenny! Can you hear me? Stay with me, Jenny ...' And then she was gone.

CHAPTER 15

She was somewhere different. The light on her eyelids. And the noises—clicking of rings as curtains were drawn, feet padding on lino.

'*Mum!*' Jenny turned her head on the pillow, opened her eyes. '*Oh, Mum!*' Melanie was sitting by her bed, holding her hand.

'How are you feeling, Mum? Oh no, don't try to say anything!'

'I'm perfectly all right,' Jenny said. She squeezed Melanie's hand back, she wiggled her toes, she savoured the clean sheet and the honeycomb blanket covering her. Everything was good. She was alive, and her lovely daughter was here with her. Now, why was she in hospital? Memories returned: her struggle to free herself from Dora, sunshine at the window, crashing, confusion, Marek's voice ...

'Did Marek tell you what happened?'

'Marek? Is he the police officer? A Detective Inspector O'Keeffe rang me—you'd listed me as your emergency contact in your diary. He said you were going to be fine, but you'd been attacked and been taken to hospital. That they'd arrested a suspect. Mum —is this to do with the bodies you found? You were very cagey about what was going on there.'

'Yes,' Jenny said. 'It's connected. The woman who attacked me—she also killed two other people.'

Melanie's eyes opened wide. '*No!* Mum, the idea was that you'd settle down to a nice peaceful life here. Not get mixed up in —*murders.*'

'It wasn't planned,' Jenny said. 'And it won't happen again. I'm not going to turn into the Miss Marple of the Cotswolds, darling.'

'I should hope not! Although if you had a little lace collar and a cameo brooch, you could do a mean Joan Hickson!'

'*Melanie!* She was at least twenty years older than me!'

'Wrinkly upper lip then!'

They both laughed.

'What time is it?'

'Early afternoon—just gone two.' Melanie glanced at her watch.

'Goodness, I must have been rushed here.'

Her daughter looked at her curiously. 'Mum, it's *Friday*. You've been out of it for twenty-four hours. The doctors said you'd been drugged—opioids and benzodiazepines, apparently.'

'Oh.' *A whole lost day.* While Jenny tried to get her mind round that, her daughter got to her feet.

'Ah—I see you have more visitors. I'll be off then, Mum, but I'll come back later.' She bent over and kissed Jenny on the cheek.

Jenny watched her walk away and stop briefly to chat to Neeta and Ceri, who had appeared in the doorway of her four-bed ward.

'Jenny!' Neeta flung her arms round her. 'Such an awful thing to happen! But you're all right? Marek said they were keeping you in for at least another day.'

'I'm fine! I think Marek saved my life, although I don't remember much about it.'

'I can vouch for *that*,' Ceri said. 'I've never actually seen someone kick a door down before—usually it's a hefty guy with an Enforcer—but he did it in one. And we mustn't forget Mrs Scrivens, either.'

'Ruby was there?'

'She was standing in the middle of the road when we drew up, hurling eggs at Mrs Wedderdale's window. Her arms were going like a windmill—I think she couldn't actually *stop*, because one of them hit the DI on the head as he was getting out of the car. When it was over and I'd handcuffed Dora and the ambulance had taken you away, I told him not to wash his hair in hot water or he'd end up with scrambled egg in it.' Ceri stole a glance at Neeta, and they both giggled. 'Anyway, he sends his best wishes, and he'll come and see you tomorrow.'

'He's interviewed Dora?'

'Well, no, because it isn't his case. But DCI Yardley let us observe while she spoke to her. I must say, Jenny, it was the strangest interview I've ever witnessed. She wasn't repentant; she actually seemed *proud* of what she'd done. She refused a solicitor —although the DCI strongly advised her to have one present— and she just talked and talked. About killing her husband, and then killing Avery Sykes because she thought he might inform on her. And sending round the poisoned chocolates—partly to get us all in a twist but also to hurt Pat Brudenell. In her eyes, there was a reason for everything she did. She did say she was sorry she attacked you, but, again, she insisted she had no choice. After about an hour, she was starting to repeat herself, going over and over the same ground. And she was behaving very oddly—she dipped her hanky in the glass of water we'd provided and scrubbed and scrubbed at an ink spot on the table in front of her. The DCI is going to arrange a psychiatric evaluation—I've seen criminals *pretend* to be nuts before, but I reckon this was the real thing. Although she certainly had her wits about her when she faked that footprint trail. I'm kicking myself for being fooled by that!'

'Did she tell you about Avery knocking Marek's father down?'

'Yes, she did. I was glad I was by his side then, because it was still a shock for him to learn exactly what happened. If only they'd called an ambulance ... But Avery was convinced Shaun O'Keeffe was dead, and Dora was adamant about not wanting to look at a body, so there was another chance missed.'

'But why did you suspect Dora in the first place?'

'Ah well, I'm going to leave it to the guv to explain that one. He did some pretty nifty behind-the-scenes detecting, despite not being officially involved in the investigation.'

'People who lie to the police', Marek said, 'always snag our attention. Of course, they may have a non-criminal reason for doing so, but, from our point of view, their card is marked.'

It was the following morning, and he was sitting at her bedside. In an hour or so, Melanie would be arriving, to take Jenny back to her cottage. And stay with her for the next few days, despite Jenny's protestations that she was fully recovered.

'It was when I found you and Neeta in Avery Sykes's house,' Marek continued. 'Dora said she'd seen you in the street and let you in through the front door with her key. Well, never mind the unlikelihood of her looking out at the exact moment the two of you went by, I'd spotted Neeta's car parked round the corner, and you wouldn't have passed Dora's house on your way to Mr Sykes's. In fact, it became clear you'd come in the *back* way, knocking over Mr Sykes's gnome ornament in the process. Which I'm guessing he also used as a key safe?'

Jenny nodded.

'So, I wondered *why* Dora had lied, and I decided she'd wanted to draw our attention away from something that was in the room. I didn't know what at the time, but I now think it was the photo of Avery wearing his pullover. Knitted pullover—murder with a knitting needle. A connection we should—*I* should—have pursued more thoroughly—I let it drop after Colin said he didn't know who the knitter was. Also, we were convinced by then that the killer was a man.'

'We all were,' Jenny said.

'Yes. But Dora stuck in my mind like a piece of grit in a sock, and I started to do some background research on her. What had happened to her husband? She described herself as a widow when I first met her, but I couldn't find a death certificate for a Frank Wedderdale. Ruby Scrivens said he had walked out on her, and I could believe that she'd want to hush that up, but there was no trace of a *living* Mr Wedderdale either. It's an unusual surname. And then I thought about the bones on the common. We connected them with Avery Sykes because his house was close to them—but *Dora's* house was close too. Could they possibly be the remains of the mysterious Frank? And, if so, had Avery killed him for some reason?

'*If* that was what had happened—and it was still a very big *if*—Dora must have had some involvement, at least in the burial. Were she and Avery having an affair? That seemed pretty incredible, but I couldn't stop pairing them together in my mind. We were looking into Avery's finances to see who might have benefited from his death, and I noticed that on the first of every month he withdrew a large sum in cash—£1,500. Why *cash*? He had credit cards, a debit card, the whole show. We knew that Dora cleaned for him, so some of it could have been to pay her, but surely not *all* of it? At the same time, I started to have doubts about how literate Dora was. The DC who took her initial statement—about when she'd last seen Avery, and whether he'd had any recent visitors, and so on—said he handed it to her to read and sign but she made a fuss about having mislaid her glasses, and in the end, she just did a sort of scrawl at the foot of the page.'

'That's right,' Jenny said. 'She told me she was teased at school because she had such difficulty with letters and numbers. She also had a big bundle of twenties in a drawer in her kitchen—she gave some to me to do her shopping for her, but she didn't seem to have any idea of their real value.'

'Yes, that explains why she wanted cash—she couldn't have coped with online banking—but I still didn't see why she was being paid so much—assuming she received all of it, which seemed likely, on balance. Was Avery *indebted* to her in some way? Or was he paying for her silence—to keep quiet about something that would have incriminated him? And might that something be linked to her missing husband? Now I reckon Avery paid her the money so she didn't tell us that he'd knocked down and killed my father.'

'An unobtrusive sort of blackmail?' Jenny said. 'Not that Dora would ever have used that word, of course. Or even *thought* that was what she was doing. But I wonder. A few years after your father's death, Avery knew Dora's secret too, and hers was far more serious than his. They must have ended up being locked together, each trapped by the other's knowledge.'

'Yes, that's true.'

Jenny and Marek stayed silent for a few moments, chilled by that picture of closeted, stifling intimacy.

'I don't think Avery lacked a conscience,' Jenny went on. 'He was planning to confess to Colin and, according to Dora, he said he'd do whatever Colin asked him to do. But he had *two* confessions to make, and I don't think the other one was his part in burying Frank's body. Dora told me she helped him with the plots for his novels, and I think he was going to tell Colin about her role. Of course, mentioning Colin to Dora was fatal anyway, because she became convinced Avery would *also* tell him about the murder.'

'So, Avery paid her a slice of his royalties. He doesn't give her a credit in any of his books, though—does he?'

'No, she doesn't figure in any of the Acknowledgements— and I checked through all of them—but she told me that was what she wanted: to stay anonymous.'

'And do we believe her—that she was Avery's co-author?'

'I *think* so. She obviously had an active imagination, and she could make up stories at the drop of a hat—like she did when she came into Avery's house that evening. She told me that when she was in school, the teachers rather gave up on her, and she was left to draw pictures and fantasize about them—the one she mentioned was rather troubling: it showed a baby falling out of a window.'

'H'm. Anyway, although I wasn't supposed to be investigating Avery's murder anymore, I kept on puzzling over Dora. I reread the witnesses' descriptions of the man in the library, and a detail I hadn't noticed before jumped out at me: they'd said that his trousers had been a bit too long for him. Now, why should that be? Even sloppy dressers can usually find themselves trousers that fit. Was he perhaps wearing someone else's clothes? And if he was, *he* might not be a *he* at all ... So, as soon as I got back into work on Thursday, Ceri and I went through the CCTV again that showed the man entering Lattimer's but not re-emerging. And, sure enough, about twenty minutes after he went in, out came a person looking very much like Dora Wedderdale, carrying a large bag. That was all we needed. We jumped in the car and sped off, and—you know the rest.'

Marek leaned back in his chair and smiled at her. 'But you were quicker off the mark than we were, Jenny. What made *you* suspect Dora?'

Jenny closed her eyes, retrieving memories. 'Dora was a very odd person and I thought, at first, she was lonely because she'd lost her husband, and that she also had a mild neurosis about cleaning. I worried she was becoming too dependent on me: ringing me about her so-called intruder, asking me to do her shopping for her. She contradicted herself: she said she didn't know anything about Avery's death, and then she said she *did* know something that put her in danger. I think now she was aiming to confuse us—like she did with the multiple boxes of chocolates. But I realized that she was the person in the library when I found a black face mask hanging on the back of her bathroom door. Dora as Dora would never have worn anything black —she fussed about that when she was deciding what to wear for the funeral. She preferred flowery patterns and soft colours. When I came out of the bathroom, I was still holding the mask —and Dora saw me with it. And then it all spilled out: she *wanted* me to know about everything she'd done. Funnily enough, she'd asked me to buy her a pack of ordinary teabags instead of her usual herbal mixes—I don't suppose she'd already decided to kill me, but they worked to disguise the taste of the drugs.'

'Yes,' Marek said. 'She'd been prescribed the drugs for depression and insomnia—well, *alleged* depression and insomnia—and she must have built up a secret stash.'

'What will happen to her now?'

'I don't know. After she'd made her confession to us—without a jot of remorse, as I expect Ceri told you—she clammed up and hasn't said another word since. We're getting a psychiatrist to examine her—it could be that she won't be judged sane enough to stand trial. In which case we might be looking at detention in a secure hospital.'

They sat in silence for a while, pondering the enigma that was Dora Wedderdale.

Then, 'You're going home today, aren't you?' Marek said. 'Would it be OK if I came round tomorrow morning and took a statement? Just to complete our records, tie up loose ends?'

'But tomorrow's Sunday—isn't it?' Jenny said. She was still thrown by that missing day. 'Wouldn't you rather be doing something else? You could surely take some time off now?'

'I suppose I could. But they expect you to put in the hours on these important cases. And I don't have anything else planned.'

He looked down at the floor for a moment, and Jenny remembered the break-up with his girlfriend. Then he brightened. 'Would you like me to tell you why Councillor Quigley hates me? I said I would, if you remember.'

'I do remember. Go on, then.'

'I have to warn you, Jenny, it'll make you lose any remaining respect you might have for me ... Well, here goes ... Once upon a time there was a little rabbit. His name was Mr Hoppy, and although he was a toy, he was very real to the boy who owned him. Me, as you might have guessed. He used to sleep on my pillow, and my dad would tell me stories about his adventures when he came to tuck me in for the night.

'Now, one day, when I was eight, I noticed that some of his stuffing was coming out. Which was only to be expected—he was nearly as old as I was. I came out of my bedroom and went down the stairs, holding Mr Hoppy—I was going to take him to Mum in the café and ask her to mend him. And there, on the landing, was Andrew Quigley. He was Hanna's boyfriend at the time, so he was often in and out of our house. I didn't like him at all, and he didn't like me. When he saw me, he gave a nasty grin and said, "Aren't you a bit old to be sleeping with an ickle bunny, Marek?" I swung Mr Hoppy at his head, but he snatched him out of my hand, tearing him some more, and then he whirled him round by one of his ears and threw him over the banisters. I was furious and I started punching him, but he easily held me off—he was ten years older than me. *And* he was laughing. Hanna came out of her bedroom to see what the noise was about, and all she saw was me aiming a parting kick at Quigley. She shouted at me, and Quigley grinned some more. I trailed downstairs and rescued Mr Hoppy, and Mum said she'd sew him up for me. Then I started to plot my revenge.

'I don't know if you happened to notice, Jenny, but Andrew Quigley's ears stick out from the side of his head. I heard Mum telling Hanna once that his mother ought to have taped them back when he was little—which didn't go down well with Hanna, as you might imagine. Anyway, for the next few days I busied myself in my bedroom, making a big cardboard model of Dumbo. I copied him out of a book of Disney stories, and I pride myself that the result was very good. I painted him and attached strings to him, so I could manoeuvre him like a puppet. The best thing was, I hinged his ears, so they'd move on their own.

'Next weekend, Quigley was back, and I could hear him in Hanna's bedroom chatting with her. My bedroom was directly above hers—it's the room that's now my sitting room, on the top floor—so I lifted Dumbo carefully out of the window and lowered him to their level. Dumbo rapped on the glass with his trunk to attract their attention. I'd taped a marble to it, to make sure they heard him. Hanna and Quigley both went quiet. Then I leaned out further and worked my props to waggle his ears to and fro. My hands were wobbling because I was laughing so much, but I heard Quigley shout something and then his feet came pounding up the stairs. I'd taken the precaution of locking my door, so he couldn't get at me, but he thumped on it with his fist and threatened all sorts of nasty things. Meanwhile, I'd reeled Dumbo back through my window, but there was such a racket that Dad came up to see what was going on. I let him in and told him about Mr Hoppy and what I'd done to avenge him. And I could see Dad was trying to keep a straight face—he wasn't a fan of Quigley, either ... Jenny—are you all right?'

For Jenny was helpless with laughter.

'Of course, it was an awful thing to do,' Marek continued after he'd poured a glass of water for her. 'I'd never make such a personal attack now—I might have scarred him for life.'

'I think he's survived,' Jenny gasped, sipping carefully so the water didn't go down the wrong way.

'Yes. Although every time he sees me—and we do run into each other occasionally at civic events and so on—I've noticed that the tips of his ears go the tiniest bit pink.'

Jenny's sides were aching and tears were running down her cheeks. 'And do you ... do you still have Mr Hoppy?'

'I do. He sits on one of my shelves—you probably didn't notice him when you visited. If I ever have kids of my own, I'll tell them all about his adventures. Although possibly not *that* one.'

Jenny drank some more water, wiped her eyes on a tissue, looked up—and saw Melanie standing a few feet away. Marek turned, following her gaze, and jumped to his feet. Melanie advanced, frowning.

'It's all right, darling, everything's fine,' Jenny said. 'Er—this is Detective Inspector Marek O'Keeffe. I think you spoke to him on the phone.'

Marek held out his hand and Melanie took it, still glaring at him suspiciously.

'Mel, really, I'm not upset.' Jenny tried to squeeze down the giggles that were still rising inside her.

'I must go,' Marek said. 'Good to meet you, Ms Meaden. Jenny—I'll be with you at about eleven tomorrow.'

'*Jenny*, is it?' Melanie watched him walk out of the ward, stopping to chat briefly with a nurse who was changing the sheets on one of the other beds.

'He's a good friend—he's *become* a good friend,' Jenny said. 'He was telling me a funny story. And truly, Mel, if he hadn't turned up when that woman was trying to smother me, I don't know what would have happened.'

'Oh, well—I'll be nice to him, then. Now, I hope these clothes are OK. For you to change into ...'

The next morning Marek arrived about twenty minutes late.

'I'm sorry,' he said under Melanie's freshly critical eye, 'there was an emergency at the station. Dora Wedderdale collapsed suddenly, and it appears she's suffered a stroke. She's been taken to hospital—not sure what the prognosis will be.'

'Oh.' Jenny didn't know how she felt about the news.

'I suppose that makes a trial less likely,' Melanie said.

'It depends on how her recovery goes—*if* she recovers—and also on the psychiatric evaluation we were in the process of making. But it's out of our hands now—we just have to wait and see.' Marek passed a carrier bag over to Jenny. 'Here are your shoes —they were in the hallway—and your phone. Dora had hidden it under a cushion—I don't know if you'd missed it?'

'I had,' Jenny said, 'but I thought I'd left it in Waitrose. Well, that's a relief: it shows my brain cells haven't entirely packed up.'

'Far from it,' Marek said, smiling. 'Now, if it's OK with you, we'll just go over your statement ...'

'Would you like a tea? Or a coffee?' Marek looked up at Melanie and, as Jenny watched, something seemed to pass between them. A tingle of electricity, subtle but unmistakable, as they held each other's gaze for a moment too long. *Oh, Melanie! I'll have to speak to him,* Jenny thought, *because I'm not having my daughter hurt all over again.* She recited her account of what had happened in Dora's house, she answered Marek's questions, but her mind was elsewhere.

'Thank you, Jenny.' Marek folded the sheet she had signed and slipped it into his briefcase.

'Come and look at the garden,' Melanie said. 'You can help me collect some apples.'

From the kitchen window, Jenny watched them wander down the path. Marek carried the bag he'd brought Jenny's shoes and phone in, and they started to fill it with the windfalls. She held her breath as they moved away from her, under the canopy of branches—because surely they'd stopped bending for the apples and were standing close together. *I shouldn't be doing a Ruby*, she told herself, and walked back into the sitting room with a tray for the empty coffee cups. Soon afterwards, they came in from the garden, and Melanie handed her the bag. *Not very full*, Jenny noted.

Marek had a few leaves stuck in his hair. 'Well, I'll be off,' he said. 'Thanks for the statement, Jenny. And the coffee. Of course I'll keep you informed about what happens with Dora. Oh, forgot to say we found Neeta's thingy on wheels behind a bush in the garden, and one of the PCs delivered it back to her. You'd borrowed it for the shopping, I'm guessing?'

Jenny nodded. And then, after they'd exchanged goodbyes, she crossed the room to the window overlooking the garden, resisting the temptation to watch Melanie follow Marek out to his car. Although she found herself counting the seconds before her daughter came back in.

CHAPTER 16

It took a while for Jenny to resume her old routine—for things to feel normal again. Or as normal as they were ever going to be. Val welcomed her back to the library, and she helped to decorate the Recommended Reads table with acorns and spiky-shelled conkers. She and Neeta delivered new collections of books to Mrs Pycroft, Mrs Grundy, Mr Nettles, and Ruby. To her surprise, Mrs Pycroft was extremely complimentary about the re-issued 1940s and 1950s titles she'd looked out for her.

'Now, that's what I call a *proper* mystery. Something that appeals to our *brains*, not to our ... lower senses.'

Ruby was full of questions about Dora. 'Well, always up to no good, that one. I wasn't fooled by the *hair*. Like an old bird's nest, don't you think? I was watching her with you, Jenny, and when I couldn't see you no more, I came out with me eggs.'

'It's a very good thing you did, Ruby. I'll always be grateful to you.' Jenny explained that Dora was still in hospital. Her stroke had left her unable to speak, and she was unlikely to face a trial. Sometimes, Jenny thought that was for the best, but at others she shivered at the picture of Dora aware of what was happening around her but unable to communicate with anyone. A sentence more deadly than anything a court could impose.

Melanie had returned to London and her job, but she came back to visit every weekend. Jenny didn't flatter herself that she was the main attraction. The last time she'd texted *See you in the morning!* and her mother had no doubts about where she'd spent the night. And Jenny had not *spoken to Marek*, as she'd originally intended. It would have seemed an intrusion, when they were both so radiantly happy. *Sometimes, you simply have to trust.* Like she'd trusted Colin ...

He'd texted her, asking if she'd meet him in Avery's old home, which he'd inherited along with the rest of his possessions. At first, Colin ambled through the rooms, revisiting each, smiling at the bedside book of crosswords, and at the photograph of Avery in his knitted pullover. *Of course*, Jenny thought, *he never came here when Avery was alive.*

'Is it how you imagined it would be?' she asked.

'Sort of. It's absolutely *him*. I think we could have lived very happily here. Of course, I'd have had to do something about the garden. *That gnome!* Although I'll probably keep it, to remember him by. Oh—and there's *your garden* too. I hadn't forgotten.'

'I'd love you to redesign it, but won't that be too much of a burden for you, having to travel up from London?'

'I'm not going to stay in London—I'm going to move in here. I'm sure there's an opening for the sort of services I offer, and I'm going to make a start by talking to the local gardeners—perhaps one or two of them would like to come into partnership with me.'

'That sounds like a great idea.'

'Now I know what Avery wanted to confess to me. Writing the books with Mrs Wedderdale—well, that's neither here nor there. According to Inspector O'Keeffe, she didn't want any credit for her contributions, and I'm also sure that there's more of *him* in them than there is of *her*. A lot of the dialogue, and the humour—I can hear his voice so clearly. Knocking down and killing the Inspector's father—well, of course, that's infinitely worse. If only he'd owned up at the time—he'd have been convicted, he could well have gone to prison, but he wouldn't have had that terrible weight hanging over him for years and years.'

'What would you have advised him to do?' Jenny asked gently.

'I don't know. In a way, I'm relieved it's a decision I no longer have to make. What I *am* sure of, though, is that it wouldn't have altered our relationship, our love for one another.'

Colin sighed, and walked slowly along the length of Avery's bookcases, running his fingers along the spines of the massed volumes.

'There are more books here than I could read in a lifetime. I'll have to do *some* weeding out. All the Skye Savorys, for instance—I have a complete set myself, so they could go to Oxfam.'

'I know someone who would love to give them a home,' Jenny said. 'A true fan—and also someone who helped to save me when Dora attacked me. Perhaps I could buy them from you?'

'Oh, don't give me any money! I think I know who you mean —the lady in the feather cloak? She made quite an impression on some of Avery's friends at the funeral.'

'Yes, she's Ruby Scrivens, and she lives in the bungalow opposite.'

'Goodness me!' Colin looked slightly apprehensive. 'Well, of course she can have them—I'll take them over myself. Er—later.'

After their latest library run, Jenny and Neeta stopped off in Dani's café for coffee and apple cake.

'How's Maisie's pet detective work going?'

Neeta grunted. 'It's going the wrong way. She hasn't been asked to find any more *lost* animals; she's trying to find a home for a rabbit that turned up on our doorstep yesterday morning.'

'An abandoned pet?'

'I should think so. It's a rather pretty Dutch rabbit, ginger and white. Maisie thought it had been well looked after, but I explained to her there was a reason it was so plump. A bunny with a bun in the oven—*several* buns, if I'm not mistaken. I suppose you wouldn't like ...?'

'I'll think about it,' Jenny said. She liked rabbits—although having one, or *two*, might mean she had to revise her garden plans ...

'Anyway, Jenny,' Neeta went on, 'talking about detectives, pet or not, has given me an idea.'

Was she going to comment on Marek and Melanie? She hadn't told her about them yet ...

'We found out a lot of things in our investigation,' Neeta continued. 'All right, we were—*I* was—a bit off track some of the time, but on balance we really helped the police. Especially *you* did. What I'm thinking is—why don't we launch our own detective agency? We could start small to begin with—perhaps a room in your house? Some clients might flip at the rats in ours, not to mention forthcoming multi-bunnies ...'

'But Neeta,' Jenny said, playing for time while she considered this totally unexpected suggestion, 'you have a job already. And I do as well.'

'My job is only part-time. And you told me yours is too. Also, like I said, we'll start small, see how it pans out. Even if we don't get any takers, we won't have risked anything.'

Neeta was right. And, despite her natural inclination to be cautious, to avoid leaps into the unknown, Jenny had to admit she was tempted. 'Let me think about it,' she said, smiling.

'*Good!* I have a name for us, too. The Middle Way—what do you think of that?'

'What does it mean?'

'Well, if you have a problem, you have a choice about what to do. At one extreme, you can ignore it, hope it will go away. At the other, you can involve official agencies, such as the police. But by consulting us, you choose *the middle way*.'

'Oh, I see.'

'Also, Jenny—and I'm surprised you haven't spotted this—it's a mix of our two names, *Meaden* and *Biddle*. You see, I *have* learned something from all this crosswording!'

After supper that evening, Jenny sat at her table with a glass of whisky. She got up and moved Alan's photo from the sideboard to stand in front of her. He helped her to think, to sort out everything that had happened. It had all been strange, but some parts of it stranger than others. To begin with, she remembered how she'd become fixated on puzzles, on plays on words, believing that the mystery's solution lay in some elegant manipulation of signs and symbols. When all the time, the murderer was someone to whom all of this was a closed book!

That will teach me! Jenny thought. But was it important that she should be *taught*, should learn from her experience? Yes, it was, she decided. Not only in the general way of becoming more attuned to other people, but because she'd decided she was going to go along with Neeta's suggestion. *Meaden and Biddle. The Middle Way!* She found she was already planning to convert the third bedroom—full of unpacked boxes—into an office space, where they could talk to their clients in a welcoming, relaxed atmosphere. Comfortable chairs, restful landscapes on the walls, a vase of freshly picked wildflowers … Neeta was very good at putting people at their ease, and if her ideas sometimes went off at a wild tangent, that was a necessary part of the brainstorming process—*out-of-the-sky, blue-box thinking*, she remembered, with a smile.

And no assumptions either! That was another thing she'd learned. She'd made so many along the way, from trivial ones, like the source of Ruby's eggs, to vital ones, like the identity of the person with the knitting needle. And about people too—about

Marek, for instance, who was very far from being the careless heartbreaker she'd been led to imagine.

Jenny sipped her whisky and brushed her finger over the frame of Alan's photo. It seemed right to talk to him out loud.

'I wonder what you'd make of all this, darling! You'd be glad Melanie is so happy. I think you'd like Marek. Perhaps he has a bit of growing up to do, but he has a true heart. A loving one. And he's kind and thoughtful, and he makes her laugh. If you could see them together, you'd understand. It's not up to us, though, is it, the choices our daughter makes? We just have to hope. And *trust.*'

I'll have to tell Neeta too, Jenny thought, anticipating her friend's explosive reaction. Which would probably be equalled by Marek's when they told him about the Middle Way Detective Agency. Just now, power was in her hands. Power to give each of her friends a huge surprise. And as Jenny finished her whisky and sat back in her chair, she found herself smiling.

ABOUT THE AUTHOR

Mariko McCarthy lives in Oxford, where she works as a professional editor, as well as running poetry workshops in museums and galleries. As Dorothy Yamamoto, she has published poetry, and non-fiction books about animals. Mystery stories are a new departure for her—but there will always be an animal in there somewhere!

To learn more about Mariko McCarthy and discover more Next Chapter authors, visit our website at www.nextchapter.pub.

Printed in Great Britain
by Amazon